THE
ONE
THAT
GOT
AWAY

THE
ONE
THAT
GOT
AWAY

JENNIFER
PALGRAVE

Town
Belt
Press

WELLINGTON, NZ

Published by Town Belt Press, Wellington, New Zealand: townbeltpress@xtra.co.nz
Printed by Your Books, Wellington, New Zealand
Cover designed by James McDonald: JAMESMCDONALDBOOKS.COM
Cover photograph © Constance Fein Harding: www.cfeinphotography.com

ISBN: 978-0-473-50007-8

This is a work of fiction. References to historical events, real people or real places are
used fictitiously.

Catalogue record available from National Library of New Zealand.

❀ Created with Vellum

The evil that men do lives after them; the good is oft interred with their bones.

— WILLIAM SHAKESPEARE, JULIUS CAESAR, ACT 3, SCENE 2

1

'Honour is the subject of my story'

They walked down the curved marble stairs and emerged from the theatre into bright sunshine.

'So deliciously wicked to go to a movie in the morning,' said Lauren as they stood outside on the footpath.

'I wouldn't usually spend time inside on such a beautiful day. We should be outdoors.' Pam's weathered complexion suggested she usually was. 'Hard to resist a National Theatre *Julius Caesar*, though.'

Lauren's mind was still full of the play and its images. She didn't mind squandering sunny weather for such a rich return. 'Don't you think the way the stage jutted out into the audience was brilliant? You couldn't tell which were the audience and which the actors in the crowd scenes.' Lauren shivered as she recalled how the yelling, pumped-up actors seemed to encircle the spectators, so that they were included in the mob.

'The modern dress brought it all too close to home,' Pam said. 'Creepy. The rabble. The power struggles. That guy playing Julius Caesar wearing a baseball cap. A take-off on Donald Trump. I bet he wouldn't have minded being an Emperor.'

A truck squealed to a halt at the traffic lights, drowning out their words. Lauren had to repeat herself, raising her voice. 'His career ambition, no doubt. But when will people notice he has no clothes?'

Pam laughed. 'Rich men vying for power and ultimately betraying each other. Times don't change, do they?'

Lauren agreed. 'I liked it that they had women playing a couple of the conspirators.' Pam nodded. 'But I couldn't help remembering that the real Cassius was a man. Women were kept right out of politics then. Unless they were Cleopatra, of course.'

'I guess the women knew what was going on and tried to use their influence,' said Pam, stepping out of the way of a young man walking along the pavement directly towards her, earphones insulating him from his surroundings.

'Yes, but in the play Caesar took no notice of his wife's warnings. And Brutus's wife killed herself by swallowing fire.' Pam shuddered and Lauren said, after a moment's thought, 'I think that was true historically, not just something Shakespeare came up with.'

Pam picked up her backpack, preparing to leave. 'Well, here we are in the twenty-first century on the other side of the world. At least New Zealand politics aren't that bad. I don't think our election campaign will involve murder and mayhem.'

'You might think we're more civilized now,' Lauren said. She grasped her handbag to her chest. 'But I don't call it civilized when we've got people sleeping in cars and on the street. And kids going to school hungry. And-'

A steady series of ringing tones interrupted her. Lauren groped for her phone. 'Must have forgotten to turn it off, just as well this call didn't come while we were in there.' She turned away. 'Hello, Lauren here?'

'It's Ro. Lauren, I need to see you urgently. Are you free now?'

'Not really, I've just come out of *Julius Caesar* with Pam, and I guess we're both heading home.' She turned back to Pam, raised a questioning eyebrow and Pam nodded.

'Can you meet for coffee at Clark's, then, say about three?'

'What's it about, Ro? I have a batch of editing I was hoping to complete this afternoon.' She put her hand over her free ear as the lights turned green and the traffic surged forwards.

'I can't tell you over the phone. Please, Lauren, it's really important.'

Lauren sighed, agreed and rang off.

Pam said, 'Sounds like that's your afternoon mapped out.'

'Certainly does, you know Ro, no use arguing, she can be pretty fiery. Those stereotypes about redheads being hot-headed may be right.'

Pam smiled, 'No stereotypes about people like me with mousy brown hair, alas! But with Ro, it's not so much that she's hot-headed, she's just so focused on what she's doing, she forgets about the niceties.'

'She's certainly absorbed in her current project. Women in the fourth Labour Government. I'm surprised she's got the energy to think about anything else. I wonder what it's about. An affair of the heart, perhaps?'

'Could be. That's not my area of expertise. You'll find out soon enough.' Pam checked her watch. 'I'd better run, get my bus.' They hugged goodbye, Pam hurried across the road just as the 'cross now' signal turned red and Lauren began walking swiftly up Marjoribanks Street.

SHE MADE a striking figure as she strode up the hill. Tall, sleek grey hair shaped in a neat cap, stylish black boots, blue jeans and a bright yellow top. She was still thinking about the play by the time she reached St Gerard's monastery. Brutus was the real hero, such a sad muddle of a man; wasn't the woman playing Cassius fantastic?

She paused for breath and took in the view. The city and close suburbs ringed the expanse of sparkling water before her. The red Harbour Board tugs were busy shepherding a container ship into port. It was a stunning pocket city, all spread out before her.

Halfway home and now she had the vista of Oriental Bay. The

high footpath took her past grand houses with harbour views; even their carports had views. She stepped onto a track that took her through regenerating bush, her favourite part of the walk. Another twenty minutes saw her at the apartment block, only slightly out of breath. She retrieved her mail from the letterbox, took the footpath down and the steps up two at a time, unlocked the door and once inside, switched on the kettle.

Waiting for it to boil, Lauren gazed fondly around her apartment. When she retired from full-time work, she'd finally got round to selling the family home and downsized. But she was determined not to have an apartment that constricted her. She loved hers: the living room and the main bedroom both had expansive views over the harbour, and the whole place was full of space and light. She had spread oriental rugs across a glowing matai timber floor. (And what a mission restoring the floor had been.) And built-in bookshelves everywhere–the living room, the study, the bedroom–to house her extensive collection. Well, almost. The books still tended to spill out, even encroaching on to her rimu table, the centrepiece of her kitchen-dining room, good for working at, eating at, entertaining friends.

Her home felt as right as a snail's shell does to a snail. The only lack, a garden, to get her hands into the soil. Pam's allotment on Mt Vic dealt to that–lots of Pam's friends helped with the work there.

LAUREN SPOONED tealeaves into the pot and made herself a tomato sandwich as she waited for the brew to steep. She poured tea into her favourite mug, then sat down with her lunch at the table. She flicked through the mail. Begging letters from Forest & Bird and Save the Children, an invitation to Megan's sixty-fifth (Sixty-fifth! Help! But why a letter? Even the sixty-five year olds usually sent invites by email these days...) and a letter in a cream deckled envelope. From her old Cambridge college. No doubt another plea for funds. They'd save money if they spent less on their stationery. She slit open the envelope.

Dear Alumna

You are invited to a special event from September 25th to 27th, 2017. It is the launch of Cambridge Women Ageing Well. This life course study will explore the lives of our women graduates as they age. Trinity College alumnus, Mr Brett Wilson, has generously provided support for the initial stages of the research. His kindness will allow you to travel to Cambridge, all expenses paid. The research is described further in the attached document. We do encourage all alumnae who completed their Tripos at the college between 1970 and 1975 to attend. Travel arrangements can be made using the enclosed form, which should be returned to the Bursar.

Yours sincerely

Mary Lashley, PhD

President

Lauren gasped. 'Wow. Not a begging letter after all, what a surprise!' she said aloud. What a good idea the research project sounded: baby boomers would do ageing differently.

Great that the study included her year. It meant they were all getting older, though. University days seemed a long time in the past. Lauren had been an undergraduate in Cambridge courtesy of a Girdlers' scholarship which her enthusiastic Latin teacher had urged her to apply for. Lauren was thrilled and her parents tickled pink when she was awarded one. It had been scary too, but she was a robust seventeen- year-old, up for the challenge.

What a great opportunity to see her old student friends, and her daughter Julia and the grandchildren in Brighton. And free travel! Brett Wilson though–surely that wasn't the Brett she'd known as a student–she wouldn't have picked him as someone likely to give money to a women's college, even though she'd heard he was filthy rich now. Australian, parents rich Sydneysiders (or was it a cattle ranch?), good-looking, charming, bright–but overly pleased with himself and ran through a hell of a lot of girlfriends.

Damn! The dates clashed with the holiday Kirsten and her friends were planning in Greece. Lauren saw little enough of her girlfriend, now that Kirsten had moved to Auckland. And Kirsten hadn't made it clear if she was really keen on Lauren joining them. But Lauren felt that if she didn't go, it wouldn't be good for their relationship.

She couldn't stop looking at the letter. The fourth time through she realised the dates also clashed with the general election. Damn and double damn! She wouldn't be able to help on election day. She would have to remember to vote before she went.

Hmm, all somewhat problematic. She drained her cup, looked at the time and realised she needed to hurry, to get to Clark's by three.

SHE ANGLED her jaunty red Jazz out of the tight apartment car park and wound her way down the hill to Oriental Parade. The weather held. It was still a clear crisp winter day. Oriental Bay was clogged with people out to enjoy the sun. A pair of poodles stalled her at a pedestrian crossing, their owner fitting the mould of looking just like her pets, all of them with tightly curled apricot hair.

Lauren parked in the library basement and caught the lift up to the mezzanine. Clark's was busy as always, with chatty groups and solitary readers oblivious to their surroundings. Lauren spotted Ro easily enough–her red hair helped–and waved. Ro had already got herself a coffee and had papers strewn around the table. She waved back to Lauren, a wide smile breaking out. A tall, shambling woman, she gave the impression that she had just wandered in from the paddocks. Thank goodness it wasn't the eighties, Lauren thought, or Ro would have been wearing overalls. But it was the same look. Checked shirt, blue jeans, boots made for rougher ground than Clarks or the library stacks.

Lauren was held up by the queue at the counter, which gave her plenty of time to consider adding a very large slice of lemon meringue pie to her coffee order. She thought of her waistline, fought with herself, lost, and decided she would offer Ro half.

'Good to see you, Lauren. Thank you so much for coming.' They embraced rather clumsily; Lauren was trying to put a tray on the table at the same time.

'Good to see you too. So what's all the urgency? Girlfriend trouble?'

Ro was indignant. 'Don't be silly, I haven't got time for that sort of thing. I'm getting desperate about my book, there's a deadline coming up.' She paused, took a sip of her coffee, and then plunged in. 'You'll never guess what I'm onto, Lauren.' She lowered her voice, looked around and whispered, 'Something's come up in one of my interviews. I'll bet you didn't know there was a plot to kill David Lange in 1988.'

2

'A woman well-reputed'

Lauren shook her head, then laughed. 'A plot to kill the prime minister? You've got to be joking. Surely I'd remember hearing about that. Sounds unlikely!' She frowned at her friend.

'Shh. Someone might overhear you.' Ro leaned forward again and whispered, 'Must have been hushed up. It's not on the record. Will be soon though, if I've got anything to do with it.'

Lauren stared at Ro. Surely her friend wasn't being dragged down into the dark world of internet conspiracies, that spiderweb of rumours, half-truths and outright lies. Perhaps she had been interviewing gullible people and actually believed them? 'Oh come on, Ro, you're supposed to be a historian not a fantasist. Use your judgement! We're in New Zealand, not some banana republic. We don't do political murders, assassinations or the like.'

Ro reddened, bit her bottom lip and stirred her coffee again. 'Lauren, it's true. You need to hear me out.'

'It had better be good.'

Ro ignored the sceptical tone. 'You'll know that the atmosphere around Parliament in '88 was poisonous.'

'Of course I do, I remember it well. I was around at the time, don't forget. With Government Print, the job I came back from the UK for.'

'Of course. So, it wasn't about the opposition, it was open warfare between the two different factions in government. The Labour caucus was really split–Lange thought their radical economic reforms had gone far enough–but Douglas and his mob had got carried away and wanted to keep going.'

'I know all about Douglas and his asset sales programme, Ro,' said Lauren. 'I hadn't been in my job two months when we were told Government Print was being sold to a private bidder and our jobs were on the line. Then the sale ran into delays. It was a horrible process, uncertainty for all of us staff for months and months and I was senior management, had to try to keep up morale.' She was vehement.

'It was pretty hateful,' said Ro. She slipped back into lecturing mode. 'When Lange started voicing doubts, his so-called friends didn't like it. They turned on him like wolves, tried to topple him in '88, finished him off in mid-'89, and so he resigned as prime minister. You've just seen *Julius Caesar*? It was a real *et tu Brute* situation.'

Lauren gave a wry smile. 'But, Ro, you're talking heavy politics, not assassination.'

'That's where you're wrong,' said Ro. She dropped her voice again. 'You should have been a fly on the wall when I was interviewing a woman at Karori Gardens last week.'

'Isn't that the rest home for the blue rinse brigade?'

Ro glared at Lauren. 'I think she did have a blue rinse, but no need to be sarcastic. She was well known in her time, a very lively politician. A butt-kicker of the old school.'

Lauren hmmed sceptically. She would have known at least the names of all the women in Parliament at the time, there were so few of them. 'Who was it?'

'Confidential.'

Lauren was irritated. What was the point of telling her then? Ro went on. 'I was asking her about her split life, in Wellington all week when Parliament was in session. Late sittings, all the intensity, how that contrasted with her family life back in small town New Zealand. She had a husband and teenage kids.'

'Probably no contrast, she'd have handled the male MPs just like teenagers?' Lauren couldn't resist the quip. She pulled the lemon and meringue pie towards her, sliced it in two and put a fork on each side.

Ro scarcely smiled, she was keen to get on with the story. 'Don't distract me, Lauren. Anyhow, she had an affair–it's amazing, so many of the women I've spoken to had affairs with their colleagues. Ugh, what an unprepossessing bunch most of the men were, too.'

'High pressure environment, I guess. But I agree, back then I often heard rumours and we all found them most amusing.'

'The guy was a backbencher and she didn't tell me his name–she wasn't easy to draw out, I got the impression she was still feeling guilty about it. But she made the most extraordinary claim.'

She leant forward again, brushing her elbow against the slice of lemon meringue pie that lay neglected on the table, and almost whispered. 'Apparently this guy got drunk one night–not so unusual–and started bragging to her about nearly managing to off David Lange. Her guy was right behind the so-called reforms. She was sitting on the fence–like quite a lot of the women I interviewed. Anyhow, he hung around with a lot of Business Roundtable types, and it was something to do with them. She implied that there was some kind of plot to get rid of Lange. To kill him.'

'Go on,' said Lauren. Now she was interested. 'What did she say?'

'No details, really.' Ro looked crestfallen.

Lauren was reminded of someone telling a shaggy dog story and forgetting the punch line. 'Is that all you've got? Not very convincing, just a titbit, really.' She remembered Ro's urgency on the phone. 'I can see that if it were true, it would be pretty amazing–but what was the big hurry to tell me?'

Ro ignored the question, and carried on. 'You wouldn't say it wasn't convincing if you'd heard her, Lauren. She'd been enjoying telling stories about her time in office, but when she got onto this topic you could see the emotion bubbling up. First she said something about a plot and then she clammed up. I was taken aback. It was distracting, because her revelation was off the point, in terms of my project. I pulled myself together and did try to get more out of her, but then she was off on another anecdote and I couldn't divert her back. Soon after she slowed right down and looked so tired that I had to stop the interview.'

Ro sank back in her chair, took a forkful of the lemon meringue pie. She said, 'I tell you what, Lauren. I'm getting desperate about my book, there's a deadline coming up. This plot business has surfaced and I'm very distracted. I'm not sure whether to put it in or not. It's so dramatic it could draw attention away from my focus on the experiences of women in Parliament.'

'And it might turn out to be completely wrong, if that's all you've got to go on. Imagine the bad press you'd get, the damage to your reputation.'

Ro shrugged. 'I'm sure there's something there. I could go back to her later and try to get more. Perhaps work it up into a separate piece, maybe for a magazine. But she isn't getting any younger. It would be awful if anything happened to her, or if she got too forgetful. And of course, there's lots from her story that would need checking out, more interviews and fact-checking.'

'Yes, I should say so. Perhaps you should get onto it straight away. Put your book aside for the moment?'

'No, I can't do that. The publisher is really hassling me.' Ro hesitated, took another mouthful of pie and then came out with it: 'Would you be prepared to do some work on the plot for me?'

'Certainly not!' Lauren didn't hesitate for a moment. 'So that's why you wanted to tell me. I wondered what was so urgent.' She softened her tone. 'Ro, research isn't really my thing.'

'But you did that oral history course a couple of years back, when you were wondering how to fill in time when you retired. You enjoyed the course. So, you have the know-how and you must have plenty of time now.'

'I'm not retired,' snapped Lauren. 'I have my editing work. I guess I'd describe myself as semi-retired but I'm busier than ever.'

'Right, like going to the movies in the daytime.'

Lauren glared at Ro, who tried to look contrite. 'Most of my friends, the 'retired', as you call them, are in the same boat. When you stop full-time work you think of all the things you've ever wanted to do and then you start doing them. Sometimes all at once. It makes for a very busy life.'

Ro stared at Lauren and raised an eyebrow. Lauren defended herself. 'I'm doing lots for the election campaign, now that I've joined up with Labour. It took me a long time to get over the eighties! And I'm helping with Pam's community garden and I have to get ahead with my editing hours because I'm thinking about a trip overseas in September.'

'Oh, are you? You hadn't told me about that.'

'It's just come up. Two things actually. Kirsten's been talking about a trip to Greece with some of her Auckland friends. They're a younger crowd. I feel as if she's invited me as an afterthought, but ...' she hesitated–Ro was a good friend but single and obsessed with work–'...it's been tough on us since Kirsten moved to Auckland. Getting away together might help.'

'That's what you get for robbing the cradle,' replied Ro knowingly.

'Not helpful!' Lauren tried to smile.

'Sorry,' said Ro, 'I know you fell pretty hard when you met her. She was doing some interesting work promoting public health, wasn't she?'

Lauren was grateful that Ro didn't go on about cradle-snatching. Now, she replied, 'That was when she was in Wellington. In Auckland, she's working as an account executive for Barton and Mackie. A good career move for her, but commercial advertising is a bit different.'

She sighed. She and Kirsten had met when Kirsten's agency commissioned a story for a school publication about brushing teeth, as part of a campaign around dental health. Lauren had been in a meeting where the commission was discussed, since she was to edit the piece. Kirsten's agency had persuaded a noted children's author to write to the brief, and the story was charming. Only a few days later, Lauren ran into Kirsten at a lesbian drinks function. They'd given a mutual smile of recognition...and there it all began.

Lauren realised Ro was staring at her. 'Sorry, wool-gathering,' she apologised. 'Anyway, now there's another complication. I got a letter this morning from my old Cambridge college. They're calling in former students from the years I was there to take part in some research on ageing.' Her blue eyes twinkled. 'Perhaps they made a mistake. Me, ageing?'

Ro didn't voice the hoped-for compliment, so Lauren went on. 'But the dates overlap with the Greek trip. I'd love to see my old student friends, it sounds like interesting research, and it's free. I'll talk to Kirsten about it when we have our phone call tonight.' She frowned. 'Weird, though, the Cambridge trip is being funded by someone I think I know. Brett Wilson, he must be the Australian who was my year in Cambridge. I didn't care for him much.'

Ro jerked, dropped a piece of pie on her front. 'Shit!' she said, and dabbed at it. 'Did you say Brett Wilson? *The* Brett Wilson? The money man?'

'I don't know what you're talking about,' said Lauren. 'I believe he has made lots of money, but I don't see how that makes him a money man?'

'Lauren, you were here in the eighties: he was one of the wheeler dealers busily buying assets off us–he was in and out of New Zealand, fraternising with the free marketeers, giving talks courtesy of the Roundtable and so on.'

'In that case, it's hardly surprising he didn't look me up. Well, perhaps that settles it,' said Lauren. 'Maybe I'll just go to Greece as planned, not Cambridge. I don't want to play a part in any of his enterprises, even if they are philanthropic.'

'No, you should go and corner him when you get the chance, you might be able to find out more about any high finance skullduggery from that time.'

"Ro, how often do I need to say it? I really don't have time to be your research assistant!'

Ro shrugged, tried to look conciliatory. 'Okay, okay, I understand. You can't take on anything big. But how would you feel about doing just one thing, a really urgent job?'

'What's that?' Here she goes, Lauren thought. She's incorrigible.

'Lauren, you're very good at winkling things out of people.' Ro cocked her head and smiled. 'Not that you give much away yourself. But could you do another interview with Judith Butler? She's the woman in the rest home, and I'm telling you her name in confidence. See if you can find out more about the plot, like who was the guy she was having an affair with, what did he actually do, who else was involved and so forth? And record it?' Ro contrived to look hurt. 'And that'll give you the chance to see that it's true.'

'Judith Butler? She was the one who was a mayor somewhere before she got into parliament?' Then Lauren sighed, 'Oh, Ro, I suppose I could.' The agreement was grudging, but Ro was delighted and the talk turned to practicalities. They finished their coffee and cake and took their leave of each other.

As Lauren headed out of the car park, she was thinking so hard about Ro's extraordinary claim that she didn't pay attention to her driving. There was a scrunch as she grated the rim of her back wheel along the high gutter edging the exit. A couple standing across the road grinned and gave her the thumbs up. Damn and blast. She was glad to turn the corner and leave them behind.

She drove more carefully, but was still trying to get her head round a plot to kill a prime minister. The tale was hard to credit, but what if it were true? That would go down in history. Ro was a good scholar. She clearly believed she was onto something big and she wouldn't make up a story from nothing. But someone else might have–if Lauren talked to Judith Butler, she might expose it for nonsense, get Ro back on track. Anyway, it would be churlish not to help her out. One interview, how much trouble could that be?

3

'O conspiracy!'

Lauren pulled into the visitor car park at Karori Gardens. She groped in her handbag for the voice recorder Ro had lent her. It had been a couple of years since she last used such a device and she had spent time the night before familiarising herself with the controls. An interview would not go well if she was fumbling with the equipment. So she sat in the car for a few minutes and practiced hitting record, pause, rewind and play before walking over to reception.

'I'm here to visit Judith Butler,' she informed a harassed woman who emerged from a back room some time after Lauren pushed the buzzer.

'Sorry, I was signing off something, it's always a rush around here. Judith Butler, let's see. Room 23, it's on the top floor of the next block.' She gestured vaguely towards a swing door. 'Just sign the book first and remember to sign out before you leave.'

Lauren made her way through the swing door into a rabbit warren. A corridor led to a passageway joining two blocks, where there was a fire door leading to a stairwell. Then it was up some stairs into another corridor. There must have been lifts somewhere but Lauren didn't notice any. As she walked past open doors she glanced into rooms which revealed residents resting in bed or sitting listlessly in armchairs. An occasional aide made her way past Lauren, bustling along the corridors, clutching linen or pushing a trolley.

Judith Butler was sitting in an armchair by her bed, her eyes closed and a book upside down, almost sliding off her lap. Afternoon sunshine streamed in the window making the room very warm. The elderly woman was wearing makeup, her eyeshadow and lipstick a little smeared, as if shakily applied or smudged.

'Mrs Butler.... Mrs Butler!' Lauren raised her voice and the woman startled, looking around in an unfocused way. It took a moment before her gaze alighted on Lauren.

'Hello, I'm Lauren Fraser.' She smiled. 'Do you remember Rowan Wisbech coming to see you? She's the historian working on a book about Labour women.'

Judith nodded. 'Oh yes, that's right.' She looked quizzical and Lauren wasn't sure if she really remembered, or was just being polite. 'Rowan has asked me to do a follow-up interview. Is that all right with you?'

'You may as well, dear, not a lot happens in here. I really enjoy having someone to talk to.' She was becoming more alert. 'What did you say your name was again?'

They made conversation for a few minutes. Lauren established that Judith, while perhaps forgetful in the present, was easily able to talk about the past. She began reminiscing to Lauren about her first election campaign for local government, when she was a stay at home mum with preschoolers, up to her elbows in the kitchen sink.

Then Lauren asked, 'Do you mind if I record our conversation?' and receiving a nod, switched on the machine. The red 'record' light glowed and she felt confident that everything was working as it should. Now the test would be to get Judith onto the topic of real interest. It was important not to hurry her, but Lauren didn't want her to tire of talking before they got to the plot. So after some more inconsequential reminiscence, Lauren took the plunge. 'Rowan told me you'd said something about someone trying to kill David Lange when he was prime minister.' Judith looked up, as if examining Lauren carefully. Lauren went on. 'We'd be really interested in hearing more about that.'

'It was a long time ago.'

'Yes, it was,' Lauren agreed. 'But I'm sure your memory is really good.' Judith nodded. 'What can you tell me about that time?'

Judith closed her eyes. Was she struggling with herself? Drifting? Then she looked up sharply. 'I haven't really talked to anyone about it before. You have to learn to keep secrets in politics.' She placed her book carefully on the tray table beside her and examined the silver and gold rings on her fingers.

Lauren cursed inwardly. This was going to be difficult. 'As you said, it was a long time ago. So it's history, now. Rowan is a very good historian and she wants to get things right. She thinks you can help by telling us more about what went on in the eighties.'

Was Judith convinced? She appeared to concentrate and then began to speak. 'It was a very confusing time. I came into Parliament when Labour became the government, and the government was really getting things done.' She hesitated and Lauren smiled encouragement, hoping that Judith wasn't going to lapse into political speech mode. But she went on, 'I was spending the weekdays in Wellington. The kids were in their teens, dear Tom was managing all right, and I'd be home at weekends. I was sharing a flat in Thorndon with Catherine Harris. We had late nights in Parliament, a lot of legislation being rushed through. It was a government in a hurry!'

She paused again, before continuing, 'As backbenchers we didn't have much say in anything, so there was a lot of hanging about.' She stopped and looked hard at Lauren. 'It wouldn't surprise you, dear, would it, if there was a bit of hanky panky?'

Lauren smiled. 'I'm sure that's very understandable, given the circumstances.' Privately amused, she thought that "hanky panky" was an innocuous phrase to describe the hotbed of infidelity Parliament was reputed to be in those times, and perhaps even now.

Judith seemed to be gathering pace. 'Tom and I had a very solid marriage, and I wasn't into flirtations. But towards the end of the second term, it was getting hard to be away from home so much of the time. So one night, when a lot of us backbenchers were hanging about...' She hesitated, 'I guess I'd had a bit too much to drink... anyway, I ended up in bed with Kevin.' She wrinkled her nose at the memory.

'Who was Kevin?' Lauren hoped that Judith would get to the point and not come up with a long story about her extra-marital adventures. Pursing her lips, Judith made a little moue, 'Let's just call him Kevin for now. He was another backbencher. Catherine was quite shocked to see him sneaking out of the bathroom the next morning, but she didn't say anything.'

'Was that when he told you about David Lange?'

Judith looked disconcerted and Lauren thought she had been too direct. Not good interviewing practice. But the older woman got back to the thread of her story.

'We had a brief affair. It was all very clandestine. Kevin turned my head at first, he was quite a bit younger than me. But I felt very guilty about Tom and I worried we might get caught. There were lots of journalists nosing around, politics was very exciting then. Mind you, they didn't go in for dishing the dirt on who was sleeping with whom in those days.' She paused and frowned. 'He really was a bastard, that Kevin, I found out he was two-timing me with another MP and she tipped me off to what he was really like.'

'So where does David Lange come into it?' Lauren risked trying to get her back on track.

Judith looked startled. 'David? Oh, that's right, you did ask about him. What was it you wanted to know again?'

Lauren tried to arrange her face to look sympathetic. She managed not to sigh as she prepared to go back to square one. But then Judith continued. 'Oh, yes, that's right, extraordinary really. Kevin had an obsession about Lange. He was always criticising him. I thought Lange was a good leader, he'd definitely won us the election. But Kevin was in thick with some business associates and they were getting really fed up. They were angry because there were signs that

Lange might put the brakes on the asset sales.' She looked at Lauren inquiringly. 'You do know what the asset sales were, don't you?'

Lauren nodded and Judith went on, 'I found it difficult to know what to think. The government's reform programme was really exciting, but perhaps it was going a bit far. Kevin and his mates didn't think so, though.'

'So, Kevin? What was his last name again?' Lauren's ploy was successful. Judith looked at her sharply, 'Kevin Driscoll, I thought I told you that. You really do need to pay attention, dear.'

'Sorry, so Kevin and Lange...?'

'Well, one night Kevin had far too much to drink and he started bragging to me about how he'd nearly managed to see David off for good and all.'

'Do you mean he said that he tried to kill him?'

'Oh yes, that's definitely what he meant. Apparently some of the business guys had been saying they needed to see the fat man off and Kevin must have decided he'd take it into his own hands.' Judith seemed to have forgotten her earlier doubts about disclosure and was now enjoying the story.

Lauren, though, was finding it horrific. She told herself to stay professional and make sure she got all the details straight. 'So it was a plot? The businessmen put him up to it? Or was it just Kevin acting on his own?'

'I think they egged him on, one or two of his business cronies. But what he did, he did on his own, as far as I could make sense of what he said. Wanting to please them, that's my bet. I suspect he might have been on the take.'

'Who were these men, do you know?'

Judith frowned, trying hard to remember. 'He didn't say. And I'm hopeless with names these days, so I probably wouldn't remember anyway. I didn't mix with the business types, they weren't interested in talking to women in those days, not about finance.'

Lauren leaned forward. She needed the details. 'So, tell me, Judith, what did Kevin actually do?'

'I'm not sure, I got the impression he might have slipped Lange something in a drink. I asked him to tell me more, but he clammed up. Next thing he was terribly cross with me for asking questions. In fact he took it out on me. He was a nasty drunk and I had to explain a cut on my lip to Tom the next weekend. I broke it off with Kevin then and I didn't see him after that, except when I had to.'

Judith slumped down in her chair. 'I think I'll just take a little nap, dear.' She seemed to doze off. Apparently the interview had ended.

Lauren left the room. She realised she was literally in shock. She paused in the corridor and put a hand on the wall to steady herself. She was convinced by Judith's tale—though it was frustratingly short on detail. She nearly blundered out through a fire exit door—no doubt it would have set off alarms. That would have matched her jangled thoughts. Extraordinary. An assassination attempt. A plot to murder a prime minister. Exactly who was involved, how near they came to pulling it off, all still murky. But the why was clear enough: greed on the part of the plotters, anger that they might not make the money they expected.

She got into the car and drove home on autopilot. Her thoughts were whirling around. Kevin Driscoll? Kevin Driscoll, the name was familiar to her. Ah yes, he was the son of her parents' friends. Charlie Driscoll, the trade unionist and his wife lived in Wellington for a time. They'd long left the capital, and gone back to their home in Mangere. Her mind wandered. She remembered her mother's sage plant, a special sort. Hadn't Mrs Driscoll given her the cutting? She was a great gardener, keen about herbs. Of course, they had a son called Kevin, younger than Lauren so she'd taken no notice of him, if they did meet at all.

Scary, she didn't really want any connection with a would-be murderer. At least she'd never seen him again as a grown-up. Then a memory struck. A trip to hear David Lange speak at Oxford in 1985– five in the car and one of them was Kevin Driscoll. She'd thought he was a real creep.

Lauren tried to concentrate on her driving. So, Kevin Driscoll. She wondered what he was doing now. What should she do? Her thoughts were still racing, so was her pulse. But by the time she had parked the car, she'd worked it out. She would ask Phyl O'Donnell's advice. Who better than an ex-cop?

~

LAUREN WALKED DOWN THE PATH, then up the steps towards her own apartment on the first floor. She stopped before she got there, knocked on her neighbour's door. She wasn't sure if Phyl was in, then she heard the clip clip of paws up the hallway and a voice saying, 'No, Monty.' Phyl edged the door open and looked comically horrified when she saw who it was. 'Oh, Lauren, I've just brought Monty home from a walk! Had we arranged that you'd take him?'

'No, it's not the dog, Phyl. Can I come in?' She patted Monty absentmindedly as Phyl led her into the living room. 'Tea?'

'Yes, please,' said Lauren and, while Phyl moved methodically around in the kitchen, thought how lucky she was to have her living next door. Phyl looked out for her–everyone in the group of six apartments looked out for one another, but Phyl was the nearest, the most likely to see Lauren's comings and goings. She had the extra attraction of owning Monty, her friendly mutt with a touch of Staffordshire.

Now, as Lauren waited, he came and leant against her. She was sure he sensed that she was upset. She ruffled his fur and enjoyed the weight of him. He looked up at her and she said automatically, 'Good dog, Monty.'

Lauren enjoyed walking with Monty. All the pleasure of owning a dog and none of the expense. Phyl was well retired from the police force but sharp as she'd ever been, and fit with it–except for times when her arthritis was bad. Then, Lauren was happy to step in and take Monty on outings.

She couldn't think of better neighbours than the pair of them. She still remembered how she first met Phyl. She'd just taken possession of the flat and in the bustle and stress of moving in, managed to lock herself out. She'd knocked on Phyl's door, hoping to use the phone to call a locksmith. Instead the sprightly grey-haired woman had produced a ladder, used it to balance precariously on top of a neighbour's back porch roof and pulled out the old-fashioned louvres from Lauren's lavatory window. Then she climbed in, retrieved Lauren's keys and met her at the front door. Lauren tried to thank her, but was interrupted with a lecture on security. Phyl told her to get rid of the louvres (she did) and entertained her with stories of burglars she'd known.

This was much worse than a burglary, though. She eased herself away from Monty and ran her hands through her hair. Phyl was bringing the tea and looked concerned. 'So, what's on your mind?' she said.

'Attempted murder, actually. My friend Ro and I have stumbled across something.' Phyl had just sat down, and now she half rose, interrupting. 'You need to phone the police straight away.'

'No, no,' said Lauren, 'I guess it's one of those cold cases, something that happened back in the eighties, when you were making your way up the ranks.'

Phyl sank back into her seat. 'Good heavens. Tell me about it then.'

Lauren explained what she had discovered from Ro and the interview with Judith Butler. 'Plotting to get someone out of office is one thing,' she concluded, 'Attempted murder another!'

Phyl frowned and tapped her fingers on the arm of her chair. 'Yes,' she said slowly, 'There was something about a plot. Let me think...it wasn't my area, you understand, but of course there was a lot of gossip. Apparently there was an incident at Lange's flat, when the fire brigade was called–a pot on the stove smoking and Lange there, asleep and out to it. That might have been suspicious. I think the Diplomatic Protection Service investigated.'

'Weird,' said Lauren. 'Why didn't the public hear about it?' She examined her fingernails, lost in thought for a moment. 'I don't see how Kevin Driscoll could have been involved with that. He wouldn't have been in Lange's flat. They wouldn't have been bosom buddies. Kevin was a backbencher and a hanger-on to the Douglas lot. Anyhow, Judith said she thought that Kevin had slipped something into a drink.'

'Well,' said Phyl, 'a tape from an old woman who says someone she used to know tried to off Lange isn't evidence of anything. But if there was a case, it won't have been closed. I'll tell you what, I shouldn't really do this, but I'll ring my friend Deirdre Nathan and ask if she could check. She might read through any case notes and remind me of the details. I can't give you anything, mind, but I think Deirdre would talk to me. She used to work in my section.' She added, 'She's an inspector now.'

'Thank you,' said Lauren, 'I said to Ro that I wouldn't do more than interview Judith. I'm quite busy before I head off overseas in a few weeks. But I must say, I feel like finding out more now.' She rose to go. 'In fact, now I remember Kevin Driscoll, I'm feeling really angry about it. How dare he try to get away with killing the prime minister. In New Zealand! I want to know what really happened.'

LAUREN LEFT PHYL'S, still fired up. She scarcely took the time to hang up her coat before she went and switched on her computer. She googled Kevin Driscoll. She established that he was still alive and kicking, and owned an immigration consultancy on Auckland's North Shore. It had been set up not long after he left Parliament in 1990. The website looked professional, there were several staff and it was aimed at the business sector. No doubt Kevin had made good use of his government contacts to get overseas cronies through the immigration hoops. Lauren recalled various scandals of recent years involving wealthy off-shore business people who sought to buy property in New Zealand but had dodgy grounds for residency. She wondered if Kevin had been involved in any of those.

The Wikipedia article on Kevin was brief, not surprisingly. It detailed the terms he served as MP for Birkdale. It mentioned that his father, a trade unionist, had also been active in the Labour Party, the implication being that Kevin had followed in his father's footsteps. There was a mention of his mother's involvement in a trial for illegally procuring an abortion away back in the 1960s. A journalist had dug that out when Kevin was standing for Parliament and though it had proved an embarrassment, he still won the seat.

Lauren googled Charlie Driscoll as well and recognised him, standing with trade unionist Ken Douglas in a photograph of a picket line. He had died in 1978. Perhaps Kevin's mother was still alive? She must be very old, but Lauren could perhaps use her family connection to talk to her, find out more about Kevin? The White Pages online gave her an address and phone number for a Driscoll in Mangere, where their family home had been.

That would do for now, she thought, plenty to tell Ro about.

4

'Let us swear our resolution'

Ro was about to leave the house when her phone rang. The landline. Hardly anyone used it now, she'd been thinking about getting it disconnected, but it had been there for ever. She ran back up the hall.

It was Lauren. 'Ro, I interviewed Judith Butler yesterday. You were right,' she said, 'there was a plot. I apologise for being sceptical! I'd like to come and talk to you about what next. Are you home this morning?'

Ro jigged up and down on the spot with excitement. 'Lauren, that's fantastic. Thank you so much. Who was it?'

'Steady on. I'll fill you in when I see you; this is too important to do over the phone. I can come over now?'

'I was just going in to the university library, but don't worry. I'll do that later.'

It was half an hour before Lauren arrived. She couldn't find a place to park at the top of Ro's street in Wadestown, so left the car a couple of streets away and walked down the steep public footpath to Ro's house.

She was wary as she negotiated Ro's property. A cat sauntered up to the gate when Lauren pushed it open and rubbed itself against her legs. The narrow footpath to the back of the house was mossy and overgrown and she sighed as she had to step over a fallen branch. Ro's house was a perfect example of a working class villa from back in the early years of the twentieth century, but Lauren wished she would give it a bit more attention. She wondered if Ro had done anything to it since her father died? Not that he'd done much either–the suburb gentrified around him and his daughter, and their house stayed true to its roots. And now Ro was far too absorbed in her academic work to worry about the house. At least it wasn't raining, so there was no danger of slipping.

The back door was wide open so Lauren called out. A shouted acknowledgment and Ro emerged from the living room, pushing a kitty litter box out of the way so that Lauren didn't have to step over it in the hallway. 'Come in, come in. Come and sit down. Tell me all about it.'

They went into the living room. Ro lifted another cat off a very old and scratched armchair, and they sat down. The place smelt of cat but it had a settled, comfortable feel. The walls were lined with towering bookshelves.

Lauren sat and said nothing for a moment. She realised how tired she was: sleep hadn't come easily the night before–but she knew that once she shared her news with Ro, she'd feel better.

'The interview?' Ro prompted again.

'I liked Judith; I'd say she was a pretty good politician in her day. You were right, though, it was quite hard to winkle the story out of her.'

'Lauren!' said Ro. 'Will you please tell me what you've found out.'

'Sorry, I'm not really trying to be annoying, it's just all so hard to credit.' She put her hand up to ward Ro off, as Ro looked ready to get up and shake the name out of her. 'Okay, okay, this is the story. It was a guy called Kevin Driscoll, he was the one she had the brief affair with.'

'Kevin Driscoll,' Ro repeated. She screwed up her face in thought. 'A nondescript backbencher?'

Lauren nodded, and went over the whole interview with Ro, and her web search, and Ro listened enthralled.

'That's great, Lauren, let's have a coffee and talk about what next.' They both went into the kitchen, Lauren opting for a cup of tea instead of Ro's drink of choice, instant coffee. Then they returned to the sitting room.

They both clutched their drinks, warming their hands. The room was chilly. Lauren said, 'What I haven't told you, Ro, is that Mum and Dad were friends with Kevin's parents, his father was a unionist–and I actually met Kevin years ago in the UK, when he was a backbencher.'

'That's weird. How come? What was he like?'

'He was awful, I couldn't believe he was Charlie Driscoll's son. Rodney and I were invited to go and hear Lange at the Oxford Union, the famous nuclear weapons debate. When our friends arrived to collect us in their car, Driscoll was already sitting in the back seat. He was wearing dreadful clothes, suit too bright, tie too in your face. And he kept licking his lips and his mouth looked wet and flabby. I had to sit next to him and he smelt of stale sweat and alcohol.'

'Good heavens, he clearly made a lasting impression.' Ro grinned. 'But I guess we can't condemn the man for his taste in clothes or his appearance.'

'I suppose not.' Lauren was almost reluctant to agree. 'But it was all of a piece. I asked him if he was kept busy with his constituency work and he said they were a pack of moaning Minnies!'

'What a bastard!'

'At least we didn't have to put up with him on the way back. He was staying in Oxford for a day or two, and we managed to avoid him for the debate. We were invited to drinks and then the official dinner before the debate. Even got to meet Lange and he made one of his jokes.'

'Oh?'

'Yes, he said if another New Zealander hadn't got to Cambridge before Rodney and me, none of us would be in Oxford for the debate–you know, Rutherford splitting the atom.'

Ro nodded appreciatively, 'Typical Lange, always had a quip ready.'

Lauren continued. 'He was marvelous at the debate itself. The union hall was impressive. Big stained-glass windows and galleries upstairs, and about nine hundred people crammed in. And there was our clever witty prime minister, the star of the debate. I felt really proud and I loved it when he said New Zealand wouldn't be part of a nuclear alliance.'

'That caused huge ructions with officials back home and with the Americans,' said Ro, 'even though ordinary Kiwis loved it.'

'Well, I loved it.' They were both silent for a moment, recalling those halcyon days before all the bickering and backbiting–and perhaps worse.

Lauren shook herself and said, "So had you heard of Kevin, Ro?'

'Yes, I think so.' She hesitated. 'As I said, nondescript, insignificant. Associated with the Auckland group around Roger Douglas. Did she say who else?'

'She didn't seem to know, just talked about money men,' Lauren said.

Ro was still trying to process it all. 'Did she say when it happened?'

'No specific dates, she couldn't remember exactly but her memory of what happened was vivid. She told me all about Kevin hitting her. Anyhow, I've been talking to Phyl, the ex-cop who's my neighbour.'

'You've what? Why did you talk to her?' Ro bounced on her chair; its springs already seemed rather the worse for wear. 'Lauren, this could be a great coup for me, a piece of history no other historians know about. We have to keep it quiet until I've found out more about it.'

'Don't worry, she won't say anything. She said we haven't got enough evidence.'

'She's right,' said Ro, 'a lot more research is required. Once I've got my manuscript off to the publisher I'll get onto it. I'll mention the plot in the book, but not the specifics. You shouldn't talk to anyone else about it. It's sensational gossip and there are plenty of historians out there who wouldn't respect the fact that it's my story.'

'Ro,' said Lauren, 'that's not what I mean. It's evidence for the police that Phyl and I were discussing. This isn't a history scoop we're talking about, it's a crime.'

Her voice was stern and she kept her blue eyes firmly fixed on Ro's. She wasn't glowering, but she wasn't smiling either. 'Ro, someone tried to kill a New Zealand prime minister. And that some-one—or those someones—are probably still alive and still at large. They can't be allowed to get away with it. I'm keen to help you find out more, so that we can bring them to justice.'

'I see what you mean,' Ro looked uncomfortable. She pulled her eyes away from Lauren's and stared at her worn carpet. One of her cats was walking past and she bent to stroke it. Then she conceded. 'Well, good on you! Of course I'd love to have your help. I'll get the recording from you and listen to it carefully, and we'll work on it when you're back from your trip. I should have my book off by then. In the meantime, promise me you'll keep quiet about it.'

Lauren promised to keep it to herself, and lightened the conversation. 'I've always loved that painting,' Lauren said, pointing to a picture over the mantelpiece. It showed a lamplit street corner in the rain, with a typically old-fashioned dairy, a Cadbury's chocolate advert in its window, a newspaper dispenser outside and some figures hurrying past, battling the weather.

'Yes, it's a John Ramsay—Dad was a friend of his. It's always been here. I can't bear to get rid of the things Dad loved. I suppose I should get a declutterer in.'

'Unlikely!' Lauren looked at her affectionately. She noticed that one of the bookcases was crammed with books that surely must have been Ro's father's—novels from the 1960s and earlier, books on New Zealand birds, geology, maritime history, tales of exploration.

She changed the subject again. 'If you listen to the recording and follow up what you can, I'll see what I can find out in Cambridge. I've decided I'm going; I'm not going to be put off because it's Brett Wilson funding it. In fact, if he's there, I'll make sure I talk to him and ask what he knows about that time in the eighties. Even if he's not, I bet some of my old friends will have kept tabs, and be able to tell me what happened to him after Cambridge and how he made his money.'

'But what about your holiday with Kirsten?'

Lauren looked pleased. 'I've worked out I can probably fit everything in–being a research guinea pig, seeing my friend Rachel and my family, and then meeting Kirsten and the others in Greece, instead of travelling with them.'

'That's great,' said Ro. She looked at her watch. 'I'd better get to the library, they were supposed to be hauling out some papers for me this morning. I'll see you soon, and remember–not a word to anyone else about the plot.'

LAUREN GLANCED at the time–six-thirty, usually a good time to call Kirsten. She carried the phone to her favourite armchair, sat down and punched in the number.

'Kirsten here.'

'Hello darling, have you had a lovely day?'

'Just got in the door, I'll call you right back.'

A few minutes later her phone rang and Kirsten started talking about the account she'd been trying to land for weeks. 'Nearly there,' she said, 'the client loved our pitch with the netball team in the changing rooms. Maybe a little exploitative, but it's fun.'

Lauren suppressed a feminist response. How could Kirsten feel excited about using women's bodies to sell toothpaste! 'Do netballers *really* brush their teeth after a game?'

'Don't pour cold water, darling,' Kirsten replied. 'Anyhow, how are you? You didn't call yesterday.' (Neither did you, thought Lauren.)

'Busy. I think I told you I was helping Ro Wisbech with an interview. I did it yesterday and talked about it with her this morning. We came up with some unexpected material, and it might keep me busy for a while.' She hesitated; she would like to have told Kirsten how horrifying she'd found the discovery of the plot, but Ro had asked her to keep it quiet. Besides, she had a sinking feeling that Kirsten might not see how momentous it was; she sounded unengaged.

She changed the subject. 'I told you my Cambridge trip was being funded by Brett Wilson, and that I knew him when I was a student? I hadn't realised–he was in New Zealand a lot in the eighties–Ro told me he was one of the money men pawing over our state assets then. I still can't understand why he'd be supporting a project on women and ageing, no matter how wealthy he is. I wonder if he's got an ulterior motive.'

'Don't be ridiculous, darling. You're always so suspicious of anyone who's made a pile. He's probably perfectly nice and wants to do something useful with his money.'

Lauren doubted it, but decided not to pursue that line of conversation. They chatted on in a desultory sort of way, before agreeing to phone earlier the next night, as they both had Saturday outings planned. They signed off with their usual, 'Love you.'

Lauren reached for her book, a new sci-fi that her friend Megan had recommended. She could have been making calls to people, urging them to vote Labour in the election; or working on how she could find out more about Kevin Driscoll. But she decided what she needed was a cosy evening at home with a good book. She became absorbed and went to bed ridiculously late.

LAUREN HAD PROMISED to go to the Newtown market the next morning, to help with Labour electioneering. She groaned when she woke up and saw the time, leapt out of bed and was at the market by nine o'clock.

The market was already well under way. The Newtown School grounds were completely transformed, stalls butting close together, canvas tops to keep out the sun or rain, and fruit and veg displayed invitingly on stall after stall. Familiar fruit like apples, oranges, pears and kiwifruit, as well as mangoes, persimmons, guavas. Vegetables and herbs for Asian cooking: kohlrabi, bok choy, lemongrass–Newtown was known for its cultural diversity. Lauren made a mental note to do her own shopping before she left, but in the meantime, joined the little cluster of red-jacketed figures by one of the entrances.

'Oh Lauren, you're here! Take this – one of them passed her a clip-board–'and give out these.' The face of Jacinda Ardern, new leader of the Labour Party, looked out from the front of a pamphlet. 'And if people aren't on the electoral roll yet, get them to fill out one of these if you can, and we'll gather up the forms and get them to a PostShop. You go that way.'

Lauren obediently walked off in the direction he indicated. She gave herself a mental shake, put a smile on her face and said, 'Good morning,' cheerfully to people as they passed. 'An election coming soon,' she said, 'Are you on the electoral roll?' The reactions were predictable. A 'No thank you' from National voters taking in her red jacket, a 'Good on you' from Labour sympathisers, or a note of uncertainty from others.

One man came up to her and said, 'So why should I trust your party? David Lange promised us the earth, before they sold us down the river.'

That was an interesting mixed metaphor, Lauren thought, but she had to agree with it. 'A lot of us felt betrayed at that time, but I have faith in Jacinda Ardern. Why don't you give her a go?'

The guy harrumphed and walked off, leaving Lauren to reflect that the state of the government under Lange was even worse than people realised, if it had come to poison!

She finished her stint, returned the paraphernalia–jacket, clip-board and the rest–to the organiser, bought her own fruit and veg for the week, and headed home.

There was more electioneering that she'd promised to help with in the weeks ahead: pamphlets to deliver, street corner meetings, house meetings. She also had an urgent batch of editing to complete before she went to England. Any work on the Lange plot would have to wait till she returned, she decided. Ro had her head down, finishing her book; Phyl's contact in the police was in Australia on some exchange scheme; and she herself had to get her paid work done. No point in worrying about it; after all, the case had been unsolved for years. When she was in Cambridge she would try to find out more about Brett and the money men, and by the time she got home, Ro and she would both have more time.

5

'There is a tide in the affairs of men, which, taken at the flood, leads on to fortune'

The eleven-hour flight from Auckland to Singapore was as ghastly as usual. Lauren had flown from Wellington earlier in the day, then transferred from the domestic to the international airport. She had called Kirsten while waiting in the departure lounge, but had managed only the briefest of farewells since Kirsten had been in a meeting. As she settled into her seat, on the aisle with two strangers beside her, she recalled how ceremonious the departure had been on her first trip to England, back in the 1970s.

She had chosen to go the old-fashioned way, by ocean liner. Her family made the trip to Auckland to explore the ship with her before they were called off to join the crowd lining the wharf. The ship pulled slowly out from its mooring, streamers linking passengers and those farewelling them. The air had been filled with brass band music, the crowd singing along to 'Now Is the Hour'. Streamers snapped one by one and trailed in the water. Lauren's last sight was her mother wiping her eyes, her father's arm around her shoulders. Six blissful weeks ahead, time for tackling the Cambridge reading list, not to mention enjoying foreign ports and shipboard romances. Now, it seemed, your partner could leave for the other side of the world with barely a goodbye. Not worth interrupting a business meeting!

The six hours between flights allowed time to walk off those hours of sitting and dozing, but mostly it was an interval to be endured. Usually, she would have built in a night or two's stopover. Tacking the trip to England onto the original holiday arrangement had not given her the luxury of spare days.

With relief she boarded the plane to Heathrow. The thirteen-hour flight was a nightmare of screaming babies and hacking adults. She was desperate for sleep now, but her usual tricks of counting in fives or going through the alphabet, first with girls' names then boys' names, did not work. She got right through to Zachariah and then spent the hours in a fugue-like state, aware of her aches and pains and worries and distanced from the life of the bodies pressed close around her.

She dwelt on the possible meeting with Brett Wilson. What would she say to him? She tried rehearsing some opening lines, but did not have the concentration to settle on any one strategy. Thinking of Brett made her think back to Kevin and she worried away at his reported attempt to kill Lange. What did Judith Butler mean by saying she thought he might have slipped something in a drink. Slipped what? Why was Butler unsure? When did it happen? Who put Kevin up to it? Did whatever was slipped into the drink, if that was it, have any effect at all? It was all difficult to imagine and she wished the interview had been more satisfactory. Sure, she got the plot confirmed and Driscoll named, but the details were irritatingly patchy.

When Lauren was not thinking about Kirsten, or how to squeeze information out of Brett, or Driscoll's nefarious behaviour, her anxieties circled round to the election taking place in New Zealand at this very moment. She had voted before leaving and she had given as much time to electioneering as she could afford. There was so much resting on the result, but Labour's chance seemed slight. Despite coming back from the dead with Jacinda's stellar rise, they were still behind in the polls. But surely people would not vote for things to go on as they were. Lauren would jerk properly awake, horrified at the thought, then sink back to semi-consciousness. She roused herself altogether as the plane's lights went on. Breakfast came eventually and Lauren managed to adjust her off-key body clock enough to tackle bacon and eggs with surprising relish. Soon after, the plane landed.

Passengers shuffled off, red-eyed and half asleep, to join the long queue at customs. Lauren blessed her dual citizenship as she joined the much shorter queue for 'British and EU passports'. If nothing else, Brexit would make this queue even shorter. Uplifting her bag, a small one that she could comfortably manoeuvre around airports and train stations, she was through Customs quickly.

She looked around the waiting crowd and saw someone frantically waving in her direction, her granddaughter Tamsin held up high by Julia. Soon they were embracing, with Tamsin in her arms, Julia's solid hug and Adam clinging to her trousers. Lauren didn't go in for emotional displays but she felt her throat constrict. Damn, she thought, there were twelve thousand miles between them. She wished they would come home.

The grandchildren were all over her in the train from Heathrow and in the taxi to their hotel. Julia had brought them up the night before as a treat, and booked two adjoining hotel rooms. Lauren threw down her coat and bag on a bed and slumped in a chair. A weekend in London with her family–in New Zealand it had sounded like a great idea. The children both talked at once, their voices getting louder as they tried to be heard over each other; they patted her for attention, told her they were going on the Eye, and to the zoo. But right now, all Lauren wanted was a shower and a lie-down.

She pulled herself up straighter, tousled Adam's hair and said it all sounded lovely but first Gran must have a rest. Over the children's heads, Julia and she agreed–Julia would take them shopping and Lauren would meet them all for a late lunch at Giraffe, a child-friendly restaurant nearby, before taking a bus from Baker Street to the zoo. 'But before you all go, there's something even more important—we have to see what's happened in New Zealand.'

'But Gran, haven't you just been in New Zealand?' That was pretty good for a five-year-old, Lauren thought.

'Yes, Adam, but while I was flying here, there was a general election, and everyone will have voted by now. Your gran's been working hard to help try to get a new government and I want to find out if we have.' She checked the time—ten-thirty—so it would be ten-thirty in the evening back home. Usually far too late to phone people but she'd already arranged with her friends that she'd be in touch during the election night party. Though since they all voted on the left, it hadn't been much of a party the last couple of occasions. She was praying that this time it would be different. She dug in the bag for her laptop and said to Julia, 'I'm skyping, so they can fill me in properly.'

There was the usual fiddling, then they were connected. Ro's face on the screen didn't look ecstatic. 'Doesn't look like Labour can do it,' she said. 'They've got lots more seats than last time, but the Nats are still ahead. Even if Labour and the Greens went into coalition, they still haven't got the seats. I hope you voted before you went?'

'Of course I did! So we're stuck with a National Government?'

'Probably—they can't govern by themselves but no doubt they'll cobble something together.'

'With ACT and the Māori party again?'

'Nope, the Māori party's out of Parliament. Guess who's got the balance of power?'

'Oh no, not Winston again.' Lauren groaned. 'When will we know? What's he saying?'

'Nothing that says which way he'll go, but I suppose it'll be the Nats again. Now here's Pam to say hello.'

Pam's face replaced Ro's, and she waved at Lauren. 'It's not all gloom and doom,' she said, 'Labour's done really well, good on Jacinda.' She began giving Lauren the details, but Lauren could feel her attention wandering—that shower and sleep had to be soon. She finished the call. 'You heard all that?' she said to Julia.

'Yes, I'm sorry Mum, I know you've been working hard for Labour.

And I'm dying to know whether you think the new leader is as good as all the besotted journalists seem to think.'

'Jacinda? You bet.' Lauren was fervent. 'We'll have a good talk this evening, once the children are in bed.'

As LAUREN and Julia walked and the children alternately skipped and dawdled round London Zoo that afternoon, Lauren mused on the wonder of standing under running hot water and lying flat. Followed with the walk in the fresh air, it was a good cure for jet lag. It took her mind off historic cold cases too–she might have been dreaming about attempted murder on the plane, but since landing, she'd only had time to think about New Zealand politics now, not in the nineteen eighties. Even those thoughts were receding as her grandchildren swung on her hand, chatted to her, marvelled at the tiger's huge feet, giggled at the baboons' red bottoms, and pointed at a giraffe's blue tongue. She wondered how it was that one's own grandchildren were so much more likeable than anyone else's.

When evening came she still felt energetic enough to help Julia get the children to bed. Adam and Tamsin both enjoyed their baths and being bundled in the hotel's soft white towels. Lauren patted them dry and helped them into their pyjamas while Julia mopped up water from the bathroom floor. Then she sat down with Tamsin on her knee, put an arm round Adam as he leaned in to her, and read them a bedtime story. She had brought with her a picture book, a fresh new edition of *The Lion in the Meadow*, once their mother's favourite.

'THAT WAS A MISSION,' said Julia, collapsing into a chair. 'It's always harder when they're out of routine.'

'They'll sleep soundly now, and I can tell you all about the exciting times we've been having back home.' Lauren sat down on the edge of the bed.

'Great, Mum. It sounds extraordinary. One moment you were emailing me to say there's no hope and the next the whole damn world's talking about Jacinda Ardern.'

Lauren laughed. 'You've nailed it! It was exactly like that. Labour had its worst poll ever, Andrew Little leading them into an election that they should have won easily but that seemed increasingly unlikely. The Nats had a tired government, they'd swapped their leader for someone with less appeal, and there was lots of disaffection. Next thing you know Andrew stepped aside and this 37-year-old unknown is leader of the Labour Party and fighting a general election with just seven weeks to go.'

Julia stood up and swapped places with her mother. She gathered the children's discarded clothes on to the bed beside her as she continued talking. 'Sounds just like Jeremy Corbyn here. How did the party supporters react? Were they cross about such a late change?'

'Not on your life. She never put a foot wrong from the moment she took over. Said she'd be relentlessly positive and she is.'

Lauren was enthusiastic as she reminisced, but suddenly she became subdued. Goodness knows how Jacinda would be feeling now. All that hard work and they hadn't pulled it off.

'Seven weeks would have been a tall order, Mum. And I guess the Labour Party never has enough money, just like here. Fancy having to redo all its publicity stuff.'

'That's exactly what I thought, so I sent them a donation and so did thousands of other people. They got this huge influx of funds.'

Julia folded the children's clothes as her mother continued.

'Money's not everything, though, and they got lots more volunteers. We were all out there door-knocking, phoning, running house meetings, public meetings, street corner meetings. She had a rally at the St James Theatre in Wellington and the queue to get in stretched right along to the Taranaki Street corner. People were so excited! And she made a great speech!'

Julia put her hand gently on Lauren's shoulder. 'Sounds like a bad case of Jacindamania, Mum.'

Lauren had to laugh. 'It's true, I guess. But if you'd been grown up in the eighties when Labour just about wrecked itself with the Lange-Douglas goings on, you'd understand how wonderful it is to have something to believe in again. It's just such a shame that they won't get in.'

'I learnt about the Lange years at school,' Julia said.

'Knowing about something isn't the same as living through it.' Part of her life, Lauren thought, but just history to her children. 'It might seem like ancient history. But it's not to me.' She hesitated, Ro had asked her not to tell anyone about their discovery–but Julia was a long way away, and she could trust her daughter to keep it to herself. 'My friend Ro, you've met Ro...'

'Oh, yes. The redhead with the flannel shirts. Good historian, but her dress sense!'

Lauren ignored this and went on, 'Ro's discovered a plot to kill David Lange back in the eighties. Seems like it was money men egging on a really nasty backbencher. The surprising thing is that I once met the guy. His parents were friends of Grandma and Grandpa's.'

'How extraordinary. What's she going to do about it? Is the guy still alive?'

'Yes he is, he's an immigration consultant in Auckland. I've promised to help Ro investigate when I get back.'

'Mum! Why would you get involved in Ro's obsessions. You know what she's like. And if she's right, it might be dangerous.' Julia frowned at her mother. 'Don't get yourself into anything you can't handle.'

Lauren was offended but made a joke of it. 'Don't you remember the time I accidentally tossed your little brother across the room? When I'd done a self-defence course, I asked him to rush at me. Then I stepped quickly aside and helped him on his way. He didn't really come off the worse for wear.' They both laughed and the topic was closed.

For the rest of the weekend Lauren didn't have time to brood on the election and what was likely to happen back home. Nor on the Lange plot. She enjoyed her grandchildren and when she said goodbye to them early on Monday morning, she was pleased that she'd see them again so soon. They were taking the train back to Brighton. Lauren decided to catch her train to Cambridge early in the day, well before the beginning of the alumnae event. She was looking forward to it immensely.

6

'Yon Cassius has a lean and hungry look; he thinks too much; such men are dangerous'

T he London-Cambridge journey felt familiar, although in the old days Lauren wouldn't have taken a taxi from the station. Her college had offered rooms for alumnae in a new accommodation block. The taxi dropped her and she checked in at the porter's lodge. She was directed to a grey concrete building which had all the charm of student accommodation anywhere. Unlocking the door to her room, Lauren tossed her unopened suitcase onto the floor, pulled off her shoes and trousers and lay down flat on the single bed. The bliss! So the jet lag hadn't completely gone. As her eyes shut she decided that everything could wait. Meeting up with old friends, finding her way to the first event. Unlikely to be getting around on a bicycle, she thought, as sleep overcame her.

She woke just in time to get to the briefing, making her way down a winding cobbled street to a modern building and then following the hubbub to an upstairs lecture theatre. There was no time to look around for old friends. She spotted an empty seat and squeezed past a couple of women, both wearing silk scarves flung over their jackets and discreetly expensive jewellery. With her tailored trousers, collared shirt, pinky ring and short hairstyle, Lauren supposed she might be the odd woman out. Mind you, there might be a silver lining, perhaps she'd show up on someone's gaydar.

'Lauren!' The woman she found herself sitting next to turned towards her. 'Goodness me, I hardly recognised you.'

Lauren was at a loss. Peering beyond the dyed hair and makeup, she said, 'Ginny, is that you?'

'Of course it's me, darling and don't say you haven't changed at all since the seventies.' Ginny cast an eye over Lauren, registering the difference. No longer long hair tied back into pigtails, the short, shapely cut with its streak of purple accentuating the grey perhaps sent a signal about Lauren's lifestyle.

A shushing went round the room as a young man walked up to the podium. He began fiddling with the screen display, prompting another outbreak of chattering.

'Where are you staying?' whispered Ginny loudly. 'At the college?' Lauren nodded.

'See you outside the porter's lodge at 12.15 tomorrow. We've arranged to go to Fitzbillies for lunch. All the old gang will be there.'

A smartly dressed woman, probably in her forties, walked up to the lectern and tapped the mike to get their attention. 'Welcome to the first meeting of participants in the Cambridge Women Ageing Well Project,' she said.

'Ageing?' Ginny whispered loudly, 'I'm trying very hard not to.' Her words were loud enough for those around to hear and giggle.

Takes me right back, thought Lauren, giggling in lectures. How awkward she'd been as a teenager, newly arrived from New Zealand with her outlandish accent, clothes and demeanour. But her fellow students had been friendly and it hadn't taken long for her to fit in and become one of the gang.

'Today I'm going to introduce the study to you and I hope by the end of the session you will agree that this is a wonderful opportunity to capture the lives of a group of well-educated women. You're mostly from fortunate backgrounds and we think we can learn a lot from you about ageing well in the twenty-first century.' Hmph! thought Lauren, we didn't all go to English public schools.

The study did sound interesting. Lauren realised they were going to be busy all of Tuesday and on Wednesday morning, what with physical examinations, photographs, all kinds of measurements, bloods, DNA sampling, various tests and questionnaires and an interview. There was a long lunch break on the Tuesday, so the date at Fitzbillies would work.

THE FIRST NIGHT RECEPTION, after the briefing, was in the Great Hall of Lauren's college. It looked splendid. The chandeliers were sparkling and the wooden floors sported a high polish. Portraits of bygone women scholars, hung around the walls, looked down impressively at the graduates who were all dressed up. The wine was sparkling too, and Ginny and Lauren were drinking and chatting when one of the sprinkling of men in the room came to stand by Ginny.

He smiled at Lauren. 'You're looking pretty good after more than forty years.'

Brett! She had been hoping to run into him. Now was her opportunity and she still hadn't decided how she could steer the conversation. And he was definitely flirting. For sixty-something himself, he looked pretty good too. Still a full head of hair, now streaked with grey, still those arresting pale blue eyes and full mouth twitching into a smile. More lines on his face, but an imposing presence with his height and heft, his air of self-assurance–and his beautifully tailored grey suit.

'Hello, Brett.' Lauren couldn't bring herself to return the compliment. Had he never realised she thought he was a ratbag? They'd had a lot of fun in that run of *Julius Caesar*, it was esprit de corps, she supposed. But she had tried to warn Charlotte against having a fling with him, and it hadn't been long before she was mopping Charlotte's tears.

Back then Lauren had noticed how Brett used his smile and his height on his next victim. Victim might have been an odd word for girlfriend but there was always an air of held-back menace about him. Still, she needed to recognise his generosity on this occasion.

'I believe we have to thank you for our airfares. That was extraordinarily kind of you?'

The implied question was clear. Why would you help women come to a women's event? He chose not to answer, instead began to ask her about Kiwi and Aussie friends and acquaintances who had hung out together in those old days at Cambridge. His reaction was revealing. He seemed most interested in those who had made money or been successful in business. Academics, scientists, public servants, he didn't dismiss exactly, just didn't want to hear more. Competitive still, thought Lauren, and very pleased with himself for his wealth.

He did enquire politely about Lauren's career, but was more interested in telling her about himself. 'After Cambridge I worked in the City–lucky for me they were prepared to take on a brash young Aussie. It was a great job, they sent me to do some more study in the States, and I got into the new economics. After that, I did international monetary policy for the firm. So I spent some time in New Zealand in the eighties, all eyes were on New Zealand. I met up with...'–he named a couple of people that Lauren thought of as captains of industry. 'Gave a couple of talks, too. Your Business Roundtable invited me to speak at a seminar in Auckland. They were exciting times, your Finance Minister was a remarkable man!'

Well! She didn't need a conversational ploy to introduce the topic, here it was! So Brett had definitely been pursuing business interests in New Zealand at the time of the Lange era, just as Ro had suggested. She had no need to feign interest in his self-congratulatory spiel. She smiled and murmured something like assent and that encouraged him to go on.

'Your government was very bold, selling off so many state assets and getting streamlined–not many countries were as committed. Actually, that's where I made my first real money. Struck out on my own, borrowed a bundle from the old man. It was easy to get loans and I hooked up with the Americans to buy a couple of the state-owned enterprises being sold off.' He smiled reminiscently. 'But I don't think you were around at the time?' he asked.

What a bastard he was, thought Lauren. He'd made money off a misguided policy in her country–and probably got his hands dirty doing so. She contained her anger, but thought she probably sounded acid as she said, 'I was, but I clearly wasn't moving in the circles you found yourself in. I don't think you bothered to look me up. I imagine you were a young man in a hurry.' Not that young, though. He must have been in his 30s, he was the same age as her. She elaborated. 'I told you I was working in publishing after I graduated. I got back to New Zealand in the mid-80s. Headhunted to take up a senior role in the Government Printing Office in Wellington.'

Brett smiled politely but a flick of his eyes across the room showed he was a little bored. Lauren went on. 'Government Print was one of those assets that government decided to sell, not long after I arrived, in fact. Exciting times mightn't be the phrase I'd use about the period.'

'All for the good, though. I bet you found something else. A Cambridge degree wouldn't leave you beached for long. Not in a small place like New Zealand.' Lauren couldn't believe the cheek of the man. But she needed to get to the point before he moved on to some other woman he'd seen across the room. She was thinking rapidly. Was Brett one of the business types that egged Kevin on? He may well have known him, but surely Brett wouldn't have.... He might be greedy and unprincipled, but urging on a murderer is a different matter entirely. She tried to sound casual as she said, 'By the way, did you know Kevin Driscoll? He was a backbench MP at the time, I believe he was moving in the circles you describe.'

For no more than a millisecond, Brett went completely still. Then he wrinkled his forehead as if in thought and answered just as casually, 'Doesn't ring a bell. I knew some of the main players. Why do you ask?'

Lauren was put on the spot. She had a strong feeling that Brett was lying. 'No reason, really. Someone was talking to me recently about Lange's Oxford Union debate. I drove over with a bunch of Kiwis, and Kevin was one of them. He was on a political junket, something to do with banking, and so he came along with our friend who worked in the High Commission. It was when Lange got offside with the Americans.'

Brett didn't seem interested in New Zealand's nuclear policies. Lauren didn't feel she could pry any further without it seeming odd. She needed to get away. Her skin felt prickly and she was sure she was breathing fast. Ginny, bored with talk about people she hadn't known well, had already drifted off. Brett seemed ready to do the same. Lauren had just spotted her old friend Rachel across the room and so she took the cue and escaped. As she skirted around groups of women chatting noisily and happily, she wondered why she felt certain that Brett had been lying. And why did she feel so uneasy?

THE NEXT MORNING was as busy as the briefing had suggested. The student common room was taken over by the research team and each woman put through a comprehensive physical. This involved blood and saliva samples and running on a treadmill to measure heart performance under stress. Knees were tapped for reflexes, hand grip strength was measured with a device that looked like a bicycle brake and balance was tested by walking around tippy-toed and then on heels. As well, there was a full medical history that took at least an hour. They were given appointments for CT scans at Addenbrookes, the university hospital, the next morning. It was a relief when they broke for lunch.

Passers-by may have been surprised by all the sixty-something women spilling out onto the footpath outside the college gates. Lauren made her way to Fitzbillies with her friends. They were lucky to find a table for seven. Out of term time, but the place was still crowded with tourists. As they spread around the table, Lauren sat herself next to Charlotte.

'Hi Charlotte, it's lovely to see you again. How's life treating you?'

She was disconcerted when Charlotte's eyes filled with tears. 'It's not been a good year. William, my husband, died of lung cancer eight months ago and I'm in the process of packing up the house. Probably I'll move to Falmouth, one of my children is teaching there and I'll be close to the grandchildren.'

Lauren thought that could be a mistake. Uprooting herself, moving away from her network of friends. Lauren herself had been sure that she wouldn't follow Kirsten to Auckland. And who knew how long Charlotte's family would stay in Falmouth anyway? Was she going to follow them around anywhere they decided to go?

She was murmuring her sympathy when Ginny called the group to attention, tinging a glass. She had always wanted everyone to listen to her latest pronouncement or plan. This time she said how special it was to see them all together again. 'I never thought we'd need to be grateful to that self-styled heartthrob Brett Wilson,' she said, glancing at Charlotte, 'but you never know what life has in store.'

She continued, 'So tell me, girls (Lauren flinched, but decided Ginny was being ironic), what evil things are they going to find out about us this afternoon, when we have our one on one interview? Having bloods and measurements taken is one thing, but trawling through our student records is another. I do remember Rachel arrived at college swearing all her immunisations were up to date and then got whooping cough. The whole college had to have booster shots!'

Rachel laughed and said, 'But Ginny, you took your gown to be mended and they swore the most likely way it could have got that huge rip in it was from a piece of barbed wire on the top of a college wall...'

There was a shout of laughter and they all began talking at once, trying to trump one another's stories of misdeeds. Even Charlotte cheered up and joined in. 'They did almost discover Brett in my room once. By the time they were knocking on my door, he was hoofing it out the gate and they couldn't prove he'd been with me!' She added, 'I know you're all snide about him, but he was actually a lot of fun and behaved well nearly all the time. He was just young and wanting to sow his wild oats.'

There was a pause. Lauren thought that if they'd been friends back in New Zealand, someone would have said, 'Yeah, right.' No one did and the conversation turned to other topics.

THAT AFTERNOON LAUREN had her interview. It began with a request that she scan through her own student records, and she was relieved to find there was nothing there to embarrass her–unless it was the personal essay she had had to write, giving her reasons for wanting to study at Cambridge.

'Goodness, my handwriting was much neater then,' she said to Ayida, the young graduate student conducting the interview, 'But I thought I knew everything when I was young. Listen to this!' She read an extract aloud. '"I plan to use my Cambridge degree back in New Zealand, engaging in some occupation useful for my country." I didn't do that, I stayed in England for quite some years.' She grimaced and the student laughed.

There were several other papers on file, including an application for a hardship grant, a request to take leave before a term had finished to return home to an ill father–she had got there just before he died, far too young–and a photo of a very youthful Lauren, her hair in plaits, looking determinedly at the camera. And what a find, a photo from the performance of *Julius Caesar*, all that time ago. A crowd scene. Lauren spotted herself at the edge of the stage. She examined it further but couldn't see spear-holder Brett.

'No problem if you want to use any of this. I'm sure it's all very boring.'

'Not at all,' Ayida replied confidently, tossing her long black hair away from her face. 'Good baseline stuff and we'll flesh it out now with a life events interview. That'll join the dots between you at eighteen and where you are now.'

Lauren felt positively wrung out at the end of the interview:

career, marriage, children, coming out–life in a nutshell. What would Ayida make of it? Such a different generation. And what would her younger self have thought if she could have seen a life so different from her parents' settled existence? A fortunate life, Lauren was well aware.

SHE DIDN'T SEE Brett again until the final tea party in the Fellows' Garden. It was a warm day, and she was enjoying a quiet moment, standing in the shade of one of the carefully cultivated trees, when she saw him making his way through the crowd towards her. She glanced round. Perhaps that confident smile was aimed at someone behind her, but no.

'Hello again, Lauren, have you enjoyed taking part in the study?'

'Yes, thanks,' she replied and smiled, a glint in her eye. She'd keep it light for the moment, but somehow she'd get him talking some more about the eighties. 'But I'm surprised to see you here again. I wouldn't have thought that ageing women were your thing, even if we were your contemporaries.'

He laughed. 'Oh, come on, don't act like a feminist harridan. That's not the girl I remember. Although you always had a line in disparaging remarks.'

She winced but Brett seemed jovial rather than offended. He went on, 'I'm very pleased to have helped the college with a few projects. I'm honoured that they're naming the new library after me.'

Lauren was stunned. She almost dropped the tea cup she was holding. The library, the very heart of scholarship, and her women's college was naming it after a man. And a man like Brett! Of course, it had to be that they needed the money, but how could he be so insensitive as to accept the honour. He probably pressed for the naming rights. She still hadn't framed her reply when he carried on.

'I was sorry our conversation was cut short at the reception the other night.' Another lie, Brett had been as ready to end the conversation as she had. He appeared to have forgotten all that now. He went on, 'I was going to say that my wife and I are buying a piece of land in New Zealand. I've always liked your country, it did me well in the nineteen eighties. We're flying over soon and expect to spend some time there while we're putting the deal together. Darya would enjoy meeting you, might we get together?'

Coming to New Zealand! Lauren's normal instinct would have been to refuse. She didn't really want to meet Brett's wife, nor have anything to do with him socially. But for the sake of their investigation, she should agree. Back in New Zealand, she'd have the chance to talk to him more about the financiers he hung out with in the eighties. She wasn't going to find out much at a sedate Cambridge afternoon tea.

She urged herself to be friendly and replied. 'Certainly,' she said, 'It would be nice to meet your wife. I'll give you my card.' She walked over to one of the trestle tables set up in the garden and put her cup down on the pristine white tablecloth. Then she hunted in her handbag and handed him one. 'But I'm not going back immediately,' she said, 'I'm staying with a friend here for a couple of nights, then after I've visited my daughter, I'm off to Greece for a bit.'

'That's fine, it'll be a month or so before we arrive. By then you should have a new government? How do you read the signs? Stability or a lurch to the left?'

He would put it like that, wouldn't he, Lauren thought. She picked up her cup again, and smiled at the college servant refilling it for her. She said, 'I think it's likely that Winston Peters...'–she stopped to see if he knew who she was talking about, and he nodded–'I think he'll almost certainly go into coalition with the National Party. Odd that his tiny party is calling the shots.'

'That's politics. Good for the economy, good for business, if the National government carries on.' He continued, oblivious to the fact that Lauren might not agree.

She couldn't resist a pointed remark. 'Some of your old cronies still around? No doubt you'll be hooking up with them?'

Brett gave her a quizzical look. 'It's a long time since I had business dealings in New Zealand. I went on to pastures new. But I have kept a few contacts from that time.' I bet you did, thought Lauren. Brett continued, 'Don't know their wives, though, and it'll be good for Darya to meet you. She's a very cultured woman.'

Lauren was pleased when the conversation finished. She hadn't anticipated that the Lange plot might infect her social life.

7

'They are portentous things'

On Friday Lauren wasn't sorry that Rob, Rachel's husband, was out of Cambridge on a work trip. It felt like one of their far-off student sessions. They'd met as students, best friends at a time of life one could tell all. Long conversations covering everything from boyfriends to putting the world to rights. Later, of course, it was talk about the children–they'd both married and had babies in Cambridge before scrabbling their way back into the paid workforce.

After their meal, they sat with glasses of wine in the living-room. Rachel nestled in one of her big comfortable armchairs with its faded Jacobean coverings and said bluntly, 'So how are you and Kirsten, all going well?'

The question made it *just* like one of their student sessions. Lauren made a little grimace. 'I've told you she moved to Auckland for a job in a big advertising company? That makes it harder–commuting relationships aren't much fun. She gets to Wellington for work occasionally and I make sure I get up to Auckland every four or five weeks for a weekend. I book ahead and get cheap flights.' She sighed and toyed with her glass, then went on, 'It'll be great to have extended time together on this Greek holiday, though ten days isn't that long.'

Rachel looked sympathetic. 'It'll give you more of a catch-up than a weekend does. You're not thinking of moving to Auckland?'

Lauren shook her head. She wasn't. She loved her apartment, loved her network of friends–and who knew when Kirsten might move somewhere else for promotion? She'd had the same thought on Charlotte's behalf.

Rachel tactfully changed the subject. 'What did you think of the get-together?'

'Oh, I loved catching up with all those old friends–Ginny's gone mother of the bride to look at, don't you think? But still behaves like a teenager! And the research project seemed worthwhile. It was amazing to look at our college records, wasn't it? No great surprises, but it was weird to read my admission essay again–I was such a know-it-all teenager.'

'So what's changed?' said Rachel.

Lauren made as if to throw a cushion at her, then continued. 'But what about Brett Wilson funding it? I couldn't believe it. He was such a pain as a student. Just because he was tall and could turn on a big smile and lots of charm, he thought he was the cat's pyjamas. And far too self-centred to be giving money away.'

Rachel was refilling her glass. She leant over and poured more into Lauren's. 'Self-centred all right, spoilt rotten is what I'd say. You know how Charlotte was almost defending him when we were at Fitzbillies? She mightn't have been so kind if she'd known about the way he treated some of his other girlfriends.'

'What do you mean?' Lauren was puzzled.

'He hated being crossed, so sure he was always in the right. Didn't you know he beat up Barbara Bagstock when she told him she was ending the affair? He broke her nose. In those days it wasn't any use complaining to the police, they never did anything. Anyhow, he's incredibly rich now.'

'Yes, he is,' said Lauren. 'He went on to me about how great it was that the New Zealand government sold lots of assets in the eighties. Didn't have any thought that I might find it offensive. They sold off stuff cheap that had always been publicly owned–assets like railways, airlines–and my place of work.' She realised she still felt bitter about it. 'He probably bought half of them.' She was tempted to tell Rachel about the Lange plot and how Brett might have been involved. But the moment passed.

Rachel said, 'You may not be so wrong, I know he made his money wheeling and dealing on a big scale. A lucky man from a lucky country. I didn't see as much of him as you did in student days, because you Antipodeans hung together.'

Lauren laughed. 'Safety in numbers–we had to protect ourselves against your English superiority.'

Rachel refused to take the bait, and they turned to reminiscing about their lives when the children were young, and their setbacks and successes as they reentered the workforce. 'I really enjoyed my work in publishing,' said Lauren. 'My life would have been different if I'd stayed.'

'You might still have been with Rodney,' said Rachel.

'Not a hope,' said Lauren, 'I'd have worked out one way or another who I really was. Anyway, that Government Print job back in New Zealand was tempting. My mother was getting on and not very well. And it looked at that stage as if we had an exciting socialist government. Duh!'

'Oh yes, you went over to Oxford to hear your prime minister, didn't you? You came back raving about it.'

'Yes, David Lange was great. But it was soon after that that I was back in New Zealand, realising that the government was in the grip of the free marketeers. The business sector loved the Labour government. And when Lange tried to put the brakes on, wanted them to stop for a cup of tea, they hated it. That's when Brett was there.'

She'd said enough, getting onto dangerous territory. She shouldn't let the Lange thing spoil her enjoyment of talking about old times with Rachel.

'You were such a Labour stalwart in the early Thatcher years here,' Rachel mused. 'You didn't consider getting involved with politics when you got home?'

'I'll say not! I was new to the public service and took their rules about neutrality quite seriously. And I was busy outside of work–Homosexual Law Reform activism, that seemed allowable, the campaign was full of public servants. And then I was coming out myself. Whew!'

'Oh yes, your letters then–and it was letters then–were full of revelations. It sounded as if you spent your time either with the new girlfriend, or at meetings or on marches!'

Lauren sighed. 'I did and the children just got the time that was left over. They were pretty young–but Rodney was good with them. He got that job at the University of Auckland and we dispatched them up and down the North Island. Hard, but they're great grown-up people now. And life has certainly calmed down for me.'

She thought again about her privileged life. 'Julia's always saying how easy our generation had it. But I don't think we should feel guilty about it.'

Rachel agreed. 'It's not that we should have had more hardship, it's just that politicians were under the spell of right-wing economists in the eighties–over here, as well as in New Zealand. It's meant that inequality's got worse in ways we couldn't imagine.'

RACHEL RAN Lauren to the railway station late Friday afternoon. The two women hugged and waved at the turnstile and promised to keep in touch. Arriving in London, Lauren negotiated the underground, settled herself on the train for Brighton and texted Julia her arrival time.

Andrew, her son-in-law, met her. 'Julia's cooking dinner and the children are having their baths,' he explained as he drove her to their terraced house, modernized but otherwise not too different from the one Lauren had owned in Cambridge when the children were young. By the time they arrived the children were in their pyjamas and ready for bed. As soon as they saw her, they were clamouring for a story from Gran.

There was just time for Lauren to hang up her clothes in the spare room. 'Enjoy it while you can,' Julia advised. 'It won't be long before the children will want a room each. Then visitors will have to have a divan in that cubbyhole Andrew calls his study.' Andrew's study was an ongoing bone of contention. He had it stuffed full of files, and piles of books and papers on the desk that overflowed onto more piles on the floor.

'It's ridiculous,' Julia said, 'in the middle of all that mess he's got a powerful computer with a big screen, and that should be all he needs. A lot of their investigative work is done online now, and he should keep electronic files, not paper ones.' Andrew was a forensic accountant. He worked for a government office concerned with white collar crime, especially tax fraud, and lots of his work could be done from home. Julia went on, 'Look at me, I'm an academic and all I need is the kitchen table to work on.'

Lauren murmured sympathetically but took care not to take sides. The children scrambled for space on her lap and argued about which book their Gran should read.

It was a busy weekend. On Saturday it was amusement for the children, starting with the beach. 'I know, I know,' said Julia, 'you think Brighton's not a beach. All stones and deck chairs for hire, not like New Zealand's long empty strands with their wild surf. But if it's all you've got...' In the afternoon they drove to Middle Farm, where the children enjoyed petting lambs, calves and a pony ride.

Sunday was for the visitor to choose, and Lauren decided on Charleston farmhouse, home of the Bloomsbury artists Vanessa Bell and Duncan Grant. She loved the way they had decorated any available surfaces, walls, doors and furniture. And she enjoyed the walled garden, with its sculptures, mosaic pavements and tile-edged pools, its flower gardens a riot of colour. Inherited wealth, she mused, had the advantage of giving talent and innovation an opportunity to flourish. The children were not troubled by any such speculation. They liked running around the garden, but more especially the tea room.

By Sunday evening, Adam and Tamsin were tired. They were giggling foolishly in bursts at a private joke, rolling their eyes, hands over their mouths. In the coming week Tamsin would stay home from child care and together she and Lauren would pick up Adam from school. Lauren did wonder if she was still up to nursemaiding, but she pushed the thought away.

At dinner Andrew said, 'Has Julia asked you about the Cambridge event? That was the reason you came over, wasn't it?'

Lauren thought what an annoyingly nice man he was, as she helped herself to a serving of Julia's ratatouille. Not who she would have picked. She had reckoned Julia needed someone more exciting. Accountancy never looked like the most interesting profession, but perhaps forensic accountants were another breed.

She told Andrew about the College project, and mentioned Brett, the 'great man' who was responsible for her trip. She made no secret of her surprise that Brett was imposing his name on the college library.

'You wouldn't want a building named after you, would you, Andrew? Don't you think that's really arrogant, given that it's a women's college?'

'I should be so lucky,' he said, helping himself from the large dish of brown rice while Julia shushed the children.

'How do they get to be so bloody rich, anyhow?' Lauren asked.

Andrew laughed. 'He's probably on file with us. We have a wall of filing cabinets that we call "the ones that got away". Practically every one of those billionaires has something shady, but we can't usually track it down—they're protected by shells, hedges, small ex-colonial jurisdictions. That's just the UK citizens. Then there's all the Eastern European oligarchs and so forth from a bit later.'

'Brett's Australian, but he's lived in England forever—went to Cambridge here when I was a student and never went home. He had family money to play with. He boasted to me that he bought New Zealand assets in the eighties. He may not have done anything unlawful, but he was certainly one of the vultures hanging about when we foolishly sold the family silver. Sorry about the mixed metaphor,' she finished.

'It's not a bad metaphor,' said Andrew. 'A lot of them did hang about–and birds do like shiny things–and even if they weren't on the wrong side of the law, they often had offsiders who were. After dinner I don't mind having a look in the study. I can't tell you confidential stuff, but there might be something there.'

Meal over and cleared away, children in bed, Lauren and Julia settled themselves in the living room. Lauren declined rooibos in favour of conventional tea. Andrew disappeared into the cubby hole and emerged twenty minutes later holding a wodge of papers. 'Well, how about this,' he said. 'Brett Wilson was one of the tycoons investigated when the government held its enquiry into money laundering, remember–about ten years back? It's all in the public domain. These are news clippings, so you can have all this, they're spare copies. We have everything online at the office now, I just haven't got round to tidying up here.'

Julia rolled her eyes as he handed Lauren the papers. 'Like I say, he's in our category of the ones that got away–so squeaky clean it's suspicious. Nothing on him, but I'd bet my last dollar that an awful lot of spring cleaning went on to make it look like that. Now he can afford to be philanthropic–he won't even miss what he's donating to your college.'

Andrew sat down in his favourite armchair. He looked like a man who would have enjoyed a pipe and slippers. He went on, 'Nothing necessarily wrong with getting rich. But it too often involves not paying taxes–that's my agency's business. And the constant mergers and acquisitions make life very hard for us, as well as for people who thought they had secure jobs.'

'Thanks, Andrew.' Lauren began reading through the reports. She was quiet for about fifteen minutes, then sighed and said, 'I don't really understand all this financial stuff. I can see I was right, though, Brett does have an interest in several New Zealand companies that used to belong to everyone. The rotten sods.'

Julia wasn't sure if her mother was cursing the Bretts of the world or the government that sold the assets. It reminded her. 'Mum, you'll have been following the coalition talks in New Zealand? Isn't it extraordinary how long it's taking Peters to make up his mind. Perhaps he won't go with National.'

'Oh, he probably will,' said her mother gloomily. 'At least I won't have time to worry about it this coming week while I'm looking after the children.'

That wasn't altogether true, Lauren made sure she looked at New Zealand news online at least once every day. By the end of the week, when she was due to fly out to Greece, she couldn't quite believe that there was still no new government. She'd enjoyed her week; time with Adam and Tamsin was precious–but she was tired, and looked forward to a real holiday.

THE RYANAIR JET touched down in Athens. It had been a good flight, despite the 4am awakening, the pre-dawn taxi to Gatwick, the hustle onto the plane and the run for the best of the unallocated seats. The cheerful cabin crew disturbed the peace by announcing football results, and trying to sell raffle tickets. Lauren had pounced on a window seat and was transfixed as Europe unfolded below her–the Channel, the flat fields of northern France and the Alps with early snow on the peaks and in the mountain valleys. Then across Italy, and the blue of the Mediterranean, and a smooth landing into Athens.

She cleared Customs and made for the exit. She did not expect Kirsten to meet her, but couldn't help scanning the small crowd of greeters. No Kirsten, of course. She found her way to the Metro, boarded and changed for Piraeus following instructions she'd printed out from the internet.

Alighting from a taxi onto the wharf, she saw Kirsten in the distance, immediately recognisable by her curly blonde hair. Crouching down, fiddling with her suitcase, she had not yet spotted Lauren, who came up behind her and tapped her on the shoulder.

Kirsten startled, turned, looked up and nearly lost her balance as she stood. They both laughed, then embraced.

'It's great to see you. Good trip?' Kirsten gave her an affectionate smile.

'Splendid outlook all the way from London. I was a bit nervous about getting to here from the airport but it all went smoothly. How about you?'

'I'm still jet lagged. Bali was a hoot. Got to Athens yesterday morning and fitted in some sightseeing. But the hotel was noisy and I couldn't sleep with the time difference. Now with sea air, four hours on the ferry, I can snooze on your shoulder.' She poked Lauren playfully. 'And then of course there's one way we can ensure a good night's sleep.'

'What on earth could you be talking about?' Lauren pretended ignorance.

'Snuggles,' smirked Kirsten. They batted each other again and Lauren started to relax. Kirsten seemed in a good mood. It was going to be a good holiday.

A boom from the ship's funnel and they made their way towards the gangway. It was a sizeable ship and once inside Lauren was reminded of the Cook Strait ferry, except there were Greek families loaded with shopping and a table full of Orthodox priests nearby, with their long black garments and faces hidden behind beards.

The sailing was smooth and the pair caught up on news. 'The others went across yesterday. They'll have got themselves established in the rental. They were going to hire a car, too,' Kirsten said.

The island came in sight, the intense blue of the harbour contrasting with the city's white buildings sprawling up a hill, an ancient Greek temple on the headland, a glimpse of mountains behind glowing red in the setting sun.

Kathy met them at the wharf. They piled into the small car, and she drove them carefully through the streets busy with pedestrians. The Airbnb on the outskirts of the city looked exactly as pictured. Kathy unloaded their bags onto the doorstep.

'The others are at the beach for sunset and I said I'll join them. I'll leave you two to get reacquainted.'

'This must be our room,' said Kirsten. They'd looked through the house, comfortably large and modern, four bedrooms, three with rumpled bedding, clothes, books and suitcases spread out. Theirs was at the end of the hallway, a huge bed with a blue and white bedspread. The room was dim and Lauren opened the shutters, revealing a terrace outside and a glimpse of sand and sea beyond. It was suburban, but neighbours not too close. Kirsten came to stand beside her, and Lauren closed the shutters again. They kissed, tentatively at first, then more sensuously and a hunger grew in Lauren. It had been so long, and she'd had her doubts, but here they were and everything felt right.

Kirsten pulled her towards the bed, they stripped the cover off and plunged in between the crisp white sheets. Lips, breasts, limbs, stroking, Lauren reached a pitch of arousal very quickly. When it was over, they laughed at their urgency. 'I can see you've been on the straight and narrow, too,' Lauren teased. Kirsten smiled, though Lauren sensed a cloud passing, a slight awkwardness. She wondered what that was about. But they held each other and Lauren drifted into a doze.

She felt someone shake her. 'We have to get up!' Kirsten kissed her again all over. 'Jump to, we're expected for drinks. Let's get dressed and wander down to the beach.'

LATER, Lauren recalled it as a magic holiday, a holiday out of time. Naxos was so much more than a tourist place of beaches and bars. Their group explored the whole island. The small farms looked as if the land had been worked in the same way for centuries. Villages had winding passages with turnings made for people and donkeys, just about impassable by car. Churches made from rough-hewn stonework fitted seamlessly into the landscape. And the early Greek ruins were so different and marvellous that they might have been constructed by a race of gods. Their ten days flew by and at the same time stretched out for years.

Lauren enjoyed getting to know the group. There was one woman she found irritating, though. It was a shame that Kirsten was particularly friendly with her. Bee seemed to talk about nothing but clothes and décor and money. She was also obsessive about fitness, an annoying characteristic in Lauren's view. On their last day in Naxos things came to a head.

'Still no decision about our new government,' Lauren had said over lunch. She'd continued to keep up with the news.

'The Nats have been doing a good job,' said Bee, reaching for the salad. 'I for one won't mind if they stay on.' Lauren had been forthcoming about her hopes for Jacinda, and she felt as if Bee was baiting her. 'I admire John Key,' Bee carried on. 'A pity he's not standing again as prime minister. He was really supportive of netball, pretty exceptional for a guy.' (Bee had been a star player in her youth, and she wasn't shy of mentioning it.)

Lauren couldn't help herself. 'I guess he liked pulling the players' ponytails,' she said, knowing Bee would remember the strife he'd got into over pulling a waitress's ponytail.

Bee flushed and tightened her lips.

That evening, Lauren and Kirsten were strolling home through the winding lanes, both slightly tipsy after a particularly delicious dinner. Lauren was thinking about the meal, and at the same time licking the sticky sweetness of baklava off her lips. She reached for Kirsten's hand and was surprised when Kirsten moved it away.

Then Kirsten said, 'I'm disappointed at how you were hassling Bee at lunchtime.'

'I wasn't hassling her,' Lauren replied. 'Was she offended? Surely she isn't such a fan of John Key that she'd stick up for him over the ponytail thing?'

'That's not the point. It was your tone. You clearly wanted to take her down a notch. We're on holiday and you should keep your politics out of it.'

Lauren was taken aback. 'My politics? What do you mean, *my* politics? I thought they were your politics too! You've certainly changed. I thought you enjoyed working to help communities, I thought you liked doing worthwhile ad campaigns. So now you've become a fan of the Nats, have you?'

'You know that's not true–but they haven't done that badly.'

Lauren had been campaigning on behalf of Labour too long to let that go by. 'So you don't mind that people can't find houses? That they're sleeping in cars? That lots of children turn up for school hungry?' She stopped and added an insult. 'What's Auckland doing to you? Are you a Jafa? Just another fucking Aucklander!'

'That was uncalled for!' Kirsten was hurt. 'But you don't have to be so'–she hesitated and searched for a word–'so doctrinaire! So sure you're right. So patronising. Not everyone in the world has to agree with you.'

'No,' said Lauren, 'but I thought you did.' They'd been walking as they spoke, but now she stood still. Kirsten stopped too, and Lauren faced her. 'Kirsten, I've loved our holiday here, but I don't think our relationship is working well. You do seem to have changed.'

Kirsten bristled. 'Why shouldn't I change? I'm not a stick in the mud and my career is taking off. I'm enjoying Auckland and the girls have been really warm and friendly.' She waved an arm in the direction of the house as she spoke.

Lauren went silent. Both tired and tipsy–probably not a good time to discuss relationships. Not that they ever had talked about how they were doing, they'd just floated along. She swallowed. 'OK, let's forget it, it's time we went to bed. An early start in the morning.'

They walked on home silently, and once there, Lauren immediately made ready for bed. Kirsten came to bed too and reached over to touch her, a placatory gesture. Lauren moved away. She couldn't let go of her anger.

In the morning, packing up, things were awkward between them. By now, Lauren felt in a more conciliatory mood. She said to Kirsten, 'After the plane lands in Auckland, shall I put back my Auckland-Wellington flight by a day? We could have another day together and perhaps we could have a bit of a chat about where we're heading.'

But Kirsten had promised to pop into work on the Wednesday afternoon and couldn't or wouldn't change her schedule. So after the usual gruelling flight (with a pause for a few hours at Singapore) Lauren flew back to Wellington on the Wednesday morning. Nothing was sorted. She didn't know how she felt about it and she didn't know what Kirsten was thinking. Time would tell.

8

'On such a full sea are we now afloat'

The phone rang. Lauren was still asleep. She mumbled, 'Lauren here,' into the receiver and opened one eye. It was 10am.

'Welcome back.' Her friend Megan's voice. 'It's a lovely day and we're doing coffee, then spending the rest of the morning at the garden. Come along!'

'Ugh,' said Lauren. 'Jet lag, don't you hate it? Tell you what, I'll give the coffee a miss and meet you there.'

England had been turning towards autumn when she left. Now, late October, New Zealand was bursting with spring, people preparing their gardens for summer. Megan and Pam were already at the plot by the time she arrived.

'Here's a spade, we've got a bag of Rua for that patch–dig it and you'll have new potatoes by Christmas.'

Lauren took the spade and began to work along a row, loading up the soil to one side of the trench she was digging, and adding a generous amount of compost before she sowed the potatoes.

It was Pam's plot that they worked in. It was only three by four metres, but over the year, Pam produced enough vegetables for herself and several others. Her friends marvelled at her energy. She was small, wiry and tireless. The plot was often a riot of colour, marigolds round the edges to keep insects off the vegetables, borage with its tiny purple flowers, dock springing up just because it did, a lavender bush, rosemary, basil in season. The array of vegetables she grew was impressive: a row of dwarf beans, peas held up with bamboo stakes, a variety of lettuces, spinach, carrots and beet that needed thinning at just the right time, a skyscraper of an artichoke, a clump of rhubarb, a little patch of strawberries on the edge.

And the potatoes. The sun warmed Lauren's back, a blackbird hopped along pecking the ground at each turn of the spade. She breathed in the fresh air. The hours of confinement receded and the recycled air of the plane retreated from her system.

They all worked busily, but found time to chat as well. 'You're not working today?' said Lauren to Megan. 'No, I'm starting late,' said Megan cheerfully. 'Last night was a big one, I was organising a reception after the concert. People who work in the arts have funny hours.' Lauren looked at her friend affectionately. No one could grace the art scene better than Megan, with her impeccable dress sense. Even her gardening clothes were presentable.

'So, Lauren,' said Megan, pulling on a stubborn weed, 'did you realise you'd be home on the day we find out what government we're going to get?'

'I did know, but it had slipped my mind,' said Lauren. 'I kept up with the news on my phone while I was away–even when I was on holiday on Naxos. It's been a very long time to wait, hasn't it! When I went, I thought it would all be settled by the time I came back. What do you two think?'

'Goodness knows, Winston Peters is playing his cards close to his chest. Hard to believe he'll go with Labour and the Greens–never forget that he was a member of the National Party once.'

'That doesn't necessarily mean a thing.' Pam chimed in. 'After all, Roger Douglas started off as a Labour MP and ended up founding the ACT party. How far right can you get?'

It was as if a cloud swept across the sun. Lauren said, 'And he behaved as if he were already in the ACT party while he was still in Labour. That government destroyed the New Zealand we knew–we had an egalitarian society and now we don't. And it's only people of our age who know that. And what's more–'

Megan interrupted, clutching a handful of weeds. 'Steady on, Lauren, we all agree, but the campaign's over now and we're about to have a new government, of whatever stripe.'

Lauren leant on her spade, looking sheepish. 'Blame it on the jet lag if you like–but it's been on my mind–I met a bloke I used to know while I was away. The bastard got rich on New Zealand's assets, and he's just one of several. Enough of that–is it about six thirty that Winston Peters will be doing the great reveal?'

'It is,' said Pam, 'and a few of us thought we should watch together. Haven't sorted out where yet.'

'Can it be at my place?' said Lauren. 'I don't know that I feel up to going out this evening.'

'Sure,' said Megan, 'we'll come early, about quarter to six. We'll make it a pot luck–nibbles before the speech, dinner afterwards. Rowie will come and so will Sally and Rebecca. And Pam of course.' She glanced at the small figure bent over a tray of seedlings. 'Don't you do anything, there's sure to be enough food.'

ABOUT SIX THIRTY, the six of them were gathered in Lauren's apartment in front of the television. Lauren winked at Ro when she came in the door, whispering that there was much to tell and she'd speak to her later. She made drinks for everyone, wondering whether after the speech they'd be quaffing champagne or needing a stiff whisky. Reporters were rhubarbing as they waited for Winston Peters to emerge; Lauren muted the channel. Finally the camera showed him walking along to the Beehive theatrette and stepping up to the podium. Lauren waved the remote and brought up the sound.

Ro was holding forth and didn't seem to notice.

'Shh,' said Megan and they settled. Winston began, thanking both parties for their maturity during the negotiations, saying his whole party made the decision, and mentioning that he'd been in coalition twice before. He talked about assumptions made by journalists during the campaign about what his party would do, and how people thought he might go with Labour and the Greens, but that was mere speculation and his party was never consulted.

'Oh no,' groaned Ro, 'he's going with National.'

'Shh!' said Pam. Winston was now saying that he thought New Zealanders wanted change.

'It'll be Labour,' shouted Ro.

'Be quiet,' Lauren said, 'Listen!' Then Winston amazed them by arguing that many New Zealanders had come to view today's capitalism not as their friend but their foe. And saying they were not all wrong.

Pam gasped. 'He's saying capitalism isn't working!'

'I don't believe it,' said Sally. She and Rebecca were a couple both immersed in trade union activities.

Winston continued briefly, then said quietly that his party chose a coalition government with Labour.

Any questions from the reporters on the screen were drowned out by the babble of voices in Lauren's living room. So exciting, fantastic, wow, good on Jacinda, amazing! The exclamations rubbed up against, overpowered, drowned one another out. They were hugging and jumping up and down, an absurd gaggle of older women.

Pam said more soberly, 'I hope they don't muff this chance. We need to get that pie cut into even pieces.'

'What?' They all looked at her.

'The pie chart, it's astonishing! One percent of New Zealanders own a quarter of the wealth and the bottom forty percent own less than two percent.'

'That's why I got involved in politics this time,' said Lauren.

Sally interrupted, 'That was pretty surprising, wasn't it, when Winston said capitalism isn't working.'

Ro frowned. 'It was great, but scary.'

'How come scary?' Sally looked doubtful.

'Because all those people who benefit from the status quo will be massing again. The way they did when they thought Lange was going to upset the apple cart.'

Ro couldn't really put a dampener on the gathering. They talked over one another about what might be fixed, and how quickly, as they ate their meal. When they were leaving, Lauren said to Ro, 'Can I drop by tomorrow?'

'Sure,' said Ro. 'I'll be working at home. Come over mid-afternoon. It'll be good to catch up.'

WHEN LAUREN ARRIVED, she had to call out twice before Ro emerged from her study. 'Sorry,' she said, 'I was miles away–desperately trying to get the book off.'

'Oh?' said Lauren. 'I thought it was due while I was away?'

'It was.' Ro groaned. 'But I didn't meet the publisher's deadline so I'm on borrowed time. I've just *got* to get it in before the end of the month. The Lange plot was a major distraction and I've just come back from the summer conference circuit in the States.'

'Of course,' said Lauren, 'I was cavorting in Greece while you were heads down with your scholarly friends.'

Ro grinned. 'Not all heads down. Why do you think conferences are still so popular in this digital age? The Berkshire one was really fun this year. We were at Hofstra on Long Island. The surroundings felt quite decadent, though not quite *The Great Gatsby*. I did put in time on the book when I could.'

'I'll bet! Well,' –Lauren paused, 'I've found out more about Brett Wilson. You thought he might fill us in on some of the wheelers and dealers at the time. It's better–or worse–than that; I'm starting to think he could have been involved. It's hard to believe, though.'

Lauren told Ro about her meetings with Brett, and what Rachel and then Andrew had said about him. Ro listened intently. 'I told you he was one of the biggies, didn't I,' she said. She smirked. 'So now we know: he was personable but self-centred, had a nasty temper when crossed, really into making money, and good at hiding his tracks.'

'Yes,' said Lauren. 'But that could apply to a lot of the business people around at the time. Much as I hate the thought of socializing with him, I hope I'll find out more by having agreed to meet his wife.'

'I'm sure you will, Lauren, you're good at social chit-chat.'

Lauren screwed up her face and said, 'It doesn't mean I enjoy it.' She sighed, and absentmindedly stroked the cat that had just jumped on her lap. 'What shall we do next on the Driscoll angle? We need to get up to speed on that.'

'You should hear from your neighbour soon, shouldn't you?' Ro seemed reconciled to Lauren having talked to Phyl about the plot.

'I'll remind her,' said Lauren, 'and meanwhile I've got other things on my mind.' She needed to mend fences with Kirsten, but she didn't mention that to Ro.

9

'A very pleasing night to honest men'

Lauren walked into Whistling Sisters and pushed through the Friday night crowd jostling around the downstairs bar. She spotted a Rainbow Wellington sign pointing up to the first floor. This was their end of year gathering and the one meeting a year Lauren made sure to attend. It was where she caught up with gays and lesbians she had known working in the public service. She was relieved to park the Lange affair, with its troubling complications, in exchange for an evening that promised to be convivial.

At the top of the stairs the noisy group spilled out of a function room. Lauren made her way through towards the drinks table, nodding at a few people as she went. She began to wish she had come with a friend. Many of the faces were younger and unfamiliar and those she recognised so far were not people she knew well. Mostly they had been junior colleagues.

It was nearly time to be seated. The MC, camping it up in a band-leader's costume covered with spangles and silver stars, began to call out names from a list and hand people name badges with table numbers on them. This was a new way to allocate seating, Lauren thought. It helped when you didn't know where to put yourself, which was what she was starting to feel.

Lauren's badge said Table Six. She found a seat next to a man who looked African, who was wearing a colourful shirt. He welcomed her with a wide smile.

'Hi,' she said, 'I'm Lauren. And you are...?'

'Kiano.' Tall and lean, he towered over her even when seated.

'I love your shirt. Is it a dashiki?'

Kiano inclined his head with a smile. 'Yes, how clever of you. Have you spent time in Africa?'

'Just once, years ago. A work trip to Nairobi, it was very brief. But when I could get out, I wandered through the markets. I loved the fabrics. And the jewellery.' She nodded at Kiano's hands. An ornate silver ring glinted on the fourth finger of his left hand and silver chain bracelets adorned both wrists.

'I'm hoping that Michael is assigned the same table,' Kiano said, fingering the ring. 'We've just arrived in Wellington and I know hardly anyone.'

'I'm sure that won't last. People are friendly here. And it's good to brave social gatherings like this. What brings you to Wellington?'

'Michael is a Kiwi. We've been together twelve years.' Lauren thought she could discern a blush suffusing his dark skin. 'I'm Kenyan but we were living all over Africa. I met him on a development project in Burkina Faso, but most recently we were in Cape Town. Michael's just retired. I saw a job that would suit me with your Ministry of Foreign Affairs and Trade, so it seemed a good idea to return him to New Zealand.' His eyes sparkled. 'I'm a bit of a fish out of water, though.'

'I'm sure your knowledge of Africa would be snapped up in Foreign Affairs.' Lauren liked the man, she decided. There was something about him, direct and honest.

There was little time for more conversation before others joined their table. Some of them Lauren knew, so the drought was broken. A man who was once Lauren's subordinate sat down on her other side, greeting her warmly. Two exes who were allocated seats next to each other attracted a lot of teasing, especially when someone noticed that their current partners, no love lost between them, also ended up next to each other at a nearby table.

Once they were all settled, conversation flowed easily. The new government had been sworn in just the day before. There was speculation about the raft of new ministers, mostly inexperienced. This was a subject of intense interest to many in the room. Senior public servants would be working with ministers directly.

The man on Lauren's left said, 'So Winston Peters has got himself Deputy PM, the wily old fox.'

'I doubt he'll ever be called to act as PM for any length of time, though. Jacinda would want to keep her eye on things,' said a woman from across the table.

'What about Andrew Little? I'm sure he'll do well as a minister. He may have been an unimpressive leader but what a great queen-maker.' Someone whooped at the unintended double-entendre.

Lauren chimed in. 'That was splendid of Little to stand aside, there's not many leaders prepared to do that.' Her mind darted to their investigation–if a leader won't stand aside, you don't try to kill them. She wanted to find out everyone who was involved, but it was so frustratingly slow, no wonder she had never been drawn to research. She made an effort and pulled herself back to the present. Someone else, world-weary, cynical, or just an experienced government-watcher was saying, 'The next thing there'll be lots of strikes. All those pent-up demands. They knew it was a waste of time striking under the Nats but Labour is more sympathetic, they'll find it hard to say no. There'll be lots of unrest.'

Everyone had an opinion and the voices got louder. As a newcomer to the country Kiano hadn't said much, just listened with interest. Then he said quietly to Lauren, 'We'd better ask Michael what he thinks. He'll have an insider view.'

'Really?' Lauren wasn't sure what he meant.

'He was a young Labour MP in the eighties, won a safe seat in the Wellington area. Petone, I think it was called.' He stumbled over the unfamiliar name and looked questioningly at Lauren, who nodded.

'He didn't get as far as being a minister. There were a lot of old hands around, not like now. But he did hold associate roles, I believe, mostly to do with overseas aid. That's where he got interested in development work.'

'What's his surname?' Lauren asked.

'Peston, Michael Peston.'

'That does ring a bell.' What a lucky break, thought Lauren. Maybe he'd be able to tell her more about the atmosphere around the Beehive at the time. He may have heard whispers about the plot. She thought hard. He must have known Kevin Driscoll, too, perhaps even worked closely with him. Ugh, fancy having that sod as a colleague.

A free-for-all began, with dessert and coffee arriving at a side table and people changing places to sit with friends. Kiano brought Michael over and sat him next to Lauren. A man in his late sixties, she guessed, balding with reddish curly hair and a freckly tanned skin somewhat the worse for wear. Too much sun, Lauren thought. He was nicely dressed in a dark green shirt, black jeans and wore a ring that matched Kiano's. He did look vaguely familiar. She would have seen photos of him as a younger man in the public eye.

'Nice to meet you, Lauren.' They started to chat and Michael talked about their decision to make New Zealand their home. He had reservations after so many years away. 'I loved Africa. It was such a wrench to leave. New Zealand has always seemed so dull in comparison.'

'I know what you mean.' Michael had said exactly what Lauren had always thought. 'I lived in the UK from university days on into my thirties. I was completely ambivalent about coming home. New Zealand seemed small and stultifying, stuck at the end of the world. But it's really not the same place now and I've fallen in love with Wellington. Coolest little capital, gay-friendly, such a lively arts scene, great coffee. I'm sure you'll find your feet.'

Michael explained that he and Kiano were renting an apartment in the central city while looking around for somewhere to buy. His sister, recently widowed, still lived in Lower Hutt. He looked forward to spending time with her and taking an interest in her grandchildren who often stayed with her. 'I missed out on seeing my niece and nephew grow up, so I can have the pleasure of taking an interest in the next generation.'

'What sort of place are you looking for?' Lauren asked. 'I hope you're not going to be one of those retirees who escape up the coast.'

'We have looked up there. I want a garden and the climate is better. But it's a long way for Kiano to commute and we want to enjoy the city life. There's a place we're considering in Hataitai. It's just within our budget. The garden has potential even though the section is hilly, and the house is roomy with great views over Evans Bay. A bit dilapidated, but I've got plenty of time for renovating.'

'And the neighbours aren't in your face,' chipped in Kiano, 'so when I get going on the sax they won't be banging on the door.'

'Sounds wonderful,' Lauren said, 'You'd be just down the road from me. Make sure it's watertight though. I had a friend who bought there and found that the southerlies bring horizontal rain, so it was a constant battle with water getting under the eaves.'

'Good point,' said Michael, digging Kiano in the ribs, 'I'll get the lad to crawl up there when we take another look at it next week.'

Coffee over, a band started up and tables were cleared for a dance floor. Lauren decided to leave and began to say her goodbyes. She was about to tell Michael that she would like to talk to him about his time in government, when he said, 'Take my card. We're having drinks this Sunday, part of our getting-to-know-people mission. Six o'clock on. Do you know the Seiko apartments? Just one street back from Clyde Quay.'

THE COCKTAIL PARTY at Michael and Kiano's was lively. Lauren had persuaded Pam to come with her and there was a sprinkling of people she knew slightly. It wasn't a large apartment and the place was crammed. The guys seemed to have been doing their networking efficiently. She guessed that some were new colleagues of Kiano. They had that public servant off the leash look.

After cocktails, which were strong enough to go to Lauren's head immediately, Kiano picked up his sax and Michael sat down at a compact keyboard in a corner of the room. They launched into 'Graceland', Michael riffing on the piano with a drumbeat set in the background. Then Kiano joined in, a quick succession of notes pouring off his instrument followed by a mellow jazzy solo.

'Wow,' Pam shouted into Lauren's ear, 'You do know how to pick them.' The song was one of Lauren's favourites and she pulled Pam into the small space where people were already moving rhythmically. It was fun, she felt much more like dancing than in the bigger crowd at the Rainbow function. The men played a few more numbers and then put down their instruments despite hand clapping from the group. Kiano bowed dramatically and said 'It's great to be here and I hope you'll all become friends.'

Lauren hoped so too; she liked them both. But she still hadn't managed to approach Michael about getting his take on the eighties. The party hadn't been the right place to bring it up.

ON MONDAY MORNING Lauren felt seedy. She cleared her breakfast things and decided to ask Phyl if she could take Monty for a walk. Fresh air would help. She was strolling along Oriental Bay with Monty on a leash when who should she run into but Michael, walking in the opposite direction. 'Well, hello,' he said, 'Who have we here?' as he bent down to pat the dog, who responded by jumping up enthusiastically.

'Down, boy,' Lauren said. 'He's being naughty. But he's anybody's. Anyhow, what are you doing? Clearing your head after last night?'

'Yes, this is my usual beat. But I needed this morning's walk more than usual.' He smiled at her.

'Me too,' said Lauren 'It was a great party, but I do take longer to recover than I used to. Why don't we have coffee, I'm sure that would help.'

Lauren often patronised a beachfront café nearby, where owners and their dogs were welcome at the outside tables. Its northerly aspect caught the sun, making it pleasantly warm. Michael went in and ordered for them both. Monty shuffled around a bit, then curled up into a contented heap.

After some brief chat about Wellington's housing market, Lauren got to the point. 'You looked familiar when we met at Rainbow Wellington. Kiano said you'd been an MP in the eighties. When I came back to New Zealand in 1985, I was with Government Print. Initially, at least, until they sold it from under us. I must have seen your photo in the newspapers but I don't think we met in person? Though we may have, it was a long time ago.'

Michael shifted uncomfortably in his seat. 'It was a pretty hard time for me, Lauren. I don't really talk about it. I came into Parliament a young man on fire, an idealist, and then found myself in the most dreadful atmosphere around the Lange-Douglas quarrel. I stuck it out till the end of the second term and then I bailed.'

Lauren nodded, encouraging him to go on. Damn, it might be quite hard to get anything out of him. He seemed more at ease when he talked about his subsequent career.

'I met a lot of people involved in development through political oversight of New Zealand's aid programme. So when I left Parliament I got a job with an international aid organisation. It wasn't the traditional way of missions, "helping poor people in Africa" '–he made quotation marks with his fingers–'raising money for food and clothing and so on. Development projects were undergoing an exciting phase, becoming politics in action. They gave me the opportunity to do the sorts of things I'd wanted to do when I got elected. And as well, I learned to love Africa.'

Michael had a faraway look in his eyes. Lauren was impressed by his fervour. She found herself drawn to the man; she thought they could be friends. But it was going to be hard to get anything out of him. She took a deep breath and plunged in. 'Michael, you say you're not keen on recalling your time in politics. I understand that, but I'm on a bit of a mission.'

Michael looked wary. 'And what would that be?'

Lauren began to tell him about her friend Ro's work on women of the fourth Labour government. He winced, but signalled her to go on. 'It's strange to realise that the times you went through are now history,' he remarked. 'Though it doesn't always feel that way. Anyhow, what is it about your friend's work that has you on a mission?'

Lauren had by now decided Michael's reluctance to recall those times meant that he was certainly a man to keep their secret. She went on to tell him about Ro's discovery and how she had been reluctantly drawn into Ro's investigation.

Michael looked more and more uncomfortable. He heard her out, then said nothing. His knuckles were white as he gripped his coffee cup. 'So....' He paused, seeming to struggle with himself. 'OK, Lauren,' he said. 'I might have something for you. I do hate to talk about that time but Kiano's been nagging me. He reckons that I need to make peace with the past or I'll find it hard to settle down here.' He looked thoughtful. 'Kiano says that perhaps I should go to a counsellor, but hey, Lauren, if you really do want to drag me through these memories, I'm willing to have a go.'

'That's really kind of you,' said Lauren. 'Can't say I've ever pretended to be a counsellor. People tell me I get impatient when other people run on about their problems.'

Michael laughed, this time genuinely. 'We're the perfect match, then. I don't want anyone to ask me how I'm feeling and you don't want to supply the tissues.'

'Quite so.' Lauren laughed too. 'Can we talk further on Thursday? I'm free then if you are.' They arranged a time, and both carried on with their walks in opposite directions.

As LAUREN GOT home from the library later that afternoon, juggling a pile of books and her door key, Phyl stepped out from next door.

'I've just heard from Deirdre, she's back in New Zealand,' she said. 'And I've got news. How about you take Monty for another walk tomorrow afternoon and then come in for a cuppa?'

'Thank you, Phyl, I'm dying to know whether the police thought there was a plot.' She paused, looked hopeful. Phyl ignored the look. 'Tomorrow then,' she said and she bustled back inside.

10

'Make me acquainted with your cause of grief'

Monty had a shorter walk than usual the next afternoon. When they returned Lauren seated herself at the dining table where Phyl had cleared a space, taking care not to break the jigsaw she was working on.

'What is it this time?' said Lauren, peering at it upside down.

'Just another sailing ship,' said Phyl. 'They're fun to do, all that sea and sky is a challenge.' She put their mugs of tea on the table, and sat down opposite Lauren. Lauren looked at her expectantly.

'Deirdre's turned up trumps,' said Phyl. 'She was always one of my best staff. She'll make police commissioner some time. She'll be the first Māori woman to get there.' She smiled and for a moment Lauren thought she was going to get a tale about Deirdre, but no.

'First, I must apologise. I probably put you wrong about Lange's flat nearly catching fire. That did happen and the Diplomatic Protection Squad was called. It turned out Lange had taken a sleeping pill and fallen asleep so heavily in his armchair that he didn't smell the smoke from a pot he'd left on the stove. The investigation went no further.'

'No need to apologise.' Lauren sounded flat. 'We haven't got far enough yet to be put on the wrong track.'

'The real story,' Phyl continued, 'was that he was having constant bouts of pain over a number of months. His staff noticed and were worried. He'd break out in sweats and was obviously suffering, but he always brushed it aside when anyone asked him if he was all right.'

'Yes?'

'In the end he got desperate enough to take himself to hospital. He'd dismissed a suggestion that it might be angina because of where he had the pain but the hospital said that's what it was. An angio-plasty fixed it.'

'Oh,' said Lauren, slumping in her chair, 'so there was nothing suspicious about any of those episodes either?'

'Yes, there was.' Phyl paused. 'They took blood samples and found he had poison in his system.'

'Poison?' Lauren sat up straight again. 'Judith Butler thought Kevin might have slipped something into his drink. What sort of poison?' She was all ears.

'Deirdre said it was aconite–I was surprised when she told me; police often want to keep a few details back to throw at a suspect if they're interviewing someone.'

'But is aconite a poison? I thought it was some kind of herb.'

'Deirdre said it's a herb often used in alternative medicine.' Phyl wrinkled her nose, she didn't hold with such nonsense. 'Harmless in small doses but it's a poison if you have too much.'

'A poison if you have too much?' Lauren echoed.

'Yes, so the hospital referred their findings to the police and that's the question that's never been solved. They couldn't work out how it got into his system. Its effect was masked by his other problems but the aconite was enough to make him sick on its own and much more would have killed him.'

'Extraordinary, and it was all hushed up? But if it was Kevin, how would he have got hold of aconite, and how on earth would he get it into Lange's system?'

They sat at the table, talking around the topic, speculating to little effect. When Lauren went back to her apartment, she googled 'aconite' but that wasn't much help. An old-fashioned method of poisoning, seldom used these days, even though widely available and very potent in powdered form. A few cases were described on the internet but nothing very useful. Lauren wondered why it would have occurred to anyone at the hospital to test for aconite.

She wandered about her apartment, fretting. Her meeting with Michael the next day wasn't likely to throw up anything in particular, but it would be useful background. She wondered if she should tell him about Kevin and aconite, but perhaps that wasn't wise. She hadn't thought to ask Phyl about confidentiality.

ON THURSDAY MICHAEL arrived early for their appointment, and Lauren ushered him into the living room. He wandered around, admiring the spectacular view and her renovations. He was clearly quite tense, so Lauren steered him to a comfortable chair and they both sat down. Then she said, 'Let's get on with it, shall we, then you can relax.'

Lauren had expected Michael to describe the tensions within the government at the time, but what she got was surprising. As a gay man Michael had struggled with being in the closet. 'It wasn't a secret to my close colleagues,' he said, 'but no one spoke about it and gay male sex was illegal when I first got into Parliament.' He shifted in his seat.

'The Colin Moyle affair was still raw. When Muldoon was PM, he had used parliamentary privilege to say that the opposition MP was "picked up by the police for homosexual activities". It was an era when media did not revel in digging up stories about politicians and their personal affairs, and Muldoon was widely despised for it, but it resulted in Moyle's resignation.'

'That was so disgusting,' said Lauren. 'And ironic, when you consider that 'Piggy' Muldoon was known to have a roving eye–and hand. Not that that got into the newspapers.'

She chuckled. 'I wasn't here then, but a friend wrote and said one of the feminist groups had pasted up around the city a fake newspaper billboard that said 'Rooting Pig Caught in Ngaio: PM Safe.'

Michael gave a wan smile, but she could tell he was reliving what happened to him when he was in Parliament.

~

HE WAS WALKING along to his office in the old Parliament Buildings when someone called out through an open door, 'Have you got a minute?'

Kevin Driscoll! Michael had no time for him, and couldn't imagine what he wanted. 'Sure,' he said and stepped inside. Kevin began with chitchat, the weather and polite inquiries about how Michael was. Michael wondered where the conversation was going, Kevin couldn't care less about him. He eyed Kevin's unfortunate blue suit and ill-chosen tie with distaste. Kevin rubbed the back of his neck, awkwardly adjusting his collar.

'You voted for the Homosexual Law Reform Act, didn't you?'

'Sure,' said Michael. 'I remember you didn't.'

Kevin was one of the few Labour members who'd voted with MPs like Norman Jones who notoriously told homosexuals to "go back in the sewers where you come from".

'I can see why you would,' Kevin said, with some distaste. 'You're good mates with Don Shepherd, aren't you?' Michael thought of Don, who was so camp it was ludicrous to think of him as married, though he was in a marriage of convenience.

Kevin leant back in his chair, crossed his legs and continued. 'It's surprising that the newspapers haven't picked up on Don and his little friends. It wouldn't look good if it got out, would it?'

'If what got out?' said Michael.

'Oh, that whole scene.' Kevin wiped his hand across his mouth. He veered off onto a different subject. 'Important vote coming up in caucus on Monday, isn't it. Lange should stop trying to put the brakes on. He needs to realise caucus is behind Roger, wants the economic programme to go ahead.'

'I don't think the whole of caucus is behind Roger,' retorted Michael. 'I'm not. I think Roger has lost sight of what Labour stands for. Those reforms

are causing a lot of distress to the very people who voted us in. Anyway, I haven't time for this, Kevin, I've things to do.' He turned to leave. He wondered what the little prick was up to, he didn't trust him as far as he could kick him.

Kevin's voice stopped him in mid-stride. 'Have a look at this before you leave. I don't think you should be so gung-ho about voting with Lange.'

Michael turned round. Kevin was holding out a photo. Michael took it. He could hardly believe his eyes. The photo caught him on a footpath. He was facing another man, holding both his hands and leaning forward. Behind, Don Shepherd was smiling at them both. It looked as if Michael was about to kiss the guy. Closer up, he could see it was taken outside The Oaks, one of the city's gay bars. 'How dare you,' he said. 'You little rat! Where did you get this? Who took it?'

'Never mind,' said Kevin. You wouldn't like it to get out, would you?'

'The press doesn't report this stuff.'

'They do if someone mentions it in Parliament.' Michael's mind went back to Colin Moyle.

Kevin was relentless. 'You wouldn't like your electorate committee chair or secretary or any of those old ladies in your electorate who do all that work for you to see copies of this, and more shots like it.'

Michael froze. His entire body had turned to ice. Then he shook himself. He said again, 'You dirty little rat.' He stood up and walked out of the office. As he did, he heard Kevin: 'Say what you like. Just make sure you vote the right way.'

TELLING LAUREN, he'd relived that meeting moment by moment. Lauren couldn't believe her ears. Kevin Driscoll again. Attempted murder. Now blackmail. She could hardly contain herself. 'Gosh, that was heavy. So what did you do?'

'What could I do?' Michael buried his head in his hands, then looked up again. 'Homosexuality wasn't a crime any longer, but I'd been living in the closet for so long. I was too scared to come out. I was happy to support Fran Wilde's Homosexual Law Reform bill, but I just couldn't bring myself to say I was gay. Cowardly, I know.'

'Those times were so different. Really hard for a public figure like you. Compared to you, I had it easy. Hugely disruptive for my family, but when I was coming out the tide was turning and there was much more acceptance. I can hardly imagine how difficult it must have been for you.'

'I'm ashamed now at my lack of courage.' Michael rubbed his face. 'I voted against my principles. It was humiliating.'

'But did your vote make a crucial difference?' Lauren wondered.

'Not necessarily,' replied Michael. 'That wasn't the point. There was terrible tension right through Cabinet and the caucus at that time. I was a Lange supporter and sceptical about Rogernomics, but many in the Parliamentary party saw it as the only way forward. Lange's hesitation was completely appropriate, in my view, as Douglas got more and more extreme and ideological. Of course the Douglas crowd mostly got what they wanted, and then they forced Lange out. End of the fourth Labour government, which I'd been so proud to serve in, to begin with.'

He slumped in the chair. Lauren thought it best not to try to comfort him, so she gave him a moment to recover and then said, 'Tell me more about the blackmail.'

Michael sat up again. 'There's not much more to say about Kevin, he threatened me only the once but I could tell that he was keeping an eye on the way I voted. There was no further conversation, I just knuckled down. I was really worried that the way I voted would affect my relationship with Lange, but he was such a good man.'

'How so?'

'He called me into his office late one afternoon soon after I'd voted against him. He had been something of a mentor to me and I expected him to give me a real bollocking, but he was so nice about it. He said that he understood how people could be convinced by Rogernomics, it's just that he thought it was all going too far and too fast.'

Michael got up and looked out of Lauren's window again. Then he turned to her. 'I was embarrassed because of course I wasn't convinced by the economics either, I was just scared for my own reputation and for my seat in Parliament. In any event, when the term expired I didn't stand again, I was so devastated by what had been going on.

'It's amazing that you think there was a plot to kill Lange, though,' he continued. 'The day Lange called me in, he seemed quite cheerful, even offered me a drink.'

Lauren was surprised. 'I thought Lange didn't drink?'

Michael was recovering himself. He laughed. 'On that occasion, he was sipping a glass of some ghastly looking greeny concoction. I thought for a moment that's what he was offering me! I must have looked horrified. He told me not to worry, he wasn't going to share it with anyone, it was a tonic one of his constituents sent him every week.'

Lauren stiffened. 'A tonic he drank every day?'

'That's what he implied. Poor sod, he had a lot of pain, his gut, I think, and he said he thought the tonic helped. You know his father was the local GP?'

Lauren nodded.

'Lange said the woman was famous for her concoctions, and his father used to point patients in her direction.' Michael smiled at the memory. 'Then he went on to offer me a choice of drinks from the liquor cabinet. It was a myth that he didn't drink. His cabinet was quite well stocked and we each had a whisky and chatted about how things were going for me. He never tried to persuade me to change my views. That's the thing about Lange, he was never an ordinary politician. He wasn't a hustler, didn't put pressure on people to support him. The tonic can't have been that good, though, he did go downhill in the next few months and often looked quite unwell. It was a terribly stressful time.'

'Must have been.' Lauren agreed absently. 'Michael, who did you say gave Lange the tonic?'

Michael looked surprised. 'One of his constituents–his father had a lot of time for her. In fact, now I think about it, it was the ghastly

Kevin's mother. Not that Lange called him the ghastly Kevin. Though I bet he preferred the mother to Kevin.'

LAUREN WAS BACK in her apartment, thinking over the interview. She couldn't believe her luck. Never mind Michael's description of the general atmosphere, he'd implicated Kevin in blackmail and shown how aconite could have got into Lange's system. All the pieces added up. If Kevin's mother was the herbalist who sent Lange bottles of tonic, Kevin could have spiked one of them with deadly quantities of aconite.

It seemed unlikely that his mother had helped to prepare the spiked medicine, but that couldn't be entirely discounted. Surely she wouldn't have colluded with her son in a plot to kill Lange? She might not have cared about economic ideology, but perhaps she was motivated to do something to help her son. And to lie for him if there had been wrongdoing? She'd broken the law before, Lauren remembered: the abortion prosecution. But that was to help women in need.

Lauren was going to Auckland the next weekend, the first time since her return from Naxos. She decided she would visit Kevin Driscoll's mother. She phoned and a woman answered, identifying herself as Gwen Driscoll. Her voice was a little quavery but she sounded alert.

'Mrs Driscoll, it's Lauren Fraser here.'

'Yes?'

'You won't remember me, but when you lived in Wellington briefly, you were friends with my parents.'

There was silence and Lauren thought she'd better give some prompts. 'Carmen and Jim Fraser. They lived in Seatoun.'

'Oh yes, I do know who you are now. They've passed on, haven't they, quite some time back?'

'Yes.' Lauren wanted to get straight onto the topic. 'Mother said you knew all about herbs and I wondered if I could come and talk to you. I'm looking to advise a friend who is interested in taking a naturopathy course.' It was a lame excuse, but Mrs Driscoll agreed, though it sounded grudging. Ten thirty, Monday morning.

She and Kirsten had papered over the cracks in their relationship, still called each other most nights, and seemed set for Lauren to continue visiting for the occasional weekend. But she was nervous asking if she could stay over on Sunday night as well. 'There's someone in Mangere I need to see on Monday morning.'

'I didn't think you knew anyone out that way?' Kirsten queried. Lauren hesitated. Then she decided she needed to let Kirsten know what she and Ro were up to. After all, Kirsten was her partner and the investigation had become a big part of her life. So she relayed the whole story as succinctly as she could. Kirsten was a good listener. At the end of Lauren's tale, she said, 'I had no idea what you'd got yourself into. I don't know what to say.'

'I'm sorry I didn't tell you earlier. But Ro put such an emphasis on keeping it all a secret. And it still is very important that you don't say anything about this to anyone else.'

It was hard to read Kirsten's reactions over the phone. She didn't sound thrilled. Perhaps she was offended about being kept out of the picture till now? But she agreed readily enough to Lauren staying longer.

'It will be good to see you, darling, but I'm not sure what I think about what you and Ro are up to. It certainly does explain a few things. You've seemed quite distracted lately.'

Lauren put down the phone and picked up her drink. Disappointment swirled through her, a lump in her throat making it difficult to swallow. She had so wanted Kirsten to understand her passion for getting to the truth of the attempt on Lange's life. No, even more, she had wanted Kirsten to encourage her, barrack for her, cheer her on. She sighed, pulled her laptop towards her and opened up a game.

11

'He loves me well'

Lauren enjoyed the flights to Auckland. She had it down to a fine art. Check in on-line the day before, arrive at the gate twenty minutes before take-off with just an overnight bag and then spend the hour in the air reading her emails and drafting replies. Today she also wanted thinking time before her visit with Kevin's mother on Monday. She mentally rehearsed a few opening remarks and mulled over how to extract any useful information.

At the terminal she looked about expectantly for Kirsten who had said she would meet her, surely a mark of affection. Her phone pinged. The text read 'Sorry, Lauren, held up at work. Get a cab? See you at my place. Kx.' Was she really held up, Lauren wondered. Or was this another sign of things falling apart? Certainly she was in two minds about whether the relationship had run its course, and probably Kirsten was too. That argument in Greece. Her own fault, really. But surely Kirsten had changed. She sighed, they would certainly have to address it over the next few days. She went outside and bought a bus ticket to the city. She couldn't bring herself to pay four or five times as much for a taxi.

A bus came almost at once. It dropped her in Mt Eden. From the stop it was only half a block to Kirsten's rental and by the time she got there Kirsten was home. The front door of the old villa was wide open and Lauren called out. Jane, one of the flatmates, popped her head out of her bedroom door. 'Oh, hello Lauren, Kirsten's in the back garden picking spinach. Go through.'

Lauren walked through to Kirsten's room at the back of the house, an annex that was long ago built on behind the kitchen. It made the space very private, which Lauren liked. She dropped her bag on a chair and went down the back steps towards the garden. 'Hello, darling,' she called as she walked. 'Are they working you to the bone?'

'What?' Kirsten looked puzzled, briefly. 'Oh no, just had to finish something. Sorry about not meeting you.' She stood up from the spinach patch, clutching a bunch of leaves and walked over to Lauren, kissing her briefly on the cheek.

'Not good enough,' Lauren gave Kirsten a big hug. She felt a burst of affection as Kirsten responded and her doubts melted away. They walked together up to the house. Kirsten was cooking for Lauren and two flatmates, a spinach and bacon salad and poached salmon. She poured Lauren a glass of wine and sipped one herself.

They settled down after dinner in the comfortable living room. The others were going out. Once it was a point of pride for Lauren to be busy on a Friday night. Now she wanted an early night with Kirsten. They were sitting together on the sofa, fingers interlaced, glasses in their free hands, chatting about the Greek holiday–the best parts of it–when the phone rang.

'Oh bother,' said Kirsten. She pulled her hand away, put her glass down and retrieved the phone from the coffee table. She checked the name of the caller and answered, 'Hi, how are you?' There was a warm lilt in her voice. Lauren looked up. Surely that tone was just for her? Kirsten was saying, 'Sorry, I'm busy tonight and over the week-end.' A pause, then 'Sunday night? I'll see.' She turned to Lauren. 'What time does your flight leave on Sunday?'

'Don't you remember,' said Lauren. 'I'm not going till Monday evening, I'm seeing Kevin Driscoll's mother on Monday. I talked to you about it yesterday.' Kirsten lifted the phone again, walked about the room, and said 'No, I'm tied up then too. Let's get together during the week. A drink after work, or even dinner.' She smiled as she finished the call and slid the phone into her pocket.

'Who was that?' said Lauren. She hoped it sounded casual but she could not help feeling nervous.

'Oh, just Bee.' Kirsten hesitated. 'We're trying to organise a get-together in a week or two, the gang from Greece.'

'Give my apologies,' Lauren said coolly.

Kirsten flushed. 'I didn't think to talk to you about it since you're not usually up here.' It was clear that Kirsten didn't see Lauren as one of 'the gang.' Fair enough, but why did Lauren feel that there was more to it than that. Recalling Bee's manner in Greece, as well as their little spat, Lauren smarted. Still, may as well keep the peace.

'Sounds like fun,' she said lightly and changed the subject. 'Kirsten, about my visit to see Mrs Driscoll, can I borrow your car? She still lives down in South Auckland in Lange's old electorate.'

Kirsten was unusually snappish. 'Of course you can borrow it. But I've been thinking about what you told me. I don't know why you want to go on a silly wild goose chase.' Lauren was offended and looked it.

Kirsten ignored the look. 'Everyone knows Lange wasn't well in his second term and he died a few years later. Probably because of all that weight he carried.' Kirsten prided herself on her fitness and a slim figure. 'And as for that backbencher's claim, he was probably just trying to impress the woman with what a devil he was. Surely you don't believe it? Things like that don't really happen in New Zealand.'

'Oh yes they do.' Lauren snapped back. 'What about the Trades Hall bombing in Wellington in the eighties–they still haven't found out who killed that poor caretaker.'

Kirsten snorted. Their earlier mood was shattered. She got up and said, 'Would you like tea before we go to bed? I'm pretty tired, it's been a busy week at work.'

The weekend's shaky start was forgotten when they woke the next morning. They lingered in bed, made up in a very satisfactory manner and emerged for showers late on Saturday morning. Any tensions seemed a long way off. The rest of the weekend was their usual pleasurable mix of walks, meals out and music. This weekend it was a concert in the Town Hall, the Auckland Philharmonic playing Mozart, Berg and Mahler, with a wonderful guest soprano. The Mozart was frothy, the Berg songs romantic and the Mahler was profoundly moving. When they talked again about Lauren using Kirsten's car, it was just about logistics.

ON MONDAY MORNING Lauren drove Kirsten to her Parnell office. Kirsten's new car was a work one and Lauren wondered if she should really be driving it, but there seemed to be few rules these days. You had to be available at all times and in return, the company supplied you with everything you needed. Lauren could see into the glass foyer of the agency, people lounging around on bean bags and a couple of them playing pool, presumably staff, not clients. She told Kirsten she would have the car back to her by lunchtime. She hoped they could have lunch together, but Kirsten said she would be busy and would drop off Lauren at the Skybus. Lauren was hurt but didn't say anything.

She pulled out of the entry way into the Auckland traffic, making sure she was in the correct lane at the Grafton on-ramp. Once she had driven over the harbour bridge by mistake. A tense moment or two while she wondered if she'd pulled it off and then she was on the southern motorway.

Kirsten had advised her to use the GPS, but Lauren was too impatient to sit parked, learning the unfamiliar technology. Kirsten should have set up the GPS for her. Too late now, she just followed the old route towards the airport exiting at Gillies Avenue, crawling through Epsom, Greenlane, Onehunga, and across the Mangere Bridge. As she crossed it she looked down at the old bridge, now used by walkers or folk fishing. It always reminded her of the famous strike over building the new bridge, which went on for years. Her father used to reminisce about it, and Kevin's father was one of the hold-outs.

Mangere itself was a puzzle to Lauren. She usually went straight through on the motorway to and from the airport. The volcanic cone was to her right and the main part of the suburb was on the southern side. She exited and drove past streets of near derelict state houses before arriving at the new town centre.

Mrs Driscoll had given her directions from there. They were not hard to follow. She turned right at the street, original state houses which looked in good shape, mostly owner-occupied after a generous buy-back scheme in the sixties. No kids out and about, one man with a walking frame, no cars rusting on the lawns. Nice shrubs and flower beds in the front gardens.

She pulled up at number eleven. The Driscoll house was distinctive. The front was a mass of planting, no lawn, just a pathway winding up to the front door. A climbing plant practically obscured the garage on the right.

She pushed the doorbell but could hear no sound within the house. Remembering her recent spell of door-knocking for Labour, she thought yet again that no Kiwi doorbells ever worked, they must just have been a 1960s fashion. So she tapped on the glass and soon heard footsteps.

Mrs Driscoll was spare and slightly stooped. She wore a shabby green cardigan over a shapeless dress, despite the warm summery day, and stockings with her scuffed moccasins. Her face was wrinkled, with white hair pulled back into a bun. She greeted Lauren less than effusively but was polite enough. 'Come into the kitchen and I'll put on the jug.'

She turned and set off at a good pace, Lauren following her through the gloomy hallway and the living room, into a sunny kitchen and dining area. The place was run down, original wallpaper bearing the marks of time, scuffed carpet and dusty venetian blinds. The living room looked as if it was frozen in the seventies, with its vinyl covered lounge suite and chrome ashtray, although there was a softer cushioned chair facing a newish flat screen television.

They sat down at the kitchen table with their cups of tea, lemon balm it tasted like, though Mrs Driscoll didn't say so and obviously expected her to drink it without comment. They exchanged a few pleasantries, the older woman recalling how accomplished a gardener Lauren's mother had been, noted for her lavenders. Lauren raised the topic of naturopathy courses. Mrs Driscoll was not too keen on them. 'Healing with herbs is a gift. If you don't have it, you won't learn it from doing a course.' After ten minutes of this, Lauren steered the conversation to Kevin.

'I was talking to someone back in Wellington about the Lange era when your son Kevin was an MP at the time. Did you see much of him then?'

'He was always a good boy.' Mrs Driscoll smiled fondly. 'Charlie died after Lange became MP for Mangere and Kevin continued Charlie's activism, working for the party.' She looked proud. 'After school Kevin got a management training job in a factory on the North Shore. He took a flat over there and seemed very settled. Then he put himself forward for Birkdale. He worked very hard and the party liked him.'

She pondered, rattling her cup down on the saucer. 'Though he always worried he was getting places on Charlie's coattails. The dear boy, he had plenty of talent himself.' Lauren murmured encouragingly, hoping she'd get on with it. She was having a hard job pretending to be impressed by the young Kevin Driscoll's achievements.

Mrs Driscoll continued. 'He won in 1984, I think it was, when Labour got in. Then he had to spend a lot of time in Wellington. He came back to his electorate Fridays and Saturdays and always came to lunch on Sundays.'

So far, so good, thought Lauren, but how could she raise the matter of the tonic? She persevered with the discussion about Kevin. 'It must have been tiring for him, all that travel, and good to have a decent meal cooked by his mum on Sundays.' Abject flattery, somehow the kitchen didn't look as if Mrs Driscoll spent much time on meals. There were herbal preparations and glass jars on every surface.

Mrs Driscoll accepted the compliment. 'Yes, they spoil their appetite for proper meals, all those functions and the alcohol flowing. Kevin has a delicate constitution, not like his father.'

Delicate constitution–Lauren had a heaven-sent memory, a moment of inspiration. 'I expect you gave him some of your tonic,' she said. 'When my mother was poorly, you gave her a bottle.'

'You've got a very good memory, dear.' Mrs Driscoll looked a little suspicious, though it was hard to tell. That seemed to be her natural demeanour.

'Mother mentioned it in one of her letters. We used to write every week when I was a student at Cambridge.'

'You were the bright one, weren't you?' Once again, Mrs Driscoll had a slightly disparaging tone. Sometimes, thought Lauren, you just have to push harder or you won't get anywhere. She steered the topic away from her mother and the unsuitably academic daughter. 'You must have been concerned about how poorly David Lange looked during his second term in office?'

'I was. He was a dear man and he so often didn't look well. I asked Kevin to take the tonic to Mr Lange.'

'Really? And did he appreciate it?'

'Oh yes, he told Kevin it gave him a real boost and asked for more. Kevin took it to him regularly over a few months. Then Kevin told me that some doctor told him to stop taking it.' Lauren was puzzled, she wondered if someone knew what was going on? Mrs Driscoll went on. 'Silly fool, doctors can be so narrow-minded. Such a pity he was taken so soon. I put that down to conventional medicine.'

The older woman got up and looked in a cupboard for something, but apparently did not find it. A bottle of tonic, perhaps? She came back to the table and started talking again. 'Mr Lange came from a fine local family. His father was a GP. He delivered my Kevin.' Lauren smiled with some effort. 'Dr Lange always respected my remedies and sometimes recommended them for his patients. Not like some doctors,' she added darkly. 'Dr Lange even wrote a letter to the chemist so that I could buy ingredients that you couldn't get off the shelf. The chemist had a register and you needed special dispensation to get them.'

'Gosh', Lauren said innocently, 'I've never heard of that. Do you mean poisons?'

Mrs Driscoll looked at her sharply. 'Some ingredients are dangerous in the wrong hands.'

'I can imagine,' said Lauren. 'Can I perhaps see where you make your remedies?'

Mrs Driscoll brightened. 'Come out the back and I'll show you.'

They walked slowly across brick paving where a black cat lay stretched out in the sun. The ramshackle shed was padlocked. Inside the shelves were neatly organised, neater than the kitchen. There were shelves of empty bottles, presumably waiting to be filled. Another wall held labelled jars of powders, liquids, commercial preparations and dried herbs.

Mrs Driscoll said, 'I grow most of my own herbs and gather some traditional Māori remedies from the bush.' She began to explain some of the principles of herbal medicine. Lauren tried to listen as she spoke, but at the same time, she was running her eyes over the jars. They were organised in alphabetical order, and in a moment she had spotted aconite.

She interrupted, hoping Mrs Driscoll would not find her query odd. 'Oh,' she said, 'I've just been hearing about aconite. You use it, do you? My friend was telling me that she'd got interested in naturopathy because someone had given her homeopathic doses before she had some surgery.'

Mrs Driscoll looked interested. 'Yes, I don't altogether hold with homeopathy but I do use homeopathic doses in some of my preparations. I'm not letting you into a secret, because it's the mix that's important, but aconite is the key ingredient in my tonics. It's a homeopathic dose there, it has to be measured very carefully. Even though I grow aconite, it's one of the ingredients that I get from the chemist because the titration has to be accurate. Like many plant remedies, a little is good, too much can make you sick or even be fatal. That's why I won't pass on my recipes–I don't trust anyone else to do it right.'

She ushered Lauren out of the shed, locked it and they walked slowly back to the house. Lauren thanked her and left. Poor lonely woman with her off-putting mannerisms, wasting her small supply of affection on her mean-spirited son. But she had been something of a heroine in helping out girls in trouble back in the days before abortion law reform. Would she have taken risks to help out her son? Surely not, she spoke so affectionately of the Langes. Kevin must have acted alone, taking some aconite from his mother and spiking one of the bottles of tonic that he regularly delivered to Lange. Anyway, there it was. Aconite.

12

'Tell me truly what thou thinkst of him'

At four thirty on Tuesday Lauren fronted up to police headquarters, got through security and made her way to the seventh floor. She was excited, very pleased with what she and Ro had discovered so far. When she had arrived home from Auckland on Monday and told Phyl about the tonic, Phyl had immediately arranged a meeting with Deirdre Nathan. She said the new evidence could be important.

Lauren was ushered into a small nondescript office. The walls were institutional cream and sported a calendar and year planner, the desk was utilitarian and held a computer as well as piles of paper, and there were two upright vinyl-covered visitors' chairs. The most interesting feature of the room was the woman who came out from behind the desk to greet her. Deirdre Nathan was tall with an upright stance, not in uniform but in a smart black suit. She had strong dark wavy hair with a tinge of grey around the edges and watchful brown eyes which gave nothing away. Not so much younger than me, Lauren thought.

Deirdre offered Lauren one of the visitor's chairs and instead of retreating behind her desk, took the other, and got straight to the point.

'Phyl tells me you've got something new on the Lange investigation.'

'Yes indeed,' said Lauren. 'Thank you so much for seeing me so promptly.' She poured out the story. The two recorded interviews with Judith Butler that led to Kevin Driscoll, Michael having seen Lange taking a tonic that Kevin's mother had sent, Lauren visiting Kevin's mother and confirming that she supplied the tonic, and that it contained aconite.

'So,' she finished up, 'it's clear that Kevin Driscoll tried to poison Lange, all the evidence points to him, don't you think?'

She paused and Deirdre, who had been listening intently, said, 'I'm afraid not. You see, we already suspected it was the tonic.' She reached over to her desk and shuffled through some old-looking files. 'Yes, here it is. A statement from Dr Waddell. He was the registrar who spotted something unusual about Lange's symptoms and arranged special tests, which showed it up.' She smiled at Lauren and put the paper back on the desk.

'Oh!' Lauren was gutted. She stared at Deirdre open-mouthed. 'You mean we've done all this to find out something you already knew?'

Deirdre didn't disagree. She explained that they'd asked Lange at the time what he'd been eating or drinking and a tonic with unknown ingredients was an obvious source. After Lange said Kevin Driscoll brought it for him, from his mother, they'd called in Kevin, but he insisted he just delivered the bottles. They had tested a bottle still on Lange's desk to find it had just a trace of aconite, appropriate for the tonic.

'Either we were on the wrong track, or Kevin had covered up well,' said Deirdre. It was clear that she thought it was the latter.

Lauren felt deflated. She and Ro had been so pleased with themselves. Then she brightened. 'But surely the interviews with Judith Butler are new evidence?'

Deirdre looked doubtful. 'Send them through to me and I'll have a listen, but it's just a second-hand report from an old lady who could have misremembered or made it up. And it doesn't sound as if she would be fit to testify. A defence lawyer would rip her to bits.'

She went on, 'Kevin would have to do something very silly to be brought to book. We do keep an eye on him, we take attempted murder very seriously, but nothing substantial has come up. He's an immigration consultant these days, working largely with overseas business people who want to settle here.' Her voice was neutral, but Lauren felt she might not approve of Kevin's current occupation.

'He always hung around business people, apparently,' said Lauren, 'though I guess you know that too. I know one of them–Brett Wilson–he was a student in Cambridge at the same time as I was. An Australian who stayed on in England and then had a career as an international money man, whatever that means. I expect to see him soon, he and his wife are coming on holiday to New Zealand, planning to buy a piece of land here.'

Deirdre looked interested. 'We think that if Kevin did try to kill Lange, he wasn't acting alone, and as you say, he did hang round with money men. From memory, Brett Wilson is one of the names that came up when the case was investigated. Contact me again if you should learn anything else.' She stood up, and it was clear the interview was over. She ushered Lauren to the lift and said goodbye.

LAUREN DROVE HOME, disconsolate. It was obvious that Kevin had tried to kill David Lange, and Judith Butler said that other people had been involved in the plot. How could she find out enough to persuade the police to prosecute? Deirdre was impressive, so it would have to be convincing.

She was still pondering, still feeling gloomy, when she drove over to Ro's the next day. She parked the car and walked into the property. Skirting the customary obstacles she made her way to the back door, open as usual, knocked, called out and went in. She was halfway down the hall as Ro emerged from her study. She led Lauren into the living room, still looking somewhat abstracted. Lauren knew that look: Ro was half with her, but her mind was still back in her study working on whatever she was doing.

Ro made an effort. 'Congratulations, Lauren, fantastic work. I'm sorry I was tied up yesterday.'

Lauren could hardly remember how euphoric she'd been when she'd rung Ro on Monday evening. Before she rang Phyl and the appointment with Deirdre. Huh! She'd told Ro they'd got him for sure. And then Ro had crowed into the phone, full of congratulations and appreciation.

Now, Ro was coming back into the present, her thoughts no longer on her work. She said, 'I've been thinking about your new findings. We should take them to the police, don't you agree?'

Lauren confessed. 'I know you were keen to keep it a secret till you could write up everything, but I thought the police should know what we'd found, and you were so busy. I've told them. And they knew it all already!' She gave Ro a blow-by-blow account of her talk to Michael and subsequent visit to Mrs Driscoll, talking to Phyl about it and her interview with Deirdre. She ended on a plaintive note. 'I think we're stuck. I'm not sure what to do next. And where are you at?'

Ro looked at her sympathetically. 'You've done well. The Butler interview was good stuff. And great to get that material from Michael. I'm keen to do more ferreting now that I've finally got the book in. I can chase up that little swine Kevin a bit more. I think he's mentioned several times in my interviews, not in relation to the plot of course, but what say I go and see a couple of my informants again? There's Moana, the other woman Judith said Kevin was having an affair with, and Catherine, Judith's flatmate.'

Lauren sighed. 'But how could they help?'

'You never know, he might have said something to Moana about the plot. Judith might have said something to her flatmate. I can only ask.'

'I suppose politicians are terrible gossips. It seems like a long shot.'

Ro looked at Lauren, slumped in her chair. 'Don't be so gloomy.'

'Sorry.' Lauren sat up straighter. 'I know, thinking of long shots, I could try to follow up on that registrar Deirdre mentioned, the one who picked up on the aconite in Lange's system. He might have something useful.'

'Good luck finding him, it was over thirty years ago. I'll start doing the research for what to write if we do get the details of the plot uncovered. The business end first, I think, because that's the most likely source of Kevin's fellow plotters. Do you think your Brett would have been in the Backbone Club?'

'I thought that was just Labour MPs who backed Douglas?'

Ro put on her lecturer's hat. 'No, there were Douglas's business backers as well. It turned into the ACT party.'

'In that case, he probably was. I might well hear from him soon. Damn! I really don't want to entertain his wife, I can't imagine I'd have much in common with anyone who wanted to hook up with Brett. Student days were different, but you'd expect mature women to have more sense.'

Ro laughed. 'Money talks. It also probably breeds affection, or perhaps she's a gold digger.'

'I'm just gloomy about relationships at the moment. I think Kirsten and I are on the way out.'

'I'm sorry to hear that.' Ro looked concerned but perhaps not sorry. 'What's been going on?'

'She's caught up in an Auckland crowd. They're younger, glamorous, work hard, play hard types. I'm sure she fancies one of them—Bee used to be a star netballer.'

'I don't see how anyone could compete with you, Lauren.' Ro blushed, though Lauren didn't notice.

'Oh well,' Lauren wanted to change the subject. 'Que sera, sera.'

'Maybe Brett's wife will be a new interest for you.' They both laughed. Ro said more seriously, 'Now you're not to be off-putting with Brett's wife, being friendly could help with our investigation.'

~

WHEN LAUREN GOT HOME, she couldn't settle to any editing, and she decided to follow up on the registrar who'd ordered the aconite tests all those years ago. Perhaps he was still living in Auckland.

She found it was easy to look up doctors on the New Zealand Medical Council's searchable database online. Within thirty seconds she found that Dr Anthony Waddell, whose scope of practice was cardiology, was currently in the Waikato District Health Board area. The White Pages again, and she found a likely phone number.

She phoned the Hamilton number. It wasn't right, but the woman who answered was helpful. She knew of a Dr Waddell, not related, who'd done a difficult operation successfully on a friend. Lauren listened patiently while it was described and then asked the woman if she knew his phone number.

'He lives in Tamahere, I believe,' said the Waddell woman. 'I know that because my friend lives there and helps out at the local church. She said that he came with his grandson to look at their nativity display and told her they'd recently moved onto a ten-acre block.' Lauren interrupted. 'Thanks so much, that'll be enough information to find the number, if he's listed.'

And listed he was. She dialled, not expecting to find a medical specialist at home during the day, but she got straight through. She talked of a quest to understand David Lange's illness back in 1988 - she didn't mention a plot but did refer to her historian friend who was suspicious about the circumstances. The doctor proved surprisingly forthcoming.

'I'm glad someone's looking into it after all these years. I spoke to the police at the time but it didn't go anywhere. All hush hush, I suppose. But back in those days, when I was an ambitious young man,'–there was a hint of false modesty–'I wanted to publish in scientific journals. I had just been to a conference on toxicology and cardiac events and recalled something that was said about aconite's effect on the heart and the other symptoms it produced, including unusual visual symptoms.

'Look, I'm not going to break patient confidentiality even at this distance, but I can send you an article I wrote. I was confident that

Lange had ingested a large dose of aconite. I understood that the police located a herbal tonic he was taking that contained traces of it, but not enough to make a person ill. As a young doctor, I found it all very interesting and I published a case history, anonymous of course. In a rather obscure journal of toxicology, but I can find a reprint in my files and scan it and send it to you.'

Lauren thanked him profusely and gave him her email address.

An hour or so later, the email came through. Essentially, the article concluded that because the patient already had a heart problem, it would have been easy to miss the signs of aconite poisoning. Identifying it meant that steps were taken to purge the patient's system of any residual poisons before a surgical intervention to fix the cardiac problems was carried out.

Lauren sighed. An interesting paper, she supposed, but she was still no further ahead. What she wanted was proof that Kevin had somehow got hold of a lethal amount of his mother's aconite powder and added it to a flask of Lange's tonic. And that seemed out of reach.

13

'Hearts of controversy'

Her phone chirped a few days later with a text from Brett. 'Just making contact. My wife would like to get in touch.' She'd replied civilly and shortly afterwards another text followed from a different number. 'Hi Lauren, this is Darya, Brett's wife. I'm in town on Wednesday. Could we meet in the afternoon?'

Lauren suggested Te Papa. New Zealand's national museum was where she usually took visitors when they first came to Wellington. She and her friends could not settle their argument about its architectural merit, but no one could contest the fact that its setting on the waterfront was glorious. The whole harbour frontage improved each year with sculptures, walkways and plantings.

Now Lauren hovered inside Te Papa's entrance. It was a typical Wellington day, windy, with clouds scudding fast across the sky, and patches of sunshine in between. The harbour rippled and waves slapped against the nearby wharves. Lauren looked up as an elegant woman carrying several shopping bags came through the entrance looking around. Lauren had said she could be identified by her short grey hair with a purple streak in it.

The woman inspected her and then approached. 'You are Lauren?' she said, in an accented voice, tripping over Lauren's name and pronouncing it as 'Lorne'.

'Yes. Pleased to meet you, Darya.' Lauren showed her the cloakroom where she could offload shopping bags. They took the escalator up to the information desk on the first floor, but not before Lauren had noticed Darya taking in the shop on the ground floor.

'Shall we look at an exhibition and then have a coffee, or coffee first?' she asked. 'There's New Zealand art on the top floors, permanent Māori, Pacific and natural history displays and a special exhibition of ceramics in New Zealand. What would you be interested in?'

Darya's expression was difficult to read and Lauren wasn't sure how good her English was. Perhaps she found the New Zealand accent difficult, although Lauren's time in England had ironed the Newzild out of hers. And she prided herself on speaking clearly. But it seemed Darya was considering the question, not puzzling over what Lauren had said.

'The ceramics,' she replied. 'My family back in the Ukraine manufactured china. As a child, I used to visit my grandfather's factory. Most of what they made was for the peasants, cheap and crude dishes.' Her watchful expression was supplanted as her face came alive. 'But grandmother had great taste. Nothing but the best of German fine china at her table.'

As they walked around the exhibition, Lauren noticed that Darya certainly had an eye for quality. The exhibition was organised as a series of table settings, laid out by decades and including Crown Lynn, Temuka stoneware and New Zealand's traditional craft pottery. It also featured imported Meissen, Wedgwood, Portmeirion and Rosenthal tableware. Lauren was transported through time, remembering meals from childhood. Her own grandmother, though clearly not wealthy like Darya's, had treasured some Wedgwood pieces which reminded her of 'Home'. That was how her grandmother had referred to England, Lauren recalled, even though she had been born in New Zealand and had never had the opportunity to see the villages in Kent and Sussex where her parents had been born.

Lauren couldn't help bristling when Darya made critical comments about the earthenware pottery. Although she had not been in New Zealand in the seventies, visitors had sometimes brought Lauren gifts of the artisanal hand-thrown mugs so popular then. A few choice pieces were amongst her own treasures now. 'A country of peasants,' Darya said with a sigh. 'I suppose I will feel at home.'

Lauren didn't expect conversation over their coffee to be easy, but they found shared interests. A true cosmopolitan, Darya spoke of Wagner's Ring cycle in Munich, the Bolshoi Ballet in St Petersburg and the Chinese terracotta warriors at their home site in Xian. The conversation veered to more personal topics and Lauren learnt that Darya's family had been out of favour–and hence out of pocket–under communism, but that since then, Darya had clawed her way back to what she considered her rightful sphere through at least two advantageous marriages, the second to Brett. Not that Darya put it like that; but she made it plain that she considered herself a cut above most people. She seemed prepared to give Lauren the benefit of the doubt–Lauren, too, had seen the warriors at Xian–remarking that Brett remembered Lauren from his student days as a clever, cultured girl.

Darya finished her coffee, looked around, and said almost offhandedly, 'Brett has some men friends coming over some weekend soon to the house we have hired in the Wairarapa. They are looking at the piece of land we will buy. I would be pleased if you would join us. I think there are vineyards there to inspect?'

Lauren knew that she should take this opportunity to find out more about Brett, although her heart sank at the thought of a whole weekend with the couple and whoever Brett's friends might be. She agreed that there were indeed vineyards in the Wairarapa and accepted the invitation with as good a grace as she could muster. Providing, of course, that she had no other engagements. The talk turned to what they should look at next and Darya thought she would have time before meeting Brett to inspect the New Zealand paintings.

They walked up to the fifth floor and through the New Zealand art on display. Lauren thought it would have been more helpful if the collection had been displayed by decades, so that visitors could get a sense of trends. She said to Darya, 'You need to see more of the country before you can appreciate our art. It reflects our surroundings. The light is very strong here and colours are brighter.'

Darya made her way through several of the art spaces and said little, until she stopped in front of the Rita Angus painting of two sisters. She seemed quite taken with the look of the blonde chubby children in gingham dresses and green cardigans. 'Here is an interesting work,' she said. 'Tell me about this artist. Is she living?'

Lauren said, 'No, that painting dates from the 1950s. She is an important New Zealand artist, but no longer alive.'

'I will look for her work in other places. If she has other paintings like this, I might collect her.'

Lauren was astonished.

'Brett collects books and old maps which I find boring, but he has a nice Hockney. I have a couple of Picasso sketches from a previous marriage, but I am keen to add to my collection. It would give me an interest while I am in New Zealand.'

Lauren tried not to smile at the idea of Rita Angus and Picasso displayed somewhere side by side. She wouldn't mind having a couple of Picassos, though, and then buying some good New Zealand art to go with them. She said, 'I would be happy to come with you if you are looking at art works in private galleries. There might be other artists whose work you would enjoy.'

'Thank you,' said Darya, 'I will probably hire an agent. However, I would enjoy looking at some more art with you, but please not that brown earthenware.'

Lauren laughed, promised, and they parted. She started her walk home. Darya wasn't so bad, just on a completely different planet. Though the idea of spending a whole weekend with her was unappealing. And Brett! How was she to get anything out of him about the 1980s? She thought he had lied to her about Kevin and he was such a smooth liar. Perhaps she could trip him up. But how? A seagull screeched, disrupting her train of thought. She paused and glanced over to see it diving into the water. That seagull would have more luck than she would, when she fished around to winkle something out of the smooth-talking Brett. Suddenly the harbour looked vast with its unimaginable hidden depths.

She shook her head and walked on. She wondered what Ro was up to. Perhaps she was having some success, re-interviewing the Labour women MPs who might have more to say about Kevin. But then she remembered. Ro was preoccupied.

Ro HAD BEEN SURPRISED to receive a call from John Barwood, a researcher on the Kim Hill radio show. 'We got a press release about your Stout Centre conference. Kim picked out your work as maybe worth an interview. Do you mind if we have a chat so that I can give her some background?' Ro was a fan of Kim Hill from way back. And an interview would be great publicity for her book. Many of her friends sweetened the pill of Saturday morning chores by listening to Kim.

'I'd love to talk to you–and Kim,' she said. 'I'm flattered.' She told Barwood that the theme of the conference had been gender and the history of emotions. 'Please do explain,' he said politely. 'I have no idea what that's all about.'

'Psychologists argue that emotions are socially constructed, that is, they differ across time and place depending on culture and circumstance.' Ro was in lecturing mode. 'Historians have picked up on that idea and investigate how emotions are expressed in different historical eras.' Shut up, she told herself. She'd better get to the point or the interview would be down the tubes. 'My work is on women in the Lange government, I'm writing a book about them, which will be out next year. The history of emotion angle is that the women politicians did what feminists call "emotional shitwork" '–John audibly drew breath.

'Perhaps I can't use that term on public radio,' Ro laughed. 'You can advise me on that.' She went on, 'It means that women in politics do the same kind of emotional work that they do in a marriage. They offer a listening ear, soothe the men, smooth out conflicts and so on. And men in politics seem to need a lot of emotional soothing. Sometimes that takes the form of affairs.'

'Really?' Barwood sounded interested.

'Yes,' Ro said. 'In any job where people spend a lot of their time away from home, affairs are common. And life in politics is so full of ups and downs, it's a breeding ground for affairs. And affairs are a great conduit for exchange of insider information. Historians who ignore pillow talk miss out on a lot.'

They went on to discuss specific examples of emotional labour and Barwood said he was sure that Ro would make a good interviewee. 'Don't lecture, though. Radio audiences like to hear dialogue, not monologues. Of course Kim is masterful when it comes to getting a word in edgeways.'

So true, Ro thought. They agreed on a time during the week for Kim to interview her–it would be pre-recorded, not live–and he told her it would be broadcast next Saturday, barring any big news events getting in the way. Hanging up, Ro did a little dance of glee. She would tell all her friends so that they could listen in. Not bragging, of course. Lauren would be first to know.

The interview went smoothly, although she was unaccountably nervous. Kim Hill asked her about her work and was particularly interested in Ro's point about affairs and pillow talk. Ro explained that with affairs in politics, it's the women who soothe raging egos, damping down the testosterone flying around when men are squabbling. 'Men confide intimate details to women–and my book will contain surprising revelations about what was going on at the time of the Lange-Douglas split. I can't say more at the moment. There are some matters we have to get a legal opinion on before publishing. There's a particular accusation that hasn't been made before.'

Lauren made sure she was listening when the interview came on that Saturday morning. Ro had done well. Great publicity for her book.

Lauren wasn't the only one listening. Kevin Driscoll had been sussing out some opportunities in Palmerston North for one of his clients, and was driving a rental car through to Wellington on Saturday morning. He switched on the radio. It was tuned to National Radio. He didn't care for Kim, too brash and ball-breaking. But he couldn't be bothered finding another station. When he realised what the topic was he was suddenly interested. Who the hell was this woman Kim was talking to? Politicians in the Lange government and their affairs? He squirmed in his seat and took a corner too fast. Get a grip, he told himself. The woman was spouting some rubbish about emotional labour, which he didn't understand at all. Then she dropped a bombshell. Some of the women had told her about affairs going on around the House. Confidences that were often spilt across the pillows.

When the speaker referred to a revelation that would be published in a book Kevin was so shocked that he pulled suddenly to the side of the road. A car behind him tooted and its occupant gave him the finger as it swerved and passed. He felt sick. He remembered spilling the beans about Lange to that old bird he'd had the affair with, Judith Butler, God, what a mistake. He must have been missing his mother! He'd been drunk when he told her, but the next morning he'd realised he'd said too much. He'd given her a good whack across the face to teach her a lesson and to remind her to keep it to herself. Nothing came of it, so that must have worked.

Nothing until now, that is. Had Judith been talking to that fucking historian? The interview ended and Kim said, 'I've been speaking with historian Rowan Wisbech.' Kevin turned around, grabbed his briefcase from the back seat and pulled out a notebook. He wrote the name down carefully. She was someone who needed a good lesson, too. He'd think about how best to make it happen.

14

'Set honour in one eye and death i' the other'

Lauren was packing a small bag, fussing more than usual. Surely she wouldn't need anything formal for a weekend in the country. The Wilsons were renting a place in the Wairarapa not Downton Abbey. Gumboots were the most likely prerequisites. But how could you tell with a woman like Darya, who was elegance personified. She threw in some slip-ons, black trousers and a designer top, just in case.

She had just zipped up her bag when there was a knock on the door. A man in a dark suit stood outside. 'Miss Fraser? I'm your driver.' She followed him to the road above where a large white car blocked the driveway to the apartments. Lauren chose to sit in front with the driver, a small act of rebellion to differentiate herself from the super-wealthy.

The discreetly luxurious vehicle purred down the hill towards the waterfront. 'Who do you work for?' she asked the man. If he were Brett's employee, perhaps she could pump him for information.

He gave her a friendly smile. 'Executive Chauffeurs. We don't have signs on the cars,' he confided. 'It's just a glorified taxi company. Get to meet some well-known people, mind.'

There was no point in pursuing the conversation, so Lauren sat back and enjoyed the drive. From Jervois Quay they turned into the wharf. The driver pointed a remote at some bollards that sank gracefully into the asphalt. Open sesame, she thought, private cars weren't allowed onto the waterfront. The tune 'Money Makes the World Go Round' drifted into her mind and stayed there, like an earworm.

A helicopter was waiting behind a fenced-off section of the wharf, its doors open. The pilot, dressed in overalls, stood at the entry gate. He issued Lauren with a life jacket and took her over to the machine, escorting her into the cabin via the rear door. Darya was already on board, dressed in immaculate casual clothing, although the chic impression was spoiled a little by the bulk of her life jacket. Lauren took the seat next to her. There didn't seem to be anything to say after perfunctory greetings, so the women sat in silence. Lauren couldn't make her out. She hoped the weekend wouldn't prove too awkward. She reminded herself that she was there to do a job, not to make friends.

Shortly afterwards two men in business suits clambered in and took the remaining seats in the rear of the cabin. There were no introductions and Lauren had managed only a glance at them. The one nearest the door had looked vaguely familiar, so she turned briefly to get another look. Both were occupied with their seatbelts and so neither met her gaze. Damn, who was that? She definitely had seen him before. It took a few seconds for the memory banks to deliver and the result horrified her. Surely it was Kevin Driscoll! She recalled the awkward drive they had shared to Oxford in the 1980s and how pleased she had been to be shot of his company. He must be over sixty now, but he still looked indefinably sleazy. Slightly too sharp a dresser with his loud suit and clashing tie. She was right in suspecting Brett had been lying when he had denied knowing the man.

A second pilot hoisted himself into the front left hand seat and began to examine the controls, while the pilot who had greeted them closed the rear door and jumped up into the front right. He turned and asked the passengers to check that their seatbelts were fastened and to don the headsets, which were hanging from hooks behind their seats. The pilot on the left then turned to address them. Another surprise. It was Brett. 'Everyone buckled in and...? Oh, hi, Lauren.'

Lauren nodded to him, struggling to keep her expression neutral. She had assumed that the Kiwi guy who met them would fly it. She wondered how much experience Brett had as a pilot. She hoped this wasn't a training run! Darya didn't seem worried, so Lauren advised herself to just sit back and enjoy the ride. No point in spoiling it by thinking about Kevin Driscoll, would-be assassin. Or about putting her life in Brett's hands.

The engine started with a roar, the blades whirred and the cabin shuddered as they took off. The chopper rose and seemed to hesitate for an instant before choosing a direction. Looking down through the floor to ceiling windows Lauren saw the sparkling blue of the harbour beneath her, a bit too close for comfort. They rose steadily and as they left the city and Oriental Bay behind, the coastline settlements across the harbour came clearly into view. She could see that the ranges of the Remutakas held traces of fog.

As the harbour receded and they gained height to pass over the peaks, the bush-covered wilderness seemed very close. She glanced behind again. The men seemed relaxed enough, pointing out sights through the windows. Darya also looked out the window, but with no apparent interest. It was still noisy despite the headsets, but Lauren was able to hear the pilots chatting through the intercom. There was another voice, too, identifying itself as from the control tower at Wellington's airport.

In less than fifteen minutes they were over the peaks of the mountain ranges and descending, a glimpse of farmland showing beyond the ragged edges of bush. The fog was thickening fast. She heard weather information coming through and the co-pilot speaking to someone about conditions further on. Then as he turned to speak to Brett, someone must have thrown a switch as communication from the pilots was shut off. The headsets cancelled out any noises from inside the cabin. She watched the pilots closely but all she could make out from trying to lip-read side on was the word 'fog'. Looking out again, she could see the view clearing a little. The helicopter was following a line of power poles that marched into nowhere, but remained well above them.

The power poles vanished from view as fog thickened again and Lauren's stomach tensed. Wouldn't do to tangle with power lines. A hot air balloon went down in a burst of flames in the Wairarapa a few years before. She looked at Darya who remained impassive. Looking around again, she saw Kevin and his companion exchanging glances. Kevin was fingering his seatbelt and the younger man grasped his knees together, knuckles clenched tightly. She turned back and saw the co-pilot speaking urgently to Brett who replied, shaking his head and looking angry. Lauren tensed as the fog swirled and the helicopter moved sideways and descended further. This was no longer a joyride.

Darya surprised her by suddenly unclipping her belt and pulling herself upright. She leant over and banged Brett's shoulder, lifted his headphone and yelled in his ear. The helicopter rose again and headed onwards. The fog dispersed and a small aerodrome came into view.

The 'copter landed safely. With the engine switched off and headsets removed, Lauren realised she was trembling. She tried to hide any signs of distress and her rapid breathing gradually returned to normal.

'Masterton airport, folks.' said Brett. He didn't look particularly concerned. 'I was going to take her down at our place, it would have been safe enough. We'll be late for lunch.'

'You're a stubborn man,' said Darya. 'Late for lunch is better than early for the devil.'

'He likes to get his own way,' she said to Lauren. 'So do I.' The co-pilot still looked tense. He spoke to Brett in a low voice, though he could be heard. 'You don't want to risk the New Zealand endorsement on your licence. It's not a good idea to neglect control tower advice, even though we were in uncontrolled airspace once we breasted the Remutakas.'

'Nonsense,' Brett responded. 'I was relying on my own judgement. Anyhow, call us up a couple of taxis–pronto.'

'I'm not a bloody taxi service,' said the co-pilot. 'I'm back off to Wellington as soon as I've helped the passengers out.'

BY THE TIME Brett had organised taxis they had all been introduced. Lauren thought Kevin had given her a funny look as they disembarked. Perhaps he had recognised her too, although there was no reason for him to have done so. She certainly wouldn't have if she hadn't been thinking about him recently. Travelling with Brett and Darya in the first taxi, she asked about him. 'I met him briefly in the 80s when he was an MP. I don't think he remembers. I thought you told me in Cambridge you didn't know him?'

'I may have met him back then.' Brett was casual. 'He's helping me with our residency application and with a land purchase. He and his offsider need to get some information about the land from the local council on Monday. It seemed sensible to bring you all over together. That way, you all got to ride in the 'copter.' Yes, thought Lauren, an experience she could have done without.

After a short drive in the direction of Martinborough both taxis stopped outside security gates. Brett used a remote on his key ring to open them and they pulled into the driveway of an imposing house. Darya still seemed cross with Brett who ignored the vibes and was cheerful and expansive.

'Here we are, girls.' He turned to face them. 'Let's have half an hour before we leave for lunch.'

Lauren made a complimentary remark about the appearance of the property, but Darya sniffed and said, 'This was all we could get for the summer.' The house was set in what appeared to be several hectares of land, with paddocks around and cows grazing. Other newish houses with a similar look could be seen spotted across the flat rural landscape. Over the years Lauren had known a few people living in the Wairarapa but they had usually been sampling country life in much less assuming properties.

Kevin and his colleague Jason were in the second taxi. They emerged and all made their way into the large foyer. Darya appeared to have met Kevin before, but not his companion. She said to Brett, 'Show the men their rooms and I'll take Lauren.'

Lauren followed Darya into the kitchen where she offloaded the contents of a Moore Wilson shopping bag. Condiments, sauces, olives, cheeses and specialty breads. 'We're going out for lunch and I've arranged a cook for dinner this evening. Staff have been so difficult to find here.' Lauren raised her eyebrows. It was starting to sound like Downton Abbey. Darya went on, 'Brett expects me to cook if there is no one else, which is very annoying. Just getting a cleaner to come in every day is difficult.'

Lauren wasn't sure how to sound sympathetic. 'I suppose it's not what you're used to,' she said.

Darya shrugged. 'I'll show you your room so that you can—what do you say—freshen up before we go out.'

The house was laid out with a huge living area off the entrance hall and a large bedroom wing. The hallway leading to the bedrooms was expansive; a couple of elegant little chairs sat by an occasional table holding a large arrangement of peonies. They passed the open door of a study and then what Darya said was the master bedroom. Lauren was shown into the room next door. Further down the hallway she could hear the men's voices. She put her overnight bag on a stand, Darya left the room and Lauren shut the door with relief.

It was late afternoon when they arrived back at the house after lunch at one vineyard and tastings at a couple of others. Brett had bought a dozen bottles from each. Lauren was relieved to find that Kevin and Jason weren't included in the lunch party—she felt she could hardly bear to be civil to Kevin. She had enjoyed the meal and the wine and now she felt a little sleepy. Lying on the bed in her room with a book which might drop from her fingers as she dozed felt like a great plan.

But Brett had other ideas. The wine had apparently had no effect on him and he was keen to show off his collection of antique maps.

'Come into the study and see what I've bought so far.' Lauren followed him into the large room with an imposing desk in the middle. The desk had beautifully finished oak panels on the one side and on the other a roomy space for a desk chair between a double set of drawers. It needed a large room to show itself off. Spread out on the desk top was a pile of maps of different sizes.

'Here we are,' said Brett. 'I need to put them away; I've just bought a map cabinet.' He waved at a wide old-fashioned filing cabinet with multiple narrow drawers. 'I know you'll appreciate them. Look at this, it's a late eighteenth century Italian lithograph of Captain Cook's first map of New Zealand. It's known as the Cassini map and it's hand coloured. You can see that if you look closely. Of course, Cook didn't spot Wellington's harbour on his first voyage, sailed right past it.' He pointed out the beautifully decorative features of the map, including the cartouche featuring Māori apparently abasing themselves at Cook's feet. Lauren thought that was fanciful, no doubt the mapmaker had never been anywhere near the Pacific.

Brett moved to the other side of the desk. 'And this one, right underneath, is an early lithograph, D'Urville's rendering of the Bay of Islands. That's quite a valuable one.' He was handling the maps carefully as he moved them from one pile to another.

Lauren said, 'This isn't your whole collection, just New Zealand maps?'

'Nothing like,' said Brett. 'I like to have ones that capture the country I'm in. Not that they'd be much good for finding your way around now.'

Lauren marvelled that in the brief time he'd been back in New Zealand he'd managed to acquire all these important historical maps. He answered her thoughts. 'I've had someone looking about for me for a while. And when one comes up for sale they let me know and I tell them if I want it.'

The last one in the pile was a historical map of the Wairarapa. 'This one was a real find. It's the original illustration for a book on the missionary William Colenso in the Wairarapa. He mapped this area in the early nineteenth century when the land was being parcelled out.' Lauren looked at it with interest. 'So where are we now?'

'Round about here.' Brett put his finger on what appeared to be a sizeable farming block, named in the map as the Robertson Station.

'Look at this,' Lauren pointed to the inset of Palliser Bay, 'He's called the mountain range the Rimutakas. Did you know that the original settlers got the name wrong and it should be Remutaka? It's recently been changed back because the original name has meaning and what the settlers called it was nonsense.'

Brett shrugged. 'I don't hold with all that political correctness.' Yes, Lauren thought, Brett wasn't one to have any sympathy with indigenous rights. He came from colonising stock. As if to prove her point, he continued. 'We've had plenty of trouble like that in Australia. History is the propaganda of the victor. Rightly so. However, in future years that might just add to the map's value, if it's the first mistake. Have you heard of da Verrazano's discovery of the Pacific?'

Lauren pleaded ignorance. Brett was enjoying instructing her, she could tell. 'He was an explorer who sailed from Europe to the eastern seaboard of America in the sixteenth century. Sailed into a sound and decided that when he sailed out the other end he had reached the Pacific, which was actually 3,000 miles across the continent. He mapped the mistaken passage. They're quite valuable now. Profiting from others' mistakes, that's the way to go.'

He lifted the map off the desk. Underneath there were two battered passports.

'Oh, they shouldn't be there.' He pulled open a drawer, thrust them in and shut it again firmly. 'Had to bring my old passports over. To prove a longstanding relationship with New Zealand.'

Lauren smiled politely and thought, 'Yeah, the relationship of a hawk with the roadkill it's picking over.'

15

'Cowards die many times before their deaths'

Lauren, dressed for dinner, stopped in her tracks as she reached the grand dining room. It was like a film set, a film starring Darya, whose glittering jewellery competed with the sparkling chandelier. Thank goodness she had put in some formal clothes. The high-backed chairs boasting embroidered seats and backs matched the formal mahogany table. Each place was set with heavy silver cutlery on fine linen table mats, three glasses by each setting.

Darya's "cook" turned out to be a catering company brought in for the occasion. There was lots of bustle in the kitchen and a nervous-looking young woman brought in and cleared away dishes.

Conversation was awkward to begin with. Darya showed no interest in Kevin or Jason. Brett tried to steer the talk towards subjects where all could participate but Lauren, sitting down to a meal with someone she thought was a would-be murderer and a host she was increasingly suspicious of, felt unusually tongue-tied.

Apparently for Lauren's benefit, Brett said a little about the proposed purchase, which the men planned to inspect again the following morning. 'You'll have heard of all the Silicon Valley billion-aires buying up property around Queenstown. Their private jets are just large enough to fly direct from LA in case of trouble at home. I think the Wairarapa is the coming place. Queenstown has the natural beauty, but it's being overrun and it's far from any cultural centres. Of course,' he laughed derisively, 'they haven't taken the great Alpine fault line into account when they've been building their bunkers.' He speared a piece of asparagus and swallowed it with relish.

Lauren countered, 'You do know about the 1855 Wairarapa earth-quake, the one that gave Wellington plenty of shoreline to build on?' She took a sip of her wine, looked at him over the top of the glass.

Brett laughed again. 'I'm not planning to build a bunker. Nowhere is completely safe, but this is nice countryside, close to the capital and reminds me of the farming country I grew up in. But New South Wales is just too damned hot now and there's always the bushfire risk.'

Darya had set down her glass of wine. 'Brett, you didn't tell me about earthquakes.' With that, in a truth is stranger than fiction moment, there was a sudden bang as if a truck had crashed into the house. The crystal glasses tinkled and the chandelier swayed as the room shook. Brett clapped his hands and the other men were strug-gling to look cool. Darya shrieked loudly and dived under the table.

The room settled. Lauren was astonished; she was used to earth-quakes. Darya crawled out, clutched her chair as she stood, and sat down heavily. Her face was chalk-white and she had balled her hands into fists. Her voice was unsteady. 'I have lived too close to warfare. I distrust unexpected noise and heavings.' She picked up her glass and took a long draught. 'Please let us carry on.'

Lauren's phone beeped. 'GeoNet says that was a 4.3, centred north of Masterton.' She just stopped herself from saying, 'No big deal,' instead said, 'There should be no damage or aftershocks.'

The earthquake loosened tongues. Darya's wine was drained and her glass refilled, Kevin and Jason fortified themselves with more wine, and the conversation turned to politics. No-one in the room apart from Lauren had a good opinion of the new government. Kevin said it wouldn't last. 'Winston will bring it down. He doesn't see eye to eye with Jacinda on much.'

Lauren interjected. 'He did say that capitalism is not working.' The men all looked at her and then at one another, and smirked. They didn't bother to counter it. Darya said, 'You should try communism. That certainly does not work, in my experience.'

Kevin went on. 'You can be sure there are tensions within that the public doesn't know about, and then one day it will crack.'

'Like Lange and Douglas?' said Lauren.

There was a pause. Kevin looked startled, and Brett said, 'That of course was a very long time ago.' He changed the subject, passed a bowl of trifle to Lauren, and beckoned to the hovering waiter to pour more wine.

Lauren was astonished when Darya suggested she and Lauren retire after dessert while the men sat over their port. People still did this? She went along with it, noticing that Kevin in particular already seemed the worse for wear and wasn't improved by alcohol. He and his offsider may not have been tasting wine with them earlier in the day, but they were certainly off somewhere drinking.

Alone with Lauren, Darya reverted to her usual persona: elegant, imperturbable. Lauren ventured, 'I'm sorry the earthquake was so upsetting for you.'

'It is not good when buildings shake, and sounds are like the noises of warfare. I have survived such times and have no wish to experience them again. I will not let anything destroy my life with Brett.'

Lauren was startled by her intensity. She chose to change the subject and until they were joined by the others, they chatted about opera performances Darya had attended.

It seemed a long evening. Making conversation with a group of strangers she was wary of was hard work. She wondered again about Brett. It was extraordinary that Kevin had turned up here, but Brett's explanation seemed reasonable enough. She couldn't imagine them as buddies: Brett as the student she knew was overly pleased with himself, but he did have some cause. He was good-looking and very bright. Whereas she found it hard to imagine how Kevin had appealed to enough people to elect him. The party machine, she guessed. She was glad he hadn't recognised her.

The moment Lauren climbed into bed she fell deeply asleep. She woke suddenly, disturbed by a crash in the corridor outside her room. Her reading light was still on. Completely disoriented, she took a moment to remember where she was. Now she heard voices – Kevin and Brett. Kevin was apologising for something. He still sounded drunk. She tuned in. He'd fallen over a chair in the hall. The chair and he had gone down in a tangle and Brett had come out of his room to see what was going on. He wasn't mollified by Kevin's apology. Lauren thought he'd probably been woken up too. She looked at her phone. It was two thirty. She couldn't imagine why Kevin was wandering about. Apparently neither could Brett. He wasn't whispering, no doubt assuming everyone else was still sleeping. She heard Kevin again.

'If you must know, I'm worried. God knows what that fucking woman's got on us.'

'What are you talking about?' Lauren hadn't heard Brett sound icy before.

Kevin's voice rose. 'You know what I'm talking about. That Rowan Wisbech. Didn't you listen to that Radio New Zealand link I sent you? I'm sure she knows about us.'

'Kevin, keep your voice down and come into the study. You'll wake everybody.'

The voices retreated. Lauren was wide awake now. Brett. And Kevin. She'd speculated that Brett could have been involved but hadn't quite believed it. Here was the proof. So much for that bright charming student! Her breathing had changed. It was shallow and her heart was pounding. She shut her eyes, took three deep breaths and calmed herself. She wanted to hear the rest of the conversation. Dare she? Even as she wrestled with herself, she slipped out of bed, made her way across the room and cautiously turned her door handle.

It was dark in the hall but she could see a sliver of light coming from the study where the door was just slightly open. She padded down the corridor towards it, keeping to the sides where boards were less likely to creak, an old trick she had learnt as a teenager coming home late. She leant against the wall next to the door and could hear the voices again.

'I tell you, she's talked to all those damn women around at the time. Stupid bitches most of them. Up themselves. Half of them dykes, I reckon.'

'Kevin, you're enlarging on this quite unnecessarily. What you need to realise is that nothing happened–nothing happened, remember.'

There was a pause then something between a cough, a snort and a sob from Kevin. His words were still slurred. 'I might have said something to–' It sounded like 'juth'.

'Juth?'

'Judith.' Now he enunciated clearly. 'Ju-dith But-ler.'

'Who?'

'MP I had a fling with. Kept it secret at the time.'

Another pause, then venomous: 'You stupid little bastard. Look, it's an outside chance that this historian is onto you. But if she is, I'll tell you this, man, you're on your own.'

No pause at all and Kevin raised his voice again. 'Oh no, I'm not, you buggers might think you can keep your hands clean but I know who egged me on, I know who helped me work out how to do it. And little thanks I got for it in the end, after all the promises. I tell you, Brett Wilson, if I go down you're going down with me.'

A chair scraped. 'Oh no,' thought Lauren, 'he's coming out.' A lurch and a muttered oath. She forgot about creaking floorboards and fled down the hall to her room, wrenched open the door, flung herself onto her bed and pulled up the covers. She heard them out in the hall.

'Go to bed now, Kevin.' Brett's voice. Uneven footsteps sounded outside her room and receded along the hallway. Then more footsteps. Past the master bedroom, coming towards her room. A pause. She froze, her door was still slightly ajar and her reading light still on.

'Lauren?' It was Brett's voice. She said nothing. She heard him push the door further open, advance a step. 'Lauren?' She kept her eyes shut, kept breathing. He stood. It was a very long moment. Then he walked away and she heard him open the door to his bedroom. She'd better not turn that light off, in case he came to check. Surprisingly, it was her last thought before sleep took her again.

~

LAUREN SLEPT LATE after the previous night's disturbance. When she woke she was quickly alert, shaken by what she'd overheard, keen to leave, keen to get back again to Phyl, to Ro, to Deirdre. The house was quiet so she showered, dressed and went into the kitchen, steeling herself to stay polite to Brett and Kevin. It was a relief to find Darya alone. She was sitting there nursing a coffee. 'Good morning, do you eat breakfast?'

Lauren was surprised by the question but looking at Darya's slim figure, thought it might be maintained at some cost. 'I usually do,' she said. She felt sickish and thought that this morning wasn't very usual. Too many revelations in the middle of the night.

Darya gestured towards the bench. On it were a couple of opened packets of cereal, some spilled, bottles of milk with lids off, no bread to be seen but a smell of burnt toast. 'The men have gone out to look at a piece of land, they put out some breakfast things and left them there, so help yourself. Would you like a coffee?'

'Yes please.' Lauren found some muesli, added milk and a small banana and sat down. She took slow mouthfuls while Darya busied herself with the coffee machine, making herself a second cup at the same time. She spoke in her usual slightly formal manner. 'Brett thinks it would be helpful for our residency if we make some donations. I thought of opera or ballet. Do you have some connections?'

Lauren had been wondering what Darya would think if she knew Brett might have connived at attempted murder. Would Darya stay in New Zealand, if Brett were in prison?

Darya was looking at her. 'Lauren?'

Lauren wrenched her thoughts away from plots and tried to attend to Darya. She thought of her friend Megan who worked for the Wellington Festival. 'Do you know of the International Festival of the Arts held in Wellington every two years? The next one is coming up in February. I do know someone involved in the festival management; they're always desperate for sponsorship. It might be too late, though, the programme is out soon.'

'That is the kind of thing, perhaps you could put me in touch. I cannot imagine they would turn down offers even this late.'

'They do have patrons, platinum, gold, silver and so on; that might still be available.'

'No,' Darya said, 'we were thinking of something bigger, a named event. But give me your friend's details and I will contact her.'

Lauren thought that she might have created a headache for Megan. 'There are other forms of sponsorship, not just the arts. I'm sure Rape Crisis or Women's Refuge would be able to come up with something in a hurry.'

Darya scowled. 'That's not where I'd put our money. Women should be able to fend for themselves, not go running off when they run into a spot of trouble.'

It flashed through Lauren's mind that Brett as a student had been shaping up to be exactly the kind of man women's refuges were set up to provide escape from. And what she'd heard in the night suggested that he'd stop at nothing, if something was in his way. Darya might see herself as made of sterner stuff, but perhaps this was just a front. How could she raise the issue?

'Brett has quite a temper,' she said. 'I was very grateful that you managed to persuade him not to land in the fog yesterday. I was starting to feel very alarmed.'

'You have to know how to manage men,' said Darya.

'Some men don't react well to being managed. I'm hesitant to say this, but there was talk about Brett when we were at Cambridge. I heard that he punched one of his girlfriends, and there were rumours of other incidents.'

Darya interrupted. 'Oh, English girls! You don't mess with a

Ukrainian. He tried something on me once and I pulled a gun on him. No trouble since then.'

'A gun?' Lauren stared at Darya. 'How did you come to have a gun?'

'My little handbag gun.' Darya reached over and patted her handbag lying on the kitchen table.

Lauren swallowed. 'You do know that you can't carry those weapons in New Zealand? You surprise me.'

Darya smiled. 'I left it in London. Brett said we must be "squeaky clean" here, we want to buy our land.' She rose. 'You will excuse me. I must go out for a while. I am going to the village to interview a house-keeper. Please amuse yourself. I will be back by eleven, and that will be in time to get you to the midday train.'

Lauren was pleased to be left alone, there was so much to think about. She sat slumped with elbows on the table, head in her hands. Clearly, Brett was involved in the plot to kill Lange. Even if Kevin prepared and delivered the poison, Brett and possibly others helped to hatch the plot. And Kevin had expected to be handsomely rewarded. He must have chickened out when the poison only made Lange ill and the police interviewed him. Kevin was really unlucky that Dr Waddell had tested for aconite. One thing was clear: Kevin had a lucky escape and it would have been foolish for him to make further attempts.

But what now? She chewed a fingernail as she thought. Kevin had threatened to dob Brett in if he was exposed and more worryingly, he clearly had it in for Ro. It would not take long for them to find a connection between Ro and herself...or would it? She couldn't think how, but it made her uneasy.

An idea that had occurred to her the afternoon before came back. At least she could try to get further information to pin down Brett's involvement. The old passports she'd seen would show her the dates he entered and left New Zealand in the eighties.

She stood up, left the kitchen and walked towards the study door, which was open. Then she stopped, better look around first. She was sure the house was empty, but she walked past all the bedrooms, then through the living areas, out onto the terrace, back through the hallway and out the front door. Rural sounds floated by, cows chomping grass and belching, a dog barking in the distance, faint traffic from the highway. All clear, she left the front door open as she went inside so that she would hear any car returning. She went quickly into the study, closing the door behind her. The facing door into the living room was open and she left it like that–an escape route could be useful.

She sat down at the imposing desk and opened the top drawer. Three passports with their top corners clipped diagonally to show they had expired. She opened each and put them in date order. The oldest was an Australian one stemming from Brett's student days and she quickly skipped through the multiple entry and exit stamps for Australia, various European countries which he must have visited over the breaks, and a couple of later stamps bearing American insignia.

The middle one, a British passport, took her into the eighties and she quickly spotted some New Zealand stamps. She rifled through the drawer, found pen and scrap paper and began to work her way through, noting down the dates of six or seven entries and exits. There were lots of stamps from other countries, too: mainly Australia, the United States, Britain and other European countries. Brett had travelled very widely. There were also stamps for South Africa, Kenya, Cayman Islands, Channel Islands, Bahamas, Tonga. Were these all holidays? Sun and beaches? Big game hunting? Who knew. She suspected it was more about countries offering tax havens.

She pocketed the paper with the New Zealand dates on it and put the two older passports away. Then quickly flicked through the last one which ran from the mid-nineties onwards. It looked as if there were one or two trips to New Zealand but not as many as in the eighties. Some to Russia and Eastern Europe. Quite the international traveller, thought Lauren.

'What on earth are you doing?' Brett's voice was at her shoulder. Lauren jumped up, dropping the passport. She turned to face him. He looked angry. She must have been too absorbed to hear him arrive. 'You startled me! I just–I just came in'–there was scarcely time to think–'to look for a pen and writing paper. Darya's gone to Martinborough and I thought I'd make a start on my end-of-year letters.' She was recovering herself now and the words was flowing more easily. 'But I didn't find what I was looking for.' She pulled out a drawer, picked up a pile of stationery and waved it at him. 'It's all monogrammed, I couldn't use that.

'And apologies, I couldn't resist looking at all the fabulous stamps you've got in your passport.' She scooped it off the floor, then opened the top drawer. 'Here's your others, remember? You slipped them in here yesterday. I was going to mention them to you, you should keep them somewhere safer.'

Brett looked at her narrowly, but seemed mollified. He allowed her to push the passports into his hand. As his fingers closed around them, he said, 'You want to be careful, you don't want to get a reputation for poking around in other people's studies.'

'I do apologise. But I can't imagine you've got anything here you want to hide.' The piece of scrap paper was burning a hole in her pocket. She pinned a cheerful smile on her face and moved towards the living area. 'Is Darya back too? She said she'd get me to the midday train, I should ask her when I need to be packed.'

She was aware of him behind her, she felt the back of her neck prickling, but he said nothing more. Darya wasn't back, but Lauren took the opportunity to go to her bedroom. She shut the door, sat on the bed and tried to steady herself. After a few minutes, she stood up and began to pack her bag. She didn't relax until she had said polite farewells, and Darya had left her at the station.

16

'While bloody treason flourished over us'

It was a sunny day but not very warm for December. Ro was at her desk, a tattered dressing gown over her clothes, proof-reading an article for an academic journal. Lauren had just told her about the overheard conversation between Kevin and Brett. It was disturbing, but she put it from her mind. The work was more important. When that was finished she planned to stretch her legs by walking over Tinakori Hill to the university, to meet an overseas visitor at the faculty club for lunch.

She finished up and prepared to put the computer to sleep, when a familiar blank spot appeared in her vision. Before long, lights were dancing across the screen. Damn! A migraine coming on. Nothing for it but to cancel lunch, take her medication and spend the afternoon with her head under the pillow and the blinds down. She stumbled to the bathroom, her eyes half closed. There she swallowed two paracetamol with the help of a glass of water, popped a rizatriptan with some difficulty from its pack and placed it under her tongue.

In her bedroom, she shut the door, shook off her dressing gown, unbuttoned her shirt and gingerly stepped out of her jeans, trying not to bend down. She winced as she got into bed, but with the drugs kicking in she soon fell into an uneasy doze.

She was roused by a knock at the back door. 'Oh, go away,' she groaned to herself, 'I'm not getting up to talk to a pair of proselytising Mormons or whoever.' She rolled over painfully, ignored the second knock and began to drift off again. On the edge of consciousness she was startled by a creaking floorboard. Then a shuffling sound and the ping of her computer coming to life. 'What the hell,' she muttered.

She lay there for another moment or two, then got up cautiously, holding one hand to her head. Opening the bedroom door she called, 'Is that you, Timmy?' Tim was her next-door neighbour's son. She let him come over for a quiet place to study–or to play video games on her computer, more likely. But Tim should be in school. Or had school broken up for the summer holidays? There was no reply.

Ro stepped back into the bedroom to search out her dressing gown, lying in a heap on the floor. As she did so, she heard footsteps retreating down the hall. She opened the door again, just in time to glimpse a figure racing out the back door. She called out, 'Hey!' and made for the dining room where a window overlooked the path to the front gate. There was just a glimpse as the intruder ran past. Male, tallish, skinny in a young-looking way, jeans, hoodie, dark hair poking out. Completely nondescript.

She was nauseated, her head throbbed and it was hard to think straight. She paused at the door of the study where her papers looked disordered and the computer blinked at her. All she could think of was to go back to bed. She shut the back door, left it unlocked–she couldn't remember where she had last seen the key and was certainly not up to looking for it right then. She needed to sleep and would worry about it later. As she crawled back into bed, her last thought was that she needed to talk to Lauren.

~

LAUREN WAS PLAYING a game on her laptop later that afternoon when the phone rang. She tried to pause the game, failed and watched as trains puffed along and then crashed into stations while she fumbled for her phone. Then she forgot the game completely.

'It's Ro. I've had an intruder. And I had a migraine. I still feel like shit.'

'Oh Rowie, tell me about it. Do you want me to come over?'

Ro sounded shaky but thought she'd be best having a quiet night by herself. She explained what had happened. 'And the worst thing, that young guy got away with my memory stick.'

'What was on it?'

'Everything. All my book notes, background research, notes from interviews. It's all right, I haven't lost them, it was just a copy of the documents on my computer. But it couldn't be random. Kevin Driscoll must be behind it. It wasn't just a burglary, the intruder was looking through my papers and at the computer. You can buy a memory stick for less than ten dollars. No, they want to know what I've got, and what's even more terrible'–she paused–'your Judith Butler interview was on it. Kevin's seen you recently and if he listens to that he'll recognise your voice.'

'Not just that,' said Lauren. By now, she was pacing around the living room. 'I used proper oral history protocol. At the beginning of the tape I identified myself and the interviewee and the date. Oh shit!' She paused and thought. 'You haven't contacted the police?'

'I haven't felt up to calling anyone. You're the first person I've spoken to.'

'In that case, I'll phone Deirdre at once and she'll probably send someone round. Ro, are you sure you wouldn't like me to come over?'

But Ro still insisted she'd like to be by herself. 'I'm sitting quietly with Sooty on my lap and I'm drinking a big mug of tea. I'm not concerned about him coming back. They've got what they wanted from me, I suspect. I'll just have to put up with the cops messing around with my stuff. Just what I don't need right now. But you'll need to take care over the next while.'

Lauren gave an involuntary shiver and sat down heavily. What had they got themselves into? She hadn't thought of stuff like this happening when they started digging. She was probably sounding as shaky as Ro–and nothing had happened to her. She cleared her throat. 'Well, Kevin already has the interview, and I can't think there's anything he'd want to get hold of from my place. I don't see what else we can do, other than getting the police on to it. Anyway, I'm not going to be at home by myself much. Kirsten's coming next Friday for a meeting and staying for the weekend and it won't be long before we're off with the Wellington gang to the South Island.'

Ro agreed, 'It'll be good for you to have Kirsten around.' She was starting to sound better. 'And it'll be good when we get away.'

Lauren got off the phone and looked at the time. It was well after five. She found Deirdre's card and phoned her direct line. Deirdre was still there. 'It's Lauren Fraser here. Remember we talked about the plot to kill Lange? I do now have some more information.' Her voice quavered, in spite of herself. 'And something awful has happened that we need to report.'

Deirdre was clearly busy, but listened while Lauren told her about Ro's intruder and the theft of the memory stick with Lauren's Judith Butler interview on it. Lauren also relayed what she had over-heard between Brett and Kevin in the Wairarapa. 'Hmm,' Deirdre said, 'I think you're right–no doubt it was Kevin who organised the memory stick theft, after hearing your friend Ro on National Radio.'

Lauren felt relieved that Deirdre was not dismissive. Deirdre continued, 'It does mean they'll soon know that it was Judith Butler who has been talking. They won't know she is forgetful and that any evidence from her might not stand up, even if she was fit to be a witness. I'll get in touch with Karori Gardens and make sure their security is up to scratch.'

'And, Lauren, you need to be careful too,' Deirdre went on. 'If they're trying to find out who knows what and how to get rid of evidence, you are now just as vulnerable as your friend.' She paused and then said, 'Why don't you talk to Phyl about safety?' She sounded quite concerned and Lauren felt surprisingly gratified. 'I'm going on holiday shortly, won't be back till mid-January, so we'll take another look at the evidence then to see if what you've found could bring the case alive again. And ask your friend Rowan to lay a complaint about the burglary with Central Police. Right away.'

Lauren said, 'Can't you let them know?'

Deirdre became impatient. 'You need to follow procedure, but I'll check that they are sending someone around straight away to have a look. I'd be surprised if we find any clues as to who the intruder was. Probably some computer geek working for them, no doubt he wore gloves.'

Lauren dutifully talked to her neighbour the following morning. Phyl advised her to get a burglar alarm before she went on holiday. But somehow, in the lead up to Christmas, it just didn't get done. Partly because Lauren had never fancied setting and disabling an alarm every time she entered and left her apartment. She liked her home to feel open and welcoming. It was a week of very busy days. She and her friends seemed to feel they absolutely had to catch up with everyone before the holiday season was upon them—lunch dates, drinks, evening functions came thick and fast.

Lauren even had a breakfast meeting with a publisher, teeing up contract editing for the year to come. That was the Friday morning Kirsten was flying in so she couldn't meet her at the airport. She hoped Kirsten wouldn't take that as a sign of Lauren cooling. They seemed to have patched up the relationship, and it was shaping up to be a weekend full of treats, once Kirsten had finished her work. A Friday meeting in Wellington, how convenient! After that, a pre-Christmas Christmas, with a meal out at Field and Green, an exchange of presents and other delights. She had spent an enjoyable hour prowling around Unity Books to find Kirsten some holiday reading. She settled on *Manhattan Beach*, good reviews and a satisfactorily fat novel, then Claire Tomalin's autobiography, a little guiltily because she wanted to read it herself, and the second of Susie Steiner's engrossing Cambridge thrillers, which her friend Rachel had introduced her to. The shop assistant gift-wrapped them for her and put in an exchange card.

Lauren had scarcely been back in her apartment five minutes when she heard a bag being lugged up the steps. She opened the door, held out her arms to Kirsten, who looked preoccupied. Lauren got a peck on the cheek before Kirsten walked inside and dropped her bag. She said. 'My meeting's in the Hutt at ten. Can I do it?'

Lauren looked at her watch. 'Yes, if you hurry. Take the car, I don't need it today.' She handed Kirsten the keys. 'Hope the meeting goes well,' she said, 'Don't drive too fast.'

She didn't expect to hear from Kirsten during the day. So it was a surprise when the phone went no more than half an hour later. 'I'm terribly sorry, Lauren. I'm afraid I've had an accident.' There was none of the usual zing in her voice. 'But I truly wasn't going that fast.'

'What's happened? Are you hurt?'

'No, but it was really scary. I came off the motorway and the car just seemed to skid all over the road and ended up against a power pole.' There was a sob, and she said again, 'I'm terribly sorry, the car's a bit of a wreck.'

Damn, thought Lauren, she bet she was going too fast. She said, 'Is the car blocking the road?'

'No, there's a wide verge. But I don't want to try and drive it.'

'OK. First tell me exactly where you are. Then you phone a taxi to get to your meeting. Leave the car keys just under the driver's seat. I'll phone the AA to tow it to a garage. Don't worry. Just concentrate on your meeting. Someone will be able to drop you back.'

The call ended, Lauren immediately picked up the phone again to call her insurance company and the AA. A couple of hours later she was inspecting her rather crumpled car at a nearby panel beater. 'Oh dear.' The phrase seemed inadequate. 'Is it fixable?'

The panel beater looked cheerful. 'You're really lucky. It looks bad but the major damage is confined to a couple of panels, shouldn't have to write it off. If you tee it up with your insurance, we can do it for you but we're terribly busy. Just over a week to Christmas now. You won't get the car back till after New Year.'

17

'Enjoy the honey-heavy dew of slumber'

On Christmas Eve Judith Butler was lying on a yoga mat, one leg off the ground. She was trying to rotate her ankle. She'd forgotten why she was part of this group of very old people, none of whom she seemed to know. But they were all following instructions from the young woman at the front of the room, so she should go along with it. She tried to concentrate. Then she imagined the instructor saying, 'Simon says, do this.' She remembered that from her childhood. She laughed out loud and tried to wiggle her ears. The others now had hands on heads. 'Boring,' she thought, then caught the sound of her own voice.

Then a girl in a pastel uniform was helping her manage her walker. The corridor was ugly, institutional greens and browns adorned with garish abstract paintings. It had a seventies look. This must be her room, Judith half-recognised it. Yes, a photo of dear Tom. Why wasn't he here? And her two children in the old photo frame, the colour fading. Best of all, one of herself, nicely made up, bright red lipstick, blusher, eyeshadow, well-cut blonde-streaked hair. As she pulled at a straggly tuft of grey, she decided she should get some colour run through again. The photo showed another woman, a glittering chain around her neck, pinning a brooch on Judith. That was an important day. An MNZM? She couldn't exactly remember the initials, or what they stood for, but it was a good honour presented by the Governor-General. She sank into the chair by her bed.

Darya was also in the complex that afternoon. She had been visiting Mrs Kravetz, the mother of her hairdresser. Kateryna was someone Lauren had recommended for a sophisticated cut, and she was Ukrainian too. At Darya's first appointment Kateryna had chatted on about her home life, and spoken of her mother in aged care, surrounded by other people, but still lonely. Scarcely anyone at the home seemed to have heard of the Ukraine, let alone have any inkling of the language. 'Not that it's so difficult,' said Kateryna as she snipped at Darya's hair, 'a Slavic language, related to Russian, most of us Ukranians speak Russian as well.'

Darya had said, 'What do you expect? There are hardly any Russians in New Zealand. I myself lived in the Ukraine as a child, though my parents sent me to Moscow for schooling.'

'Oh, perhaps you could visit Mama.' Kateryna clasped her hands together, though she was still holding the scissors. 'If you have time of course. She would so love to speak her own language with someone other than me. The home's not far away. It's in Karori, Karori Gardens.' A customer in a seat near by, with hanks of hair wrapped in plastic, looked up from her magazine in surprise. Kateryna was speaking in Ukrainian.

'My dear,' Darya had said, frowning at her image in the mirror, 'I'm very busy settling in.' She answered in English. She was sure she wouldn't want to spend time with some old peasant woman; she was from a distinguished family.

LAUREN HAD NOT BEEN the only one woken by Kevin tripping over in the hallway the weekend they were all staying with Brett and Darya. It had also roused Darya, ever alert to any disturbances. She stayed still as Brett got up, tiptoed out and shut the bedroom door behind him. She heard their raised voices in the hallway.

All the bedrooms had French doors leading out to a terrace and front garden. She heard Brett tell Kevin to go into the study and when the footsteps receded, she slipped from the bed and quietly made her way outside into the soft dark. The study had a window slightly open behind the curtains and she crouched against the wall with her ear to the crack. She could easily hear their conversation. It was all about some old woman in a rest home, Judith Butler, who had talked to someone about Kevin way back, something to do with politics and a plot. Kevin threatened Brett saying he would expose him if the police got onto him. Darya thought that if she had anything to do with it, he wouldn't. She swiftly made her way back to bed and pulled up the blankets, shivering slightly; she needed to be warm by the time Brett got back into bed. She heard Brett tap on Lauren's door and call out to her. He must have been checking that she had not woken and heard anything untoward. Darya was feigning sleep when Brett came in.

In the following days she checked Brett's emails as usual. Brett changed his passwords from time to time, but she knew he kept them in a notebook and she took care to find it, wherever they were staying. She would use the current password until it no longer worked, and then locate the new one. Brett was often out and about on business. Darya made sure she was up to date with all of it; she needed to know that their life was secure, that no catastrophe would suddenly loom and surprise her. She'd had enough of catastrophes in her life already.

There were several recent emails from Kevin. She listened to the podcast of the woman talking about a government of the past. It was very boring and she wouldn't normally have given it the time of day, but she paid careful attention when the scholar said that revelations would be forthcoming in her new book. Then another email from Kevin saying that Jack the Hack had found something interesting for Brett to listen to. To her surprise, the attached voice recording immediately identified Lauren as the speaker and Judith Butler as the person being questioned. Even the location of the rest home was given. It was Karori Gardens.

The same place her hairdresser had mentioned. Karori, she thought she knew where it was. A Wellington suburb up in the hills above the city. The Russian Embassy was there. Kevin had said that Darya might need to go there on a passport matter, even though she was Ukrainian and had a British passport. Darya liked to have more than one passport up to date.

She pressed 'play' again and listened right through the interview. The key point was that Judith told Lauren that Kevin had tried to kill David Lange, apparently the prime minister at the time. It was away back in the 1980s. Darya thought hard about this. The murder attempt hadn't succeeded but might still have been a crime. Lauren must be involved somehow with the woman she had heard on the radio.

So Lauren was snooping. Was that the reason she'd come to their house for the weekend? The thought made Darya furious: she'd liked Lauren and valued her advice. It wasn't as if she had any friends here. But how much of a threat was there? The old woman sounded really off, rambling at times until Lauren got her back onto the subject again. Leading questions, they probably wouldn't stand up as testimony. A well-paid lawyer could put paid to all that. But Judith was definitely trouble, the way she was blabbing. Darya wondered who else she might talk to. She decided to put the question of Lauren's behaviour aside for the moment. She would deal with Judith, and then she would think about Kevin.

DARYA BECAME a recognised visitor to Karori Gardens, dropping in to chat to Kateryna's mother, Mrs Kravetz, every day or two over the run up to Christmas. The old lady was in heaven. She relayed memories of playing with her brothers and sisters in a pine forest, romping with the family dog, ripe peaches with warm juice dripping down her chin, bread dipped in honey at Christmas time, songs and stories, a painted wooden horse and cart. It was hard to quieten her once she got going. Darya would sit by her bed and think about other things, occasionally mouthing platitudes in the mother tongue.

Karori Gardens was a complicated warren with several wings set over three levels and at angles to each other. There were lots of swing doors halting the flow along the corridors but there were many exits to the grounds outside. Darya had used the confusing layout as an excuse to wander all over the premises and had easily located the Butler room. Conveniently, the residents all had their names on their doors.

Today, Christmas Eve, the place was festooned with moth-eaten paper chains hanging from the corridor ceilings, but otherwise things seemed as usual. Judith was sitting in her Lazy Boy chair. The tea trolley was rattling away down the corridor. The uniformed attendant had just delivered Judith's afternoon tea, a cup of weak milky tea and a cupcake splattered with garish orange icing. Judith grimaced at the cupcake. Was it edible? But she picked it up and cautiously licked the icing.

She was surprised when a visitor slipped into her room. She didn't recognise the person. But her memory was bad these days. 'Do I know you?' she asked hesitantly.

'Good afternoon,' Darya said, looking around for somewhere to sit. She perched on the edge of the bed. 'How are you today? Oh, I'm sorry, wrong room, I was looking for someone else. But while I'm here, let me give you your tea. Then you can have a nice lie down for the rest of the afternoon.' Darya picked up the tea and Judith heard the clink of a spoon. 'I don't take sugar.'

When Darya gave it to her, she swallowed it gratefully. She was thirsty and it didn't taste too sweet.

Darya watched her drink it, then left the room and headed over to Mrs Kravetz in another wing.

A passing attendant heard Judith's cup crash to the floor, and came to the rescue. She started to clean up, and Judith tried to stand. She felt unsteady, and said, 'Sorry, sleepy. I'll just take a nap.'

She was helped into bed and almost immediately drifted off.

Dreams played through her fading consciousness, half memories, she was a child again in Taranaki, her father swinging her on his shoulders as he carried her towards the sea. Then it was difficult to breathe. She tried to call out, gasped, felt something pressing harder and harder on her face and the waves took her into their watery realm.

Darya put the pillow back under Judith's head and stepped out of the room. No one was around and she left by an outside door. She crossed the car park and sat in her Audi for a moment before switching on the ignition. She drove carefully around the winding road that led to the exit. She felt like flooring the accelerator but kept her tension in check. One mess cleaned up, that was easy. And the old woman's passing was of no account. Bigger fish to fry now. Such a nuisance cleaning up Brett's messes, but as least he wasn't as bad as Piotr.

18

'Common pleasures; to walk abroad and recreate yourselves'

At about the same time on Christmas Eve Lauren was preparing to leave her apartment. She looked around. Everything seemed in order. Well, it would be. There was no one else around to mess things up or misplace them. No pets to make arrangements for. Kirsten's visit felt like a long time ago. The car accident had coloured the weekend and, while there had been good moments, it was starting to seem as if any patching in the relationship was coming unstitched. Couples counselling sprang into her mind but she rejected the idea with a shudder. She knew too many of her friends for whom that turned out to be the last rite of their relationship. But even though she and Kirsten hadn't planned to spend Christmas together, being apart over the festive season seemed a bad sign.

She locked up and got a taxi to the Interislander. She began to feel more cheerful. Christmas holidays with 'the orphans' were always fun. Any of her friends counted as an orphan if they weren't doing Christmas with family, or never did Christmas at all. This year there were eight of them, including Lauren's closest friends, Ro, Pam and Megan. They were going walking on the Queen Charlotte track in the Marlborough Sounds. They planned to spend Christmas Day in Picton and the following morning take a water taxi to the head of the Sounds to begin their four-day tramp.

Cook Strait was looking a little dodgy, according to the marine weather forecast. Lauren checked it as they waited for the boarding call. The day was warm but a northerly sprang up as they drew away from the wharf. Lauren had forgotten to take seasick pills. 'I hope the crossing won't involve too much pitching and rolling,' she said to Kiri, who'd organised the trip.

'The best thing we can do is go to the café right now and get ourselves one of their roast dinners. Tummies full before we hit the Strait and everyone should be just fine.'

They ate as a group, then went out on deck to look at the striking views as they skirted Wellington's south coast. Lauren was suspicious about Kiri's advice, but although the ferry began to roll when they got out in the Strait, she was quite comfortable. 'Didn't I tell you?' Kiri gloated as she marched around checking on the group, 'no seasickness.'

'It's the stabilisers,' Megan rejoined, 'The trip is nothing like it was years ago.' They laughed and Pam said, 'At least we've all had dinner.'

They reached Tory Channel, the narrow entrance to the Sounds. The rest of the journey in the fading light was mesmerising. They cruised along the passage between close-set hills plunging fjord-like into the sea. The shoreline was dotted with little coves, each with its own jetty and a sprinkling of baches.

Lauren, now relaxing inside on a comfortable chair by an expansive window, realised that she felt safe. She breathed in the sea air. Anxiety had been taking a toll. Ro came and sat next to her. 'We need this,' she said. Lauren couldn't have agreed more.

They reached Picton before ten and found the motel Kiri had booked, two to each room. Karen surprised them by saying she would attend a carol service and midnight mass in the little white wooden church up on the hill. 'Anyone want to come?' Lauren was tempted, remembering childhood Christmases, but sleepiness overwhelmed her and she turned in.

They enjoyed Christmas Day, keeping to their no presents rule and at Kiri's suggestion skyping and making phone calls to friends and relatives within a couple of time bands. That kept plenty of time clear for a walk and a long cheerful Christmas lunch Kiri had booked at a local hotel.

In the morning, Lauren phoned Kirsten, now at Mangawhai Beach with her parents. They conversed pleasantly enough but briefly, the signal fading from time to time. Lauren was aware that Kirsten was probably within earshot of other family members. She herself would be mostly out of cell-phone coverage on the tramp. She also phoned Martin, her son, in Sydney and was relieved that he would be having a Christmas meal with the family of a friend rather than spending the day on his own in front of a screen, which was what she had feared.

In the evening, she skyped Julia and the family in Brighton. When she fell happily into bed that night, she realised she hadn't given a thought all day to plots, break-ins or her personal safety.

She enjoyed the four-day walk immensely. The well-formed track offered stunning coastal views and a wonderful variety of native bush. Lauren and most of the others found it easy in spite of the ups and downs between the little bays, but when Megan almost called a water taxi to do the second day's leg, Lauren felt vaguely responsible. Megan had had no time to do any preparatory training, she'd been working so hard in her festival job, and she had mentioned to Lauren that Darya's late request to be a sponsor had made life difficult. However, the group persuaded her to stick it out. She managed the third day with less difficulty. Lauren knew that on tramps people found reserves of strength they didn't know they had. Was that a life lesson or specific to walking?

Lauren and Ro were able to talk together privately. Ro told Lauren she'd spoken to Moana, the other MP Kevin was having an affair with and to Judith Butler's flatmate, Catherine. Catherine had supported Judith's story about the argument with Kevin and the cut lip. She even recalled that Judith had been upset not only by Kevin's lashing out at her but also because he had revealed something appalling. But Judith hadn't said what, and never talked about it again to Catherine.

'So much for that, then,' said Lauren, and hitched her backpack further up her back. 'What about Moana?'

Ro screwed up her face. 'I had trouble getting hold of her; she was already holidaying with her son's family in Central Otago, and reception was pretty dodgy. No hard evidence, but we did talk for a while. She really got to dislike Kevin, said that the Lange-Douglas split was hard for all of them, but there were times he was virtually incandescent with rage. She thought he had some money riding on Douglas's economic programme continuing unchecked.'

'Little swine,' said Lauren. 'I bet he wasn't worried about principles.'

'That's exactly what Moana said–that he was just worried about personal profit. She reckoned she finished with him because he became more and more unpleasant.'

'But he never told her anything about the plot?'

'Afraid not,' said Ro, 'but she said nothing would surprise her, especially if he were being encouraged.' She too hitched her backpack higher as they swung up a slope.

Lauren had nothing new to report. 'I'm feeling really frustrated that the police don't think we've got enough already to make a case. I'd have thought the break-in to your place is more supporting evidence? And what about Kevin and Brett's conversation that I overheard. And Brett's passport details that I got. They show he was here at the time. I'd stand up in court and vouch for all that.'

'Mmm,' said Ro. 'The trouble is, I suppose, that it's all circumstantial.'

They leant into the slope and strode out thoughtfully; they were walking well ahead of the others. Then Lauren slowed. 'Let's forget it for now, and just enjoy the holiday.'

She took her own advice and by the time they completed the track and returned to Picton, she was restored to her usual cheerfulness. The group agreed it had been one of their best ever holidays.

DISEMBARKING from the Interislander after a smooth trip across the Strait, the women ordered taxis. Pam was the first to be dropped off. Her flat in Te Aro was in a dingy noisy block, surrounded by busy roads. The only time Lauren had been inside was when she was picking up Pam for an outing, and Pam realised half way down the stairs that she'd forgotten something. Lauren had followed her back into the hall, and found the place startlingly disordered and gloomy. She marvelled how differently close friends can live: Pam's place was a burrow, a storage and sleeping place; Lauren saw her apartment as a refuge and a restful place to be. She was next to be dropped off, and as always, felt a little shiver of pleasure at coming back home.

She hauled her backpack out of the boot, checked her mailbox–a late Christmas card, by the look of things–and made her way down the pathway. With a slight start she noticed that her car wasn't in its usual spot. Of course, at the panel beater's still.

She climbed the apartment stairs, walked past Phyl's place and saw that her neighbour's windows were wide open. Phyl must be back from her relatives. Good, Lauren could keep up her fitness taking Monty for walks. She rummaged in her bag, found the house key and unlocked the door. Dumping the backpack in the hall, she went into the kitchen to put on the jug, dropping the mail on the table. There was something strange in the atmosphere, an indefinably foreign smell. Of course, it had been shut up for nearly a week. Lauren opened a kitchen window and went through to the front rooms. Opening the windows let in a slight sea breeze. Funny, it smelt as if someone had been smoking in the living room. She didn't even know any smokers.

She went back to the kitchen where the jug was now boiling and opened the cupboard to get out a mug. Something fell and shattered on the floor. Damn, that was a mug Kirsten had given her, she couldn't have put it away properly. Kirsten would be cross. Lauren wrapped the shards in an envelope that was lying on the table and slid out the rubbish container from under the sink. It held a screwed up chip bag. She stared at it. Where on earth did that come from? Something was definitely wrong. Had someone been in her apartment? Perhaps Phyl had let someone in? Possibly the body corporate had arranged for an inspection, work to be done on the outside needing checking from the inside? Not likely at Christmas, surely. There must be a reasonable explanation. She'd ask Phyl shortly.

She made her tea and took it into the spare room to her desk, mainly used for storage since she preferred to work on the kitchen table. The papers on her desk were not exactly in disarray, but something looked awry. She couldn't remember how she'd left things, but it wasn't like that. She switched on her laptop and checked emails. A few Christmas offers still coming in, five or six emails from family and friends, either holiday news or lengthy end of year letters from friends abroad. Lauren relaxed as she read them, ruminating that it takes a certain type of person to do an end of year letter. Someone who's confident or deluded enough to think everyone is interested in what their grown children are up to, or which part of Europe they visited on holiday. She chided herself, she shouldn't be so cynical.

She went to check the news on Stuff, and clicked on her internet browser. It usually took her to the Google home screen. Instead, she was confronted with what looked to be a porn site–a busty lascivious woman beckoning her to explore the site and who knew what else. Lauren gasped. Someone had definitely been in her office and been messing around on her computer. That's not a tradesman! A shiver went down her spine. Oh my God, someone could still be in her apartment. She stood up hastily.

Her pulse quickened as she walked around. She checked wardrobes and the broom cupboard, she looked behind doors and curtains. She felt absurd. Surely she would have heard a noise if someone was still there. But she needed to reassure herself.

She checked the bathroom last. 'Oh, that's disgusting!' she said aloud. The toilet had not been flushed. She had certainly not left it like that. She flushed it, then had a sudden thought: should she have saved the contents to help with a police investigation–DNA or some such? Too bad, she couldn't abide it.

She prowled around the apartment again, checking for what might be missing. She drew a blank. Then it dawned on her. This was like Ro's break-in. It must have been organised by Kevin. Probably the same young man that Ro had seen fleeing up her path. She checked the front door but it didn't look tampered with. An intruder with enough skill to snip a Yale lock. Not that hard, though, a credit card could do it. She had even used that trick herself once, breaking into Megan's boatshed when the key wasn't where Megan had said. She cursed herself for not paying enough attention to Deirdre and Phyl's warnings about security. Phyl would be really cross with her.

If the aim of this nasty trick was to frighten her, well, it did. So one up to Kevin and his criminal associates. Her mind kept returning to the bathroom, that made her feel especially violated. She was jittery, needed to take some action, so she went through to the bedroom and stripped the sheets from the bed, even though they didn't look disturbed. She threw all the towels in the hamper, then turned on the shower. Feeling shaky, she stood under it for a long time, washing away real and imaginary grime. Tears ran down her cheeks along with the cleansing stream of water and she angrily brushed them away. Bastards, they wouldn't scare her off.

19

'I do not know the man I should avoid'

By the end of the following day, New Year's Eve, Lauren was feeling more on top of things. She had rung Ro and told her all about it, and went to ring Deirdre, when she remembered Deirdre wouldn't be back till mid-January. She decided not to do anything official about the break-in until then. When she told Phyl, she was chided less harshly than she expected for not having installed an alarm system. Phyl must have seen how upset Lauren was, and she suggested that Lauren take Monty for a restorative walk. She told Lauren to call the police, but although Lauren said that she would, she didn't intend to. What could they do? She didn't want to go through the whole story with someone new. She'd save it for Deirdre. She'd had quite enough on her plate for the day. She was looking forward to the fireworks, that would cheer her up.

The friends met at a designated spot near the waterfront. Ro gave her a bear hug and fussed over her. She caught Megan glancing quizzically at them. Damn the investigation, she couldn't even tell her friends about the break-in. She resolutely turned her mind away from it.

The New Year's Eve fireworks were the best yet. As a ratepayer, Lauren was happy to see her money go up in smoke. She and her friends always argued about whether they should be right down amongst the crowds on the wharf or in Megan's apartment, handy to the harbour and with a great view where they could watch with a drink in their hand. This year the waterfront had won. Then it hadn't been so far to walk back to Megan's where they celebrated the coming of the New Year with a midnight supper. What a year it had been. What was yet to come? Lauren wasn't one for New Year resolutions: it was so silly to vow to lose weight, be less stressed, get fitter, good intentions that were broken a week or two later. But she did think to herself, as others were trotting out resolutions, that this was going to be an eventful year. What qualities would she need to cope with it? 'To courage,' she toasted her friends, raising the champagne glass high. Ro looked at her sideways.

New Year's Day saw Lauren making herself a strong morning coffee. She took it over to her laptop, scrolled down her emails and saw that someone had sent her a Jacquie Lawson card. She wondered who it was from. The New Year's card featured balloons, bubbly, fireworks and jazzy music. Those cards might be kitsch, but high-class kitsch. Then she got to the message. It was much longer than usual:

"Thanks for making your apartment easy to get into. And your computer. Had a beer, bought a discount movie ticket on GrabOne. The boss says stop nosing about if you want a Happy New Year. Jack the Hack. PS And that goes for your friend in Wadestown too."

Bought a discount movie ticket! Lauren checked her bank account–yes, it was there, 28th December, but no other withdrawals she couldn't account for. So that's when he was here. And all too clever with computers. She remembered that you could look at the browser history and clicked on to it. That was a shock–a list of unfamiliar sites all on the same date, including porn sites, Google searches, Trademe, GrabOne, Jacquie Lawson, dating sites and, as she'd already discovered, her bank's web address. He must have found where she kept her passwords on the computer. Damn it, she'd have to change them all. Clever bastards, they were trying to unsettle her, but nothing major for the police to take seriously. Anyway, it was all evidence that someone didn't want them digging up the past. She'd have a lot more to tell Deirdre when she got back from her holiday.

The next day was a public holiday too, so it was the day after when Lauren rang the panel beater. Yes, the car would be ready in the afternoon. Later on, she walked down to the workshop and could see her little red car, one of the overflow parked on the road. She paused to inspect it. Beautiful again. She was smiling as she walked into the office to pay and collect her keys. There was a young man in there, an apprentice, she presumed.

'Oh, that car,' he said. 'I'll just get the boss, he wanted a word.'

The boss emerged from the back of the workshop, wiping his hands. 'Hi Lauren,' he said. 'She's looking good. But I wanted to talk to you about your tyres. Do you have them checked regularly? Or is someone trying to kill you?' He laughed awkwardly. 'Your tyres were only half inflated, no wonder it skidded all over the road.'

'Really? I had the warrant done in November, they were all good then.'

'Let's go and take another look. I'll get Dave to come as well.' He called to the apprentice and the three walked to Lauren's car. He said, 'Dave, you inflated the tyres, didn't you? Did you notice anything else?'

'Yes, I had to put on a couple of valve caps. They were missing.'

The panel beater turned to Lauren and said, 'It is very dangerous if your tyres are let down in this way. It affects both the brakes and the steering. You were lucky no one was hurt. Have a think about how this might have happened.'

LAUREN DROVE HOME SLOWLY and parked the car. She was trembling. A mixture of fear and rage. How dare they! Kirsten could have been killed. She could have been killed. Bastards!

It was better to be angry than scared and she stamped up the stairs to her apartment. The day was like the aftermath of a disaster. Phone calls, discussions, endless reflecting and mulling over. This time Phyl did chide her for not having put in a burglar alarm. She rang Kirsten who was also horrified.

'I noticed it wasn't handling well when I drove off. But I thought, that's just Lauren's crappy little car.' Lauren was offended but it wasn't the time to say so.

'Kirsten, I'm really sorry you had an accident. Of course, it wasn't meant for you—whoever did it thought I'd be driving.'

Kirsten snapped. 'So it should have been. At least you would have brought it on yourself. I'm losing patience with your obsession. You should stop snooping. Who cares if someone tried to kill Lange all those years ago?'

Someone cared, thought Lauren. And Kirsten's advice was the same as Jack the Hack's.

Ro reacted differently. When Lauren told her about the tyre tampering, Ro came over straight away. She thought Lauren should move out of the apartment until things cooled down. Lauren couldn't see how they would cool down, but she didn't see the point of sharing her pessimism. She couldn't stay at Ro's place, which was also unsafe. Ro herself was off to a conference in Australia and wouldn't be back for a couple of weeks.

They discussed where Lauren might go. Ro was still trying to keep their discovery to themselves, though Lauren was getting tired of treating it as hush hush. For one thing, it meant not throwing herself on the mercy of Megan or Pam, the obvious choices (though Pam wouldn't welcome a visitor to her burrow). Then Ro said, 'What about Michael?'

So Lauren explained to Michael what had been happening and, with a wobble in her voice, admitted she did feel in danger. Before she could even ask he said, 'But you must come and stay with us.' By the evening Lauren had locked up the apartment—for what it was worth—told Phyl where she'd be and taken her clothes and gear down to Michael and Kiano's spare bedroom.

~

A GOOD NIGHT's sleep helped restore Lauren's equanimity, though not to her post-holiday level. Breakfast was a leisurely affair and she sat chatting with Michael and Kiano for some time. Then Kiano excused himself. He was still on holiday, but he'd undertaken to re-gib their laundry and wanted to get on with it. Michael got up to make more coffee and said gently 'So what do you think you'll do now, Lauren?'

It was the question she needed. 'I've stopped feeling scared, thanks to you and Kiano, but I tell you, I'm still really angry. I'll talk to Deirdre again but she's not back for a week. What I really want to do is nail those sods for attempted murder. And if they carry on like this, it might be for attempted murder now as well as thirty years ago.' She sprang up, eyes suddenly alight. 'Hey Michael, can I use your landline. I'd like to phone Brett. And he won't know your number. I'll take him by surprise.'

Michael looked apologetic. 'We decided not to get one, Lauren. But use my mobile if you like.' Lauren almost snatched it from his hand. She was feeling a rush of energy and needed to phone Brett before her courage dissipated. She keyed in the number from her contacts list, stood still and waited. Michael was standing nearby with a coffee in his hand, listening.

'Brett? It's Lauren Fraser. No, I'm not after Darya... No, I've already arranged a time to visit a gallery with her. Brett, it's your friend Kevin I'm phoning about... What?... Your colleague, then. I believe you have influence with Kevin. I noticed the way you were with him that weekend in the Wairarapa. You need to know that in the last three weeks my friend Ro's house has been burgled, my apartment has been broken into, my car tires have been deflated causing an accident and I have received a threatening email. As you will realise, this all relates to the work Ro and I have been doing to unravel the plot against David Lange in 1988. Your friend Kevin was definitely involved and there were others.'

She decided not to elaborate. She didn't want to get into an argument with him, so she went straight on: 'You need to let him know the police are gathering new evidence at the moment from a number of sources. And it would not go well with Kevin and whoever else is involved if anything happened to Ro or me. Get Kevin to call off his dogs... What?... Oh, I'm sure you can. After all, Brett, you've always considered yourself a cut above people like Kevin. I'm sure you can manage...No, I don't want to have a meeting. I'm very busy on this case. Goodbye.' She ended the call.

Michael laughed. 'That was telling him. I reckon you'll get a bit of peace now. Oh, by the way, did you know that Judith Butler died? I saw her funeral notice in the paper a couple of days ago.'

20

'Men at some time are masters of our fates'

Lauren was back in her apartment after a few days with Michael and Kiano. Kiano had offered to install a videocam on her front porch, but she disliked the idea. The call she'd made to Brett had settled her; she no longer felt frightened. She didn't think there would be more interference. Of course, he must be wondering if Lauren and Ro had anything on him, but he would be unlikely to think that harming them would help him go unnoticed and she was confident he could control Kevin.

It was the news about Judith Butler that she found unsettling. She'd texted Ro right away, as soon as Michael told her of the death. It was late afternoon in Melbourne. Ro, supposedly now on holiday, was actually in the State Library of Victoria, doing some research on the 1980s neo-liberalism and the struggle between Lange and Douglas.

When she saw the text from Lauren, Ro said aloud, 'Oh no!' and was glared at by nearby library users. Lauren was asking her to phone urgently. Perhaps something else had happened to her? She left her spot in the library and ran out into the street to make the call. She found a shady spot and leant against the wall.

Lauren wasted no time on niceties. 'Judith Butler died on Christmas Eve. I've just found out.'

Ro jerked upright. 'That can't be right! I saw her just a couple of days before Christmas, and she was fine.' Her voice got louder. 'She was one of my favourite interviewees. She might have been forgetful, but she was in good shape physically. This is weird. Have you seen a death notice?'

Lauren had found the notice online. 'It said she died peacefully. She was seventy-six.'

'That's not old these days. Lauren, I don't believe she would have just died. I saw her the day before we went to the Sounds, took her some soap and hand lotion. She seemed fine.'

'Well, the notice did say peacefully, not suddenly,' said Lauren again.

'Bullshit!' said Ro, 'I bet it was sudden—and I'll bet my bottom dollar it wasn't natural. It's all too convenient—she spills the beans to us and then she carks it.' Her voice rose, and a passer-by looked at her curiously. 'Lauren, you need to find out more about it. It's creepy.'

Lauren sighed. It would be easier to take it as just a sad coincidence. But Ro was adamant.

'Okay, Okay, I'll see what I can find out and let you know when you get back to Wellington.'

'Thanks Lauren—and you take care, too.' Ro headed back in to the library, picked up the books she had ordered and returned them to the desk. She needed to go for a long walk to settle her distressed feelings.

Ro's conviction rubbed off on Lauren. It was now more than a month since Lauren had visited Judith. Ro was right, the woman was suffering from a degree of dementia, and she did have a walker, but she had not seemed frail when Lauren interviewed her. Surely there couldn't have been foul play...or could there? Deirdre had said she'd ask the facility to beef up security. She wondered if Deirdre had specifically mentioned Judith?

She wondered who she could talk to at Karori Gardens. Perhaps the staff member who found Judith dead. She phoned the rest home to see if she could arrange that. She lied, said she was writing Judith's biography and it was important to include end of life material. And that she would take up no more than five minutes of their time. There was some hesitation. She held, while consultation went on at the other end of the phone. Finally she was asked to come at eleven thirty the next day, the end of Jasmine's morning shift. She arrived to find the receptionist expecting her. She was asked to wait while Jasmine was located.

'Just sign in while I'm looking for her.' The receptionist went off and Lauren began to sign in, then stopped abruptly. She glanced around–no one in sight–then leafed back to Christmas Eve and ran her eye down the list of visitors. Good heavens, Darya Wilson's signature, visiting a Mrs Kravetz. What was that about? Why did the name sound familiar? And why would Darya take the time to visit someone in a rest home? She'd said she didn't know anyone in New Zealand.

There was no Kevin Driscoll signature. She mocked herself. He wasn't going to sign in if he could avoid it–and it wouldn't be hard in this rabbit warren to slip in, even if they were being more careful about visitors. She turned back to today's date and dutifully finished filling in her arrival time, purpose of visit, person she was visiting, and put the register back on the desk.

Jasmine came in. She seemed to be Indonesian or from the Philippines, like so many of New Zealand's rest home workers. She murmured greetings, eyes downcast, voice hesitant. Lauren sat down with her in the reception area, but out of range of the receptionist's hearing.

'Thank you so much for agreeing to see me.' Lauren was effusive. She sensed that the woman wondered if she were in trouble somehow, and was not confident about speaking up. 'I am writing about Judith Butler. I would like to hear of her last hours. She had been an important person, she was a member of New Zealand's Parliament.' Now I'm talking down, she thought, and stopped.

Jasmine brightened. 'She was a very nice lady. So sad. I was surprised.'

'Surprised?' Lauren tried not to sound too eager.

'She had not seemed so sick. Then I had to help her into bed that afternoon and when I came back to get her for dinner, she was'–she hesitated–'gone.' She crossed herself.

Lauren was puzzled. 'Why did you have to help her into bed that afternoon?' Jasmine explained how she had found Judith sitting in a chair with her tea cup broken on the floor, and how wobbly Judith had seemed.

'Had she had any visitors?'

Jasmine screwed up her face in thought. 'I do not know,' she said. 'I did not see anyone, but I am not always near that room. But,' she brightened, 'a name would be in the visitors' book if anyone came. We are very careful to record visitors; we had a training session on security just recently.' She spoke again of the shock of finding Judith dead, and finished, 'But when they called Dr Kumar, he said old people just go when they are ready. He is a very kind man. But so sad, just before Christmas.' Her voice wobbled. 'I cried when I cleared her room. All those lovely Christmas cards.'

Lauren rose, said her thanks again, and left. She felt slightly sick. So Judith had been well until the day she died. She had a ghastly feeling Ro was right –it was foul play. They might have stricter security in place, but she bet that a visitor could avoid being noticed. There were always lots of people around. As she walked to her car, she thought grimly that pursuing a cold case was one thing, but this was another. All too immediate, too present. And Kevin–she was sure it was Kevin or someone he hired–wouldn't have bothered if it weren't for Ro and her.

She drove home, ate lunch and went to fetch Monty from Phyl's on autopilot, all the time thinking about Judith. 'I'll have him back mid-afternoon,' she told Phyl, 'I've got a hair appointment after that.'

She put Monty into the back seat of her car and drove over to the wind turbine track in Brooklyn West. Familiar territory for the dog.

He bounded out of the car and rushed up the track, tail waving joyfully as he sniffed for rabbits.

'Monty! Come here!' called Lauren, and she kept him in sight as she began walking up the steep track. It was a stiffish climb, one that followed the contours of a long fence snaking its way up the slope. The track emerged onto a flat area of grass where the wind turbine soared grandly upwards. The view was spectacular, with Wellington city stretched out in front, Cook Strait on the south side of the city, and the harbour on the other.

Lauren paused there, plopping herself down on the edge of the grass by the turbine. Usually she took time to admire the view, but not today. Today she was mulling over the interview with Jasmine. Judith's death just didn't seem natural. And if Kevin had murdered her, what else might he be brewing? Two break-ins and deflated tyres might have been just the start for Ro and her. She was glad she'd phoned Brett and hoped that was enough to stop Kevin.

She sat there, idly plucking the tops off pieces of grass, and wondered if she was being melodramatic. Perhaps it was a natural death. Her thoughts were still disjointed, but she decided to do some more digging. The Dr Kumar whom Jasmine had mentioned would be a good place to start. He had been happy enough to sign the death certificate.

She sighed. A pity Deirdre was still away. If Kevin had done it, of course he would have got in somehow without signing the visitors' book. Weird that Darya happened to be there. Perhaps she could contact her and ask if she'd seen Kevin that day?

She watched Monty turn on his back and, twisting from side to side, slide down a slight grassy slope. It had become a ritual act, a way of scratching his back. She let him climb up and roll down several times before they set off again down the track. Home, return Monty to Phyl, change into respectable clothes, get to the hairdresser. Lauren always thought she got a better cut if she looked smart when she arrived.

When she walked into the salon Kateryna greeted her with more than her usual enthusiasm. 'I'm very pleased that you sent Mrs

Wilson to me, such a kind woman.' For an instant, Lauren couldn't think who she meant–Darya didn't seem like a Mrs Wilson.

'Oh–Darya! Yes,' she said.

Kateryna continued, 'I told her of my mother in Karori Gardens and said that she would dearly like to converse in Ukrainian.' So that's why Darya was in the visitor's book! Kateryna chatted on. 'At first I thought I had offended her, she said she would be too busy. But a few days later Mama told me that a nice woman had been to see her and they enjoyed talking about the old days. She even visited on Christmas Eve, so thoughtful!'

Lauren stiffened. Perhaps it wasn't such a simple explanation. That was quite a coincidence. She shrugged to loosen her shoulders.

Kateryna said politely, 'Please keep still, the scissors are very sharp.'

'Sorry.' Lauren tried to relax. But Darya? Could she have set up her visits just to get to Judith Butler? No, too far-fetched altogether. Brett was unlikely to have confided in her.

IT HAD BEEN difficult to get an appointment with Dr Kumar. He was a GP at a group practice in Karori West. The receptionist tried to put her off. The practice was full and they were not taking on new patients. 'It's not for a consultation,' Lauren said, 'I just need five minutes of his time...' She searched for an explanation. 'I was close to a woman who died recently at Karori Gardens. Dr Kumar completed the death certificate and I want to ask him about the circumstances.'

The receptionist sounded doubtful, so Lauren went on, 'She was an important politician in her day and I'm writing her biography.' That seemed to do the trick, an odd way of pulling rank, Lauren thought, intellectual intimidation.

'He can fit you in just before surgery closes, at ten to five.'

The waiting room was far from empty when Lauren arrived. She resigned herself to quite a wait but it was a busy practice with several doctors present, and it was only a little after five when she heard her name called.

Dr Kumar had distinguished silvery grey hair, gold-rimmed spectacles and a well-cut dark suit. He shook her hand and invited her into his office. He looked fatigued but smiled at her politely. 'How can I help? Karen said that you were enquiring about one of my patients.'

'Yes, Judith Butler, who died just before Christmas at Karori Gardens. I believe you were the attending doctor.'

'Yes, that's right. What did you want to know? I should warn you that I cannot breach patient confidentiality.'

'Was Judith your patient, or were you called in when she died?'

Dr Kumar looked a little defensive. 'Our practice regularly attends elderly patients at Karori Gardens. It was Christmas Eve and we had been very busy that day. I can tell you that she was not my regular patient.'

'Can you tell me a little about what an attending doctor does in these circumstances?'

Dr Kumar visibly relaxed, once he realised he wasn't being asked to reveal private information. 'Our job is to ascertain that the patient has indeed passed away. We check for a pulse and look for other vital signs. We look at the patient's records and we speak to the staff about the circumstances. I can't give you specific information but I was satisfied that her death, although sudden, was not inconsistent with her medical records. Older people usually hang on till after Christmas, but to die suddenly is not uncommon.'

'I know she had Alzheimer's.'

'Death can be a relief, it's always distressing when people hang on for too long.'

'Is there any possibility someone could have hastened her death?'

Dr Kumar looked startled. 'Karori Gardens has an excellent reputation and I have never heard of any such suggestion before.' He stood to conclude the interview.

21

'I never stood on ceremonies'

Lauren bypassed Palmerston North, taking Highway 57 towards Ashhurst. A couple of days earlier she had called Judith Butler's daughter, Jen Bates, who had been named in the death notice. She told Jen that she was involved in Ro's project on Labour women and that she had recorded an interview with her mother some time before she died.

'I'd like to discuss some of the content of that interview with you. And as well as interviewing women politicians of the day, we're also talking to some of the family members to find out what it was like for them.' Lauren excused herself the fib, if it could help her find out more about what happened to Judith.

Jen seemed friendly on the phone and eager to talk about her mother. She explained how she had grown up in Palmerston North but moved to Ashhurst after marrying into a local farming family. Her mother had been disappointed, the Bates were all National voters and Federated Farmer types, like most in the district. Jen and Trevor had raised their children on the farm and the older two had left home now, just her and her husband and youngest daughter left in the house. She agreed to see Lauren and gave her directions.

The countryside Lauren was driving through looked fertile. She could see monster wheeled irrigators in the paddocks that were divided with wire fences. Her view from the road included milking sheds, haybarns and other outbuildings as well as the occasional farmhouse. Most paddocks were empty of livestock, but large herds of cows munched contentedly in some, suggesting they were to be rounded up for milking. Rolling countryside to the east gave way to the steeper bush-clad slopes of the Tararua Ranges.

She spotted the Bates' driveway by its dairy company number. The entrance had the usual rural postbox with its red flag up, as well as a patch of red hot pokers flanked by flax bushes. Her car rolled noisily over a cattle-stop and up the long gravelled driveway to the house on a small rise giving a view over the surrounding farmland. Jen came out of the front door and greeted her. She was a strong-looking, tanned woman of medium height with a warm smile.

'Come in. I've put the jug on and the scones are just out of the oven.'

Country hospitality, Lauren thought, remembering her student holiday job many years back, when she cooked for the shearing gang on a South Island sheep station. She'd become a dab hand at scones, always required in great quantities for morning smoko, though she seldom had occasion to make them now.

They sat down at the kauri kitchen table. Lauren was surprisingly hungry after the two-hour drive and was soon wolfing down a scone smothered in raspberry jam and cream, for all the world like a shearer.

She complimented Jen on her baking, swallowed the last mouthful and began. 'So, tell me what it was like for you when you were growing up in Palmerston North and your mother was elected to Parliament. She was in for two terms, wasn't she?'

'Yes, she got in on the 1984 swing to Labour, when I was fifteen and my little sister was twelve. She'd stood the time before, and before that, in the seventies, she was elected to the Palmerston North

City Council. I was born in 1969 and I can't remember a time when Mum wasn't involved in politics. She was out lots in the evening at meetings, there were always people calling in and there were often meetings at our house. I complained so much when I was twelve about being chucked out of the living room just before my favourite programmes, that I got a television in my bedroom, the envy of my friends.' Jen smiled at the memory.

'I'm making it sound as if Mum was neglectful but she wasn't at all. She was a very bright, outgoing person and she was fun to be around. When she was home she saw to everything. Dad was more the quiet type but he looked after us when Mum wasn't there.'

'Did he find you and your sister a handful?' Lauren asked, adding 'Teenagers, you know.'

Jen cast her mind back. 'Dad was at work, didn't usually get home 'til after five. Everyone came around to our house after school because there were no parents. Congregating at the house where there is least supervision, scoffing toast or cereal or icecream after school, playing loud music ...my kids have been through that stage but at least I'm around, so they couldn't get out of hand. When Dad arrived home, the other kids would scarper and he would try hard to be the disciplinarian. We had to help get the tea, do the dishes and then our homework. And off to bed by nine, lights out soon after, that sort of thing.'

'Sounds pretty normal.'

'Yes,' said Jen. She placed her cup carefully down on its saucer and looked at Lauren with a rueful expression. 'Of course, it was before the days of cellphones, so Mum was really out of touch, not like nowadays. Parliament often sat late and I couldn't usually phone her in the evenings though there were times when I really would have liked to talk to her.' She paused. 'But on the other hand, Parliament is only in session about half the year so she was still around a lot.'

'How did your mother seem over those years? Did she like being an MP, do you think? Very different from local body politics.'

'She was a born politician, she just loved it. But there was a tense time when there was all that ill-feeling between David Lange and the Roger Douglas camp. Mum was somewhere in the middle, she admired David Lange but I don't think she was close to him. And while she didn't really like Roger Douglas all that much personally, she seemed to think that was the right track to be on, until it all started to come unstuck. I couldn't follow it really.'

'Anything specific upset her, do you recall?' Lauren didn't really expect a useful answer.

Jen looked thoughtful. 'There was a time when my sister and I got really worried. We thought Mum and Dad might be headed for a divorce. Dad seemed really grumpy and once when she came home from Wellington she had a cut on her lip. They had the most tremendous row that night, we couldn't help hearing them yelling at each other. She just looked miserable around then. Actually, I started to go a bit wild.... But you don't need to know all this.' She looked away and started rearranging the cups and saucers on the table.

Lauren smiled sympathetically. 'It's just what the project is interested in, politicians and their families. But I do have a difficult subject to broach and I don't know quite how to go about it without upsetting you.'

Jen looked puzzled. 'Oh?'

'Have you ever heard of a politician named Kevin Driscoll, same era as your mother?'

'I do recall the name. I seem to remember that my mother didn't think much of him. But how is that relevant to anything?'

Lauren took the plunge. 'Kevin Driscoll was closely involved with the Douglas camp, he was their numbers man. I think he may have had a brief affair with your mother.'

Jen looked shocked. She shook her head in disbelief. 'Mum would never have!' Her face reddened. 'And that's quite an accusation to make. Is the project just digging up dirt, in which case I don't want anything to do with it!'

Lauren tried to reassure her. 'No, this is something quite serious. We have reason to believe that Driscoll was involved in a plot to kill David Lange. Obviously, that didn't happen, but we understand from talking to your mother that he said something to her about it. She first mentioned it when Ro, my colleague, was originally interviewing her, and then told me more about it.'

'That's crazy. I find that hard to believe. Did she actually say she'd had an affair with him?' Jen stood up and began clearing the table, banging dishes down noisily on the bench.

'I'm afraid so,' said Lauren, turning towards her, 'but she said it was an awful mistake. I don't think it lasted long. Politicians often run off the rails, women too, and it was the eighties, it was quite a free time.' She could see how upset Jen was, so to soften it, she said, 'Judith did say she had a really strong marriage—she said your father was a lovely man.'

Jen faced Lauren, clutching a tea towel. 'This is all a bit of a shock, with Mum only just passed away.' She began to pace around the room, trying to make sense of it. 'I suppose you noticed that Mum's memory was going. She found it hard to remember what she had for breakfast, or what happened yesterday. But she had very clear recall of earlier times, she wouldn't have been confused about that, we often used to chat about those days. I suppose she tried to protect me.' She added with a wry smile, 'Even though I am middle aged with three children.'

She glanced at the clock. 'I have to go and pick up my daughter.' She frowned at Lauren and Lauren stood up too. 'Just one more thing. New information on the Lange plot has come to light. Kevin heard an interview on the radio with Rowan Wisbech, the leader of this project, and realised that his past was catching up with him. It is just possible that he took your mother's life.'

'What?' Jen shrieked. She turned on her heel, grabbed a purse and car key from the kitchen bench. 'That's absurd. I think you'd better leave.'

Lauren said a hasty goodbye and made for her car. She reversed, the farm dogs barking as she did so. She drove off feeling a mixture of embarrassment and upset. How might she have handled the disclosures better? Jen's reaction was probably inevitable, no matter how Lauren had told her. Had the trip been worthwhile? Jen had confirmed the story about the cut lip, though Ro had already had it confirmed from Judith's flatmate. And she'd said her mother's memory for times past was good. But nothing else. Lauren drove back to Wellington oblivious to the landscape around her.

Later that evening, as she was preparing for bed, the phone rang. 'Hi, is that Lauren? It's Jen Bates here. I'm sorry I was so angry with you this afternoon.'

'I quite understand, I was the bearer of upsetting news.'

'Yes, it was indeed. I talked it over with my husband this evening and he thought I should phone you, tell you how surprised we were when Mum died so suddenly.'

'You weren't expecting it?' Lauren had reached to close her bedroom window, but she paused, straightened again.

'The thing is, I couldn't get down to see her as much as I would have liked but I do go–did go–most weeks. I last saw her on Christmas Eve, in the morning. She seemed very well. She was on and off, but that was a good day for her. We went and sat for a while out in the gardens. She didn't seem like someone who was ready to die.'

There was a long pause. Lauren said, 'Hello?' Had they been disconnected?

Jen snuffled. Her voice sounded constricted. 'My husband said to put aside the stuff about Mum telling you she had an affair and focus on what you said about the possibility of that man wanting Mum out of the way. We'd like to know more. So, how can we find out the truth? Have you spoken to the police? Should we get in touch with them?'

Lauren said, 'I've an ongoing conversation with a police officer about the Lange plot. She's back from leave next week and I'm going to see her. I've other evidence to put in front of her and I'm sure she'll want to get in touch with you. I'll give her your details.'

EARLY MONDAY MORNING, Lauren phoned Deirdre for an appointment and was delighted that she could see her that afternoon–perhaps she wasn't back at full speed yet after her holiday. Lauren arrived slightly early and they spent a few minutes on seasonal pleasantries: how was your Christmas? Decent weather during your holiday?

Then Deirdre said, 'So what do you have to tell me, Lauren?'

The story came tumbling out. The car tampering, the break-in to her apartment, her phone call to Brett to tell Kevin to lay off. How she'd gathered evidence about Judith Butler's death and Kevin or someone he'd hired might have killed her.

There was a pause. As usual, Deirdre had listened carefully. 'Did you report the break in to the police?'

Lauren was nervous. 'I was waiting for you to get back because I knew you'd understand.'

'What about the car tampering. Has that been reported?'

'No, same reason....'

Deirdre sighed. 'It's much easier to collect evidence if we get on to a crime as soon as we can. Never mind, I'll get you to go down to Central and fill out an incident report, police will get a statement from you, come and take a look at your apartment and your car. They'll probably do some finger-printing so be prepared to clean up afterwards.

'The next thing. Phoning Brett: was that wise? You've alerted him to what's going on and that could make an interview with him more difficult.' Lauren winced. 'Now, Judith Butler.' Deirdre stopped and thought for a moment.

She stood up, pushed her chair into the desk, paced from side to side of her office, came back, pulled the chair out, and sat down again. She said, 'What on earth were you thinking? If you were suspicious about Judith Butler's death your proper course was to inform the police as soon as you could. I'm not the only person in the police force. All this poking around and questioning that you've done will have just muddied the waters. And it's now far too late,' she looked at the calendar, 'two weeks since her death, for us to examine the scene in any useful way.' She paused again and then looked at Lauren, her brown eyes steely. 'I suggest you get on with whatever it is you usually fill your time with and leave solving crimes to us.'

Lauren was dumbstruck. She felt just as she had when ticked off by the headmistress of her school for some misdemeanor–and that was decades ago! Her stunned silence must have had some effect, because Deirdre relented. 'Look, Lauren, you did some useful work on the Lange investigation and I'm grateful for that.' Then she frowned again. 'But you will have realised that that possibly resulted in an early death for Judith Butler. If inquiries had been official that would have been unlikely to happen.' Lauren was aghast. Deirdre was blaming her–or her and Ro–for Judith's death.

Deirdre carried on. 'We'll follow up on this information and we may call in Kevin Driscoll for questioning, but it's still unlikely to result in any sort of charge. Meanwhile, you may think you're safe, but I'm not so certain. I would strongly advise you to be out of Wellington for the next while, and that applies to your friend too.'

'Ro's in Australia,' said Lauren, 'She's been at a conference and is adding some days' holiday before she comes back. I suppose I could go to Auckland for a time.'

'Good,' said Deirdre. 'I'll let you know if there's any outcome from all this, but meanwhile, please, no more sleuthing.' She stood up and gave Lauren a wintry smile.

22

'It is the bright day that brings forth the adder'

Darya arrived at Wellington station mid-morning. Brett had driven over early and she'd told him she'd get the train. She went to the bank of lockers and chose a free one, into which she placed a large sealed envelope. She closed the locker, chose a four-digit code to lock it, then walked briskly towards the waterfront.

Kevin was met by Executive Chauffeurs at Wellington airport. He was due to have lunch with Brett at Shed 5, a waterfront restaurant. Brett had sounded cool when they last spoke. Kevin couldn't tell whether that was because of the conversation they'd had in the Wairarapa about the Lange stuff. Naturally they couldn't talk about that over the phone. Or was it that the land transfer wasn't going well? It turned out that the best feature of the property, a small lake ringed by bush, was subject to an iwi settlement to compensate local Maori for historic land confiscation. That had escaped Kevin's notice.

As the driver pulled onto the wharf, he told Kevin there was a change of plan. He was to meet Brett at the steps down to the jetty where private boats were moored. The driver pointed out the direction and Kevin, taking his briefcase, made his way towards the jetty.

The waterfront was busy as usual on a sunny January day in the school holidays. There were teenagers on roller blades and skateboards, family groups with babies in front packs and toddlers in pushchairs. Ferg's Kayak Hire was in full swing and older people were wobbling along on e-bikes they were trying out for the first time. Kevin had no interest in these leisure activities but noticed everything. He was used to keeping his eyes peeled, especially in Wellington where there were many people he still knew. The great and the good and a sprinkling of the mean and the bad.

As he walked towards the jetty he spotted someone vaguely familiar coming towards him. A tall lean sixty-ish man, walking briskly. He looked in good shape, wearing expensive-looking leisure gear and smart boat shoes without socks. Kevin felt an instantaneous dislike in the moment before he recognised him. It was Michael Peston, he hadn't seen him since the eighties. Hadn't he gone overseas to some atrociously hot country to do good deeds? The two men's eyes met, holding a gaze briefly, before both looked away and walked on, Kevin turning towards the jetty steps.

He spied Darya standing at the top of the steps. 'We are lunching on the harbour today. Go on down, Brett will be along soon and I will wait for him here.'

Kevin descended the steps towards a catamaran. A crew member he felt he'd seen before stood at the head of the gangplank. 'Go on down to the cabin.' It was a large comfortable-looking boat. Kevin noticed that it was for hire by charter or available for one-hour harbour tours. He didn't much enjoy boats, but it was a pleasant day and he thought their meeting might be less tense in an environment where they could speak frankly. And he had a thing or two to say to Brett, who looked set to let him down again. Kevin was going to insist on being paid a full fee, even if the sale didn't go through, and another fee for the immigration work. That would make up, three decades late, for being ripped off when the poison didn't kill Lange, or even put him out of action entirely.

He slid open the glass door into the cabin and stepped cautiously down the three steps, half-blinded by the contrast between the dim interior and the strong sunlight outside. Someone grabbed him by the shoulder and pushed him further in. He was regaining his balance as he heard the door slide shut behind him.

Sitting at the table was someone who would strike fear into the heart of anyone familiar with New Zealand's small gangland culture. Instantly recognisable despite his dark glasses was the man known locally as the Chief. Kevin had seen photos of him–as now, wearing a dark well-tailored suit. On occasion he had had dealings with his associates. And dined in his restaurants. And made use of his brothels. 'Sit down' said the Chief, gesturing at Kevin with a pistol. 'Don't say a word.' They sat in silence. Kevin half turned his head, to see the hefty man who'd pushed him into the cabin standing behind him. The man's impassive face and cold stare frightened him and he turned back to see the pistol waving threateningly. He kept still, his heart pounding, a flush rising that made the back of his neck prickle. The gangway clanked as it was pulled on board, the anchor chain ground its way in noisily, there was a smacking sound as ropes hit the deck. The engine revved and Kevin could see through the high cabin windows that the boat had begun gliding away from the wharf.

After a few minutes the man, still pointing his gun, said to Kevin, 'You've been a bit of a blabbermouth. Time to shut your mouth for good.'

'Listen,' Kevin heard his voice come out as a croak. 'I don't know who's paying you, but I can pay you more. Tell them you've done it, and I'll scarper. I'll leave the country. God's truth.' It was an unfamiliar oath, and it didn't have any effect.

The man laughed. 'I don't think you could afford us.'

'Just tell me,' said Kevin. 'My old mum's got property worth a packet–I'll get it sold and give you the lot.'

The Chief gave a chilling smile that reached nowhere near his eyes. 'Say your prayers, mate. You're bound for a watery grave.' He nodded to the man behind. The last thing Kevin experienced was a burst of pain and an overwhelming darkness.

Brett was already seated at a table in Shed Five when Darya walked into the restaurant. He was looking at his phone and didn't notice her approaching. Darya smiled as she slipped into the seat opposite him and observed her husband. Brett was ageing gracefully. His height, his charming smile, his cultivated voice all could make heads turn. His wealth helped, too. It was a careful haircut, an elegant suit and beautiful Italian shoes. Darya was well pleased with him and certainly would not countenance their being pulled apart by nonsense thirty years old.

'Hello, darling,' she said. He was surprised. The endearment was unusual.

'Hello,' he said with one of those attractive smiles, 'but where's Kevin, and are you planning to lunch with us? You don't usually want anything to do with him. And Kevin and I will have business to discuss. The land sale has hit a bump, some Māori thing.'

'Kevin won't be coming,' said Darya calmly. With that a phone dinged. It didn't sound like Darya's, but she fished it out of her pocket and said, 'Oh, excuse me a moment.' She stood up, walked to the ladies', replied to the text with '3784', then dropped the phone in the special bin for sanitary products. That was a good lead Kevin had given her, but Brett was right, the man had been a fool. She walked back to the table. Brett looked at her, puzzled.

'Kevin won't be coming?'

'No, he won't be coming ever. You don't need to worry about him and his loose tongue again.' Then she picked up the menu and glanced at it. 'Shall we have oysters? Bluff oysters? They're one of the things I enjoy about this country. But Brett, I do not like the earth shaking and I think in coming days you may hear some things about Kevin. It would be better for us to leave this place. We should go back to London where we have friends of our own class.'

Brett sat perfectly still. His face whitened. Then he picked up the menu. In a tight voice he said, 'Darya, I have asked you before not to interfere in my business interests. A piece of land in New Zealand would have suited me. I am not going to ask what you've done, I don't want to know. But I tell you this, I might look instead at something in the New South Wales highlands. No problem with residency there. And if I go there to negotiate a deal I will not take you with me.'

'We'll see,' said Darya, keeping her voice steady. 'Now, oysters, half a dozen or a dozen each?'

23

'Dwell I but in the suburbs of your good pleasure?'

L auren didn't leave Wellington immediately after Deirdre suggested she should. But she found herself more safety conscious than usual. The chain secured her front door in the evening; she didn't take bush shortcuts on her walks.

By Friday she was in Auckland. She had felt reluctant to ask Kirsten if she could stay for a while and she didn't tell her why. Their phone calls recently had been stilted. The relationship was fraught. But Kirsten met her at the airport, a good start to the weekend, and it went well from there. They went to a party on the Saturday night, mostly a different crowd from the Greece group. They lay in bed late on Sunday morning, then strolled to a nearby café for lunch.

By mid-week she wasn't so sure. Kirsten had a frenetic regime. She went to work early, didn't get home till after six and was always buzzing with the latest triumph or setback. No sooner was she home on the Tuesday than she rushed out again for a Zumba class, and told Lauren she'd be out on Wednesday night as well for her workout at the gym. So they usually dined late. Kirsten would drink two or three glasses of wine, crash out in front of the television and then fall deeply asleep as soon as she hit the pillow. Lauren began to feel overlooked.

On the Wednesday evening they had a quarrel. Kirsten came in late after her workout. She seemed agitated and had hardly put down her sports bag when she told Lauren there was something they needed to discuss. Lauren was startled, she had been feeling like a spare wheel, but she didn't think Kirsten had noticed anything wrong. She made Kirsten a green tea and herself a black one and sat down beside her on the sofa, afraid of what was coming.

'What was the name of that aged care facility you were poking around in?' Kirsten asked abruptly. Lauren was offended at her tone, but replied, 'Karori Gardens.'

'Damn!' said Kirsten. 'I really wish you'd leave all this alone, you put me in a difficult position.'

'What on earth do you mean?'

'We've just landed a new account.' Kirsten mentioned the name of a well-known company whose business was aged care. 'They've just purchased Karori Gardens. They're changing the name and are tarting it up. They want to feature the makeover in a new series of ads.'

Lauren couldn't figure out what that had to do with anything. She looked puzzled and Kirsten went on. 'I was talking to their comms person today, she's doing a risk analysis, because of course you can't have any negative publicity just when a new campaign is going to air.'

Kirsten wouldn't meet Lauren's eye. She looked over her shoulder, apparently contemplating the garden, then clenched her jaw. 'I suddenly put two and two together and realised that's where you're claiming a murder happened. Though it seems unlikely. If word got out that the police are investigating, it wouldn't look good for my client. Lax security and all that.'

Lauren's cheeks went hot. She felt anger coursing through her. 'This is a murder investigation, who the hell cares about your client's reputation! A woman I respect was probably killed. Isn't that more important?'

Kirsten squirmed. 'I knew you'd take that tone. Look, I didn't bring it up with the client, I wanted to get confirmation from you first that we're talking about the same place.' Her tone changed, less pleading and more direct. 'And don't forget, Lauren, I could have been badly hurt, even killed, in your car because of your interfering.'

They were at an impasse. Lauren served up the simple meal she had prepared and they ate in silence. She was glad the flatmates were out. The evening passed slowly. They were both determinedly reading and said little to each other. By next morning the tension had lessened. But Lauren felt at a loss. No apartment of her own to mooch around in, no dog to walk, no community garden to help in, no one to go on outings with during the day. She spoke sternly to herself. Right, find a yoga class, do some long walks, visit the art gallery and the museum. Such a regime should see her through the week.

Thursday found Lauren walking up Mt Eden, determined to enjoy the stunning views across the Waitemata as far as Waiheke and the outer gulf islands. She kept remembering Kirsten's accusation. Kirsten could have been killed, and Lauren should have apologised again. She was too angry at the time. Now she shrugged and wondered again how long the relationship would last.

She made her way down by one of the tracks circling the volcanic cone, then walked into the village. There she spent time browsing at the local bookshop and decided to lunch in the café on the corner. It was crowded as usual, and she glanced around from habit, but of course there was no one she knew there. She picked up a newspaper from the pile against the window and took it to a free table, then went to place her order.

She was idly leafing through the paper when she froze. Kevin Driscoll. The name leapt out at her. Missing. Police asking to be advised of any sightings. Description: male, age 64, medium height, greying hair, no distinguishing features. An unappealing photo accompanied the story. It went on to describe him as an immigration consultant from the North Shore and a former Member of Parliament. Last known to have arrived at Wellington airport on Friday 19th January. There are fears for his safety. If Mr Driscoll sees this, will he please report to any police station. (Lauren thought that was unlikely.)

She sat and stared at the paper but she wasn't seeing it. Why would Kevin disappear? Why were they worried for his safety? Was that even true? Her thoughts raced round and round. She told herself firmly to calm down. She took a deep breath and considered if Kevin might have arranged his own disappearance. Only if he was scared of someone finding him–or finding out about things he'd done. For all she knew, he had lots of shady deals going on.

A waitress brought her an omelette and a flat white. Lauren scarcely remembered to thank her, she was thinking so hard about Kevin. She picked up a knife and fork but continued to ponder. Kevin was spending a lot of time on Brett's affairs so probably it was something to do with Brett. He was scared of Brett? She screwed up her face, took a mouthful, and thought, surely he wouldn't run from Brett? That business of 'taking Brett down with him' that she'd overheard suggested that he didn't expect any retaliation. Perhaps he was wrong. Or could he have taken his own life? That didn't seem likely. The worm was too narcissistic to take that way out of a scrape.

For a moment, Lauren attended to her food. As she sipped her coffee, she considered another possibility. Perhaps someone had made away with him–but who? The finger pointed at Brett, but she couldn't quite believe it. Dammit, that veneer of politesse that Brett's upbringing and wealth gave him made it hard to think of him as a common criminal. She'd sooner believe it was Darya.

Darya! Lauren still couldn't make her out, really. Such a surprising woman. That story of pointing a gun at Brett was extraordinary. Clearly she had Brett under her thumb. And there was no way she was going to see their luxurious lifestyle threatened. Darya might do anything to stop Kevin taking Brett down with him. But surely she didn't know anything about the Lange plot.

Lauren was so deep in thought that she started when the waitress came to clear her table. She smiled, stood up, said thank you and absently tucking the café's newspaper under her arm, set off at a brisk pace down the road to Kirsten's house.

~

THE PHONE RANG for a long time before Mrs Driscoll picked it up. She sounded quavery, but when Lauren identified herself her voice hardened. 'I told Kevin about you visiting and he said you were trouble, trying to make up things about him. I thought you said you were checking out naturopathy courses.'

Lauren thought quickly and decided not to make excuses. She replied, 'I'm sorry Kevin thought I was trouble. I was phoning to say how sorry I am to hear he's missing.' She crossed her fingers. 'You must be very worried.'

'Worried! It's beyond belief. I don't understand it at all. It's just not like Kevin to miss my birthday. He's always made sure he's home with me. Last Saturday it was and I'd made a roast dinner for us. And I waited and waited and the vegetables got cold, then I put them in the oven and they dried out.' Her voice broke. Any suspicion she had of Lauren was overwhelmed by the need to tell her story. 'And he wasn't answering his cellphone so on Monday I rang his work and he wasn't there either. That Jason Snell said he'd been in Wellington for a meeting but hadn't been in touch. Jason thought he'd be in later.

'I rang in the afternoon and he was still not there. Still nothing on the cellphone and it was making a funny noise.'

Lauren murmured sympathetically and Mrs Driscoll went on. 'It was me who phoned the police. First they told me not to worry. They said I should wait a few days. Treated me like a fussy old woman. I set them right. I told them Kevin Driscoll was an important man with all sorts of overseas clients who couldn't be kept waiting for him to turn up.'

'Absolutely.' Lauren was encouraging, though it was unnecessary. Mrs Driscoll paid no attention to her listener and continued her monologue. 'They left me hanging at the end of the phone for a very long time. Then the officer came back and said they'd start making inquiries straight away. Making inquiries! I want them to find him. And then he started asking me all sorts of impertinent questions.

How had Kevin seemed when I saw him last? Was he worried? Tense? Hmph. My boy. All they need to do is find him. Useless.'

Lauren made more soothing noises and asked if Mrs Driscoll needed any help or company (an emphatic 'no') and ended the call. What Mrs Driscoll hadn't been able to tell her was what really interested her. Why institute a full-scale search so early? Deirdre must be wanting to talk to Kevin.

Damn, she didn't want to be stuck up here in Auckland. She and Kirsten were clearly drifting apart, the good times merely obscuring the widening crevasse. She determined she would return to Wellington at the end of the weekend. She had felt unsafe because of what Kevin might do, given what she thought he had already done; now she didn't know what to think.

~

ON SUNDAY, Michael rang, calling her cell. 'Hi Lauren. You still in Auckland?'

'Yes, back tomorrow, what's up?'

'I wondered if you'd caught up with the news—Kevin Driscoll has gone missing. Had you heard?'

'Yes, and I spoke to his mother; it seems no one knows where he is. He didn't show up at work either. But I can't look into it too much—Deirdre gave me a telling-off for prying.'

'You might be surprised to know that I've met your lovely policewoman too.'

Lauren could imagine the twinkle in Michael's eye and suppressed a smile. 'I got in touch with them,' he went on, 'because I saw Kevin on the waterfront the day he went missing. Haven't seen him for years, but it wasn't hard to recognise my tormentor from those times.' He struggled to make light of the pain that had cut deep. 'Not a pretty face, and still a bad fashion sense. I think he recognised me too but we didn't acknowledge each other. He was heading down some steps onto the jetty where the pleasure boats depart. Deirdre seemed to think that was a useful lead.'

'Why on earth would Kevin be going for a cruise?' Lauren asked.

'No idea,' said Michael. 'He was wearing a suit, perhaps some corporate function. There's a large catamaran moored there that gets hired out.' He paused, 'Thinking about it again, I saw him speak to a well-dressed woman at the head of the steps, so it must have been a corporate function.'

Lauren stiffened at the end of the phone. 'Tell me about the woman.'

'Can't really, Lauren, it was only a moment and by that time I was quite a way away. Let's think.' He paused. 'I noticed she was well-dressed because she had heels, a very flash handbag–I can spot those at a hundred metres–and a short stylish cut. And I think she was loaded down with jewellery–something was flashing off her anyway.'

'Oh my God, that sounds just like Darya.'

'Your Ukrainian? I can see you're still on the case,' said Michael. 'Don't get in Deirdre's bad books, will you. Anyhow, let's catch up when you're back in town. Kiano is doing some backbreaking work this weekend and there's the bones of a rock garden emerging.'

'I'd love to,' Lauren replied. It was so good to have those two around.

Then her thoughts returned to Kevin. What was going on with Darya? There was no way Darya would have helped him skip, she'd made her opinion perfectly clear. So if she wasn't helping him, what was she doing? Her thoughts whirled. Kevin, the Lange plot, Judith Butler, Brett, Darya, Karori Gardens, a catamaran... She couldn't see how it all fitted. It was too hard. Or possibly, too awful to contemplate.

24

'I am constant as the northern star'

Monday saw Lauren happily back in her apartment, except that Kevin's whereabouts was still on her mind. If someone may be out to get you, you want to know where they are.

Fearing another dressing down, she put in a call to Deirdre. 'Any updates on Kevin Driscoll? I'm back in Wellington now.'

'We're following some leads,' Deirdre replied. 'I can't tell you too much but the police are inspecting a catamaran that was hired out on the day Kevin was known to have arrived in Wellington. With that tip-off from your friend Michael, we believe he may have been on it.'

'I talked to Michael yesterday,' said Lauren. 'He hadn't told you that he spotted a woman with Kevin who may have been Darya– Brett's wife. While we were talking he remembered that a well-dressed woman spoke to Kevin on the jetty. It sounded to me like Darya.'

'Interesting,' said Deirdre. 'When we talked to Brett, he said he was to meet Kevin for lunch at Shed Five but he didn't turn up, so he and his wife had lunch without him. We'll have to talk to Michael again, and to Brett's wife.' She sighed and said, 'At least I've had more people assigned, what with the Judith Butler investigation and now this. By the way, we've virtually no hope of finding if there was anything suspicious about her death–Judith Butler was cremated. Meanwhile, you should continue to be security conscious.'

It was reassuring that Deirdre was forthcoming, Lauren thought as she put the phone down. She was worried that she might have been permanently on the outer. She talked to Phyl, who came up with a myriad of suggestions for how Lauren could guard her house and her person. Lauren felt she hardly needed to do anything, Phyl was so hyper-vigilant. Still, she would consider an alarm system. Ro could benefit more from Phyl's advice, since she too might still be in danger. She checked her diary; Ro would be flying back late Wednesday and then they could catch up.

It was annoying not knowing what had happened to Kevin, but he did seem to have disappeared. For the time being, at least. Perhaps for longer. She had been thinking about Darya again, and how surprised she'd been to know Darya was a visitor at Karori Gardens. A death and a disappearance with Darya in the vicinity on both occasions. Her neck prickled. Things seemed to be coming to a head.

IT WAS before nine when she rang Ro on Thursday morning. A sleepy voice answered the phone. 'You have to wake up, Ro. Lots to tell you–did you keep up with New Zealand news while you've been away?'

'I know the news about Jacinda being pregnant, it was all over the news in Oz. Stunning, eh!' She was waking up quickly. 'Mostly a good press, too, apart from some of those Aussie radio jocks. They're such sexist boors. They talk as if only men are fit to run the country.'

'Yes, yes, but that's not the news I want to talk with you about. You need to get straight up and come over here. I'll make you some breakfast and a coffee. And Ro, find your key and lock your door before you leave.'

While she was waiting, Lauren rehearsed what she wanted to tell

Ro: Deirdre telling them to butt out, being sent out of Wellington, no leads to find if Judith's death was murder, Kevin going missing–and Darya being present in Karori Gardens the day Judith Butler died and then on the wharf talking to Kevin.

Ro arrived looking disheveled, as if she had thrown on whatever clothes were lying on the floor. Lauren placed muesli, fruit and yoghurt in front of her and they sat at the kitchen table, the morning sun streaming into the room. Lauren spoke while Ro ate and after Lauren had finished, Ro sat silent for a minute or two, frowning. 'Extraordinary,' she said at last. 'I've been so keen to get on with writing something about the Lange plot.' She sipped her coffee and said, 'Perhaps if I named Kevin as one of the plotters, he might turn up from wherever he is to sue me.'

'Better sued than murdered.' Lauren was tart rather than amused and Ro apologised for making light of it. 'It just seems so absurd. Things that happened in history come to haunt us. It's like a weird dream.'

Lauren looked at her. 'Get a grip. We need to think carefully about this. Judith was almost certainly murdered for talking to us.' Ro winced and put her head in her hands, as if trying to banish the thought.

Lauren continued, 'My best guess has been that Kevin was behind it. Or someone he hired. Although Kevin would have been less likely to look out of place at Karori Gardens than some thug. He could have claimed to be an old friend. Some truth in that.'

She wrinkled her nose, then stood up and started to clear the table. 'But now I'm wondering about Darya.' She put dishes on the bench, then turned around to Ro. 'Darya was on the spot and she does strike me as ruthless. And now that Kevin's disappeared....' She didn't finish the sentence. 'But back to Judith. I've been racking my brains to think how we could turn up anything that might implicate Darya.'

Ro thought hard. 'It's an off-chance, but how about we talk to your hairdresser's Mum, the one Darya was visiting? From what you've said, Darya doesn't seem the sort to bother doing acts of kindness. Perhaps the old lady can tell us something about those visits.'

Lauren thought she herself should steer clear of Karori Gardens. She had probably stretched their cooperativeness to the limit. They decided Ro should visit Mrs Kravetz. She wanted to go immediately, but Lauren advised her to go home first and get dressed more respectably. Ro took the implied criticism with reasonably good grace. 'Do you think I should get a blue rinse on the way?'

'Shut up,' Lauren replied, giving her a hug and pushing her out the door.

'LAUREN.' It was Megan's voice on the phone. Ro had not long left, and Lauren had just got to her desk. 'Are you free for a coffee? I'm at work, but there's something I'd like to talk to you about urgently.' Lauren agreed to meet her at Pandoro's in half an hour. It was turning into a busy morning.

'It's about Darya Wilson,' Megan said, after they'd ordered their coffee and found a seat. 'I told you how difficult she was, wanting a prime sponsorship during the Festival, even though the programme was just going to press. We managed something at the last minute, got them in as co-sponsors of one of the big events. Sydney Opera Company.'

'Yes, you told me. What's the opera again?'

'Tosca. Puccini.'

Lauren nodded, 'Oh yes, the one where the heroine stabs the villain who has it in for her lover.' Possibly more appropriate than anyone might guess, thought Lauren.

Megan looked irritated and impressed at the same time. 'Yes, I know you're an opera buff, but it's not the plot of Tosca that I wanted to discuss. Darya hasn't stumped up the money. It was a lot, fifty thousand. We usually get donations in before the programme goes out, but the timing was so tight. We asked Darya to pay in the New Year.

She promised she would, but when I checked after getting back to work the funds hadn't come in.'

Their coffee was delivered and Megan continued, between sips. 'I emailed her last week and got no reply. I had taken down her details, so early this morning I phoned her. She was difficult to talk to. She seemed in a rush. Firstly she apologised—not very sincerely, it seemed to me—and said she'd been very distracted. Asked me to contact her husband and assured me he'd sort it out. Told me I'd find him at home. Then she hung up without giving me his details. I thought you'd know how to get in touch with him.'

Lauren frowned. She couldn't tell Megan why Darya might have been distracted over the last few weeks. The most she could do was reassure her. 'I'm sure Brett will forward the funds. It wouldn't be in his interests to break a promise. He's quite set on being the big phil-anthropist. I can give you his number, it's still in my phone.'

'Thanks,' said Megan. 'I hope you're right. The funny thing was, I'm sure Darya was at the airport when I was talking to her. I distinctly heard one of those announcements blare out when she was speaking. I had to ask her to repeat herself. I'm sure I caught the word 'Sydney'.

Shit, thought Lauren, she's scarpering. 'What time was that?' She tried to sound casual.

'Must have been around eight thirty. I'd been putting off phoning her because she was such a difficult woman, but I thought I should do it first thing, so it wouldn't hang over me all day.'

Ro WENT to Karori Gardens later in the morning, her sombre mood a contrast to the first visit, when she got so excited about what Judith revealed in her interview. Despite the police warnings about security, there was no one at the reception desk. Just a note giving visitors an extension to phone. She picked up the visitors' book, and began leafing through it. Yes, Darya clocked in at two thirty on the 24th of December. She flicked further back, and found more visits—all around two thirty, so nothing odd there. She wrote her own name in with today's date, then rang to find out where Mrs Kravetz was.

Mrs Kravetz was sitting on a chair in her room, her walker nearby and a tray of magazines to hand. She didn't appear to be doing anything, just staring at the floor as if lost in thought. She raised her head when Ro came into the room and looked pleased to have a visitor, even though it was clearly not someone familiar. 'Good afternoon, dear. And who might you be?'

Ro had her introduction prepared. 'I'm Rowan Wisbech, I'm a friend of Mrs Wilson. I understand she's been visiting you. We're a little concerned about her, we haven't seen her lately. Have you seen her since Christmas?'

Mrs Kravetz looked worried. 'No, she last visited on Christmas Eve. I've been disappointed not to see her again, I so much enjoyed talking to her.' She looked around. 'No one else speaks Ukrainian here, did you know?'

Ro brought her back to Darya. 'But Mrs Wilson does?'

'Yes, and she's such a lady, always dressed smart, but she didn't talk about herself. Have you visited her house? Is it nice?'

Ro lied. 'Yes indeed, over in the Wairarapa, a lovely place. So how did Mrs Wilson seem to you when she last visited?' As she spoke, she perched on the side of the bed.

Mrs Kravetz looked thoughtful. 'It's funny that you should ask, she did seem out of sorts that day. She usually came a bit before afternoon tea, and stayed and had a cup with me, then left. But on Christmas Eve, I'd just heard the tea trolley clattering down the corridor when she suddenly got up and went out; I thought she'd left. But, no, she came back in and we talked some more–but she missed out on her tea. She stayed longer than usual and then she rushed off again, without saying Merry Christmas.'

The old woman lowered her voice. 'To tell you the truth, I thought she must have a tummy bug.' Then she brightened again. 'She did leave me a present.' Mrs Kravetz reached into the bedside drawer and pulled out a pretty little brooch. 'It looks very expensive, don't you think?'

Ro leant over and admired the brooch. She had no idea whether it was Cartier or crap. She said her goodbyes gracefully and left.

BY THE TIME Ro phoned again, Lauren was home from coffee with Megan. She had scratched herself together a late lunch and was wondering whether she should call Deirdre about Darya being at the airport. But Deirdre probably knew already, she'd said she wanted to speak to the Wilsons. And by now Darya would be well off on her journey, wherever she was headed. She told Ro about Darya's possible flight.

Ro was full of news, too. 'Mrs Kravetz said that Darya did behave oddly. Bolted out of the room at afternoon tea time, then stayed on late, then suddenly left. What do you think?' They imagined scenarios–all of them involving Darya spending time in Judith's room, either once or twice. What Ro reported was enough to convince Lauren that it was Darya, not Kevin, who had killed Judith. She must have set up the visits with Mrs Kravetz as an alibi. Could she really have been so devious? She must have been desperate to stop Brett being implicated in the Lange plot, if Kevin caved in to police questioning. How she could have known about it was unclear.

'It's still all supposition,' said Ro. The police might be onto the Wilsons about Kevin's disappearance, but they won't do anything about Judith.'

'And who do we care about most?' Lauren replied with a wry smile.

Ro surprised her. 'I still care about who was involved in the plot against Lange. For all we know there could have been other people spurring Kevin on, as well as Brett. It's what started all this. And it was you who went on about bringing them to justice.'

Lauren had to agree. 'I still think that's important. But now I want the perpetrators brought to justice for much more recent crimes–and more successful ones at that.'

Ro was insistent. 'We don't know that Brett was involved in

Judith's death or Kevin's disappearance. If Darya has scarpered, it leaves the way clear for me to talk to Brett about the plot against Lange. And, Lauren, I'll need you to come with me, to find the house–and to introduce me.'

'Introduce you! You want me to say, "This is my friend Ro–she's here to grill you about your movements in 1988"? And besides, Deirdre has told us not to do any more snooping. We should just let her know what Mrs Kravetz told you about Darya at the rest home.'

Ro managed to look like a child begging for a sweet. 'We can't let it rest here. Please, Lauren, can't we pretend we just happened to be in the Wairarapa, and thought we'd pop in? A social call?'

Lauren looked dubious. Then she laughed. 'There is an excuse we could make–Megan asked me to check that they'd put that donation into the Festival bank account. OK, I'll come with you.'

25

'Into what dangers would you lead me, Cassius?'

They set out before lunch the next day. They'd decided not to say they were coming. 'Surprise is a good tactic,' said Ro. Lauren wondered if Ro had been reading military history.

As they wound slowly over the Remutakas, Lauren remembered her last trip to the Wairarapa. The helicopter ride had been quite an experience, noisy and fast and great aerial views until that fog came down. That had been scary, Brett being so reckless before Darya intervened.

On this trip she was enjoying the magnificence of the ranges, as the small ribbon of road twisted and turned and slowly rose through line upon line of steep hills. At the summit she pulled over, parked the car and said, 'Let's look at the views on both sides and think about how we're going to manage the conversation when we get there.'

She paused, and then confessed, 'I still think we've been a bit hasty. I don't know that we should be going to talk to Brett in that isolated house all by ourselves. I know Brett had a temper when he was young, and I've seen him being obstinate to the point of folly lately. Stubborn and bad tempered, could be unpleasant to be around.'

Ro got out of the car and stretched, her red hair glinting gold in the bright sun. She said, 'He's unlikely to do us any harm, no matter what we say to him. Too many other people know about everything now—the cold case, Judith's death, Kevin's disappearance. I'm still really keen to see how we can tie him to the Lange plot. That's what we're missing. Let's walk up to the lookout and decide how we'll approach him.'

At the top, they took in the spectacular views before they sat down on the grass and thought about the forthcoming meeting.

Lauren said, 'I realise we'll need to be circumspect. We'll start with Megan's wanting to know if the Arts Festival money they promised is coming. Should we tell him Judith's death looks suspicious? And should we say it's strange I asked Brett to call off Kevin, and now Kevin's disappeared?'

Ro said, 'I don't think we can second-guess how it'll go. We should just be as polite as we can, but look as if we think he has some answers. I'll record the conversation on my phone. And don't forget what we really need to know: how was Brett involved in the plot to poison Lange?'

'You wouldn't get the truth if you asked him that direct,' said Lauren.

Ro nodded gloomily, and they walked back down the lookout track and got into the car. The road downhill was much quicker than the long haul up and they made good time to Greytown. It was Lauren's favourite settlement in the Wairarapa. It still had the air of a sleepy tree-lined country town, in spite of all the restaurants and shops catering for visiting Wellingtonians. They didn't want to arrive at Brett's right on lunch time, so they stopped at one of the restaurants.

'We don't want to be starving when we get there,' said Lauren. 'We may not even be offered a drink.'

'We mightn't want it if he did offer it,' said Ro, almost sounding lighthearted. 'Never know what might be in it.' Lauren was still nervous, but that made her laugh.

~

LAUREN THOUGHT she could get to the house from Masterton, the way the taxi had taken them. She had begun to think she'd taken a wrong turning when she saw the high fence and gate ahead. They stopped, Lauren pressed a buzzer.

'Is that the courier?' said a voice. It was Brett.

'It's Lauren Fraser.' A pause, then, 'Come in.'

The gate rolled back and they drove in. By the time they were out of the car, Brett was standing on the front porch. Good heavens, thought Lauren, we've caught him before he's shaved. He certainly wasn't looking as suave as usual. His hair was disordered, not artfully. He definitely had a five o'clock shadow, his shirt looked unironed and his trousers rumpled. He managed a civil greeting, though.

'Hello, Lauren. What an unexpected pleasure. And...?' He turned to Ro.

'This is my friend Rowan Wisbech.'

'Oh yes,' said Brett. 'The historian of the Lange years. I heard your interview with Kim Hill.'

Before Ro could respond Lauren said brightly, 'We're hoping to see Darya.'

'Well, you can't.' It was abrupt.

Lauren said, 'That's a shame, there were a couple of things we wanted to talk to her about.'

'Perhaps I can help. If it's about the Arts Festival, I've arranged for a bank transfer as promised. Your friend Megan has already been on the phone to me.'

'That's good news,' said Lauren. She lied. 'I'd told her that I'd follow up while Ro and I were over here—we're having a day out. Megan was getting stressed, I think she'd heard something from Darya, wasn't quite sure what was going on.'

'I put her on a plane yesterday morning.'

'Oh, I didn't know she was leaving the country. I would have made sure to say goodbye.' Lauren's voice trailed off. The conversation was already flagging. She rallied. 'Look, perhaps we can come in for a minute? It's very hot here.' They were still standing on the porch and the heat of the day was becoming uncomfortable.

'OK,' said Brett, 'but I'm in the middle of packing.' He waved them in ahead of him and as she passed Lauren caught a strong whiff of whisky. He showed them into the dining room. The whisky bottle and glass were sitting on the elegant long table. It was now piled up with various items and half-filled boxes, and there were more boxes on the floor.

'Do sit down.' He waved them to the table and sat down himself by his whisky glass.

'Can I get you a drink?' He poured more into his glass and held up the bottle inquiringly.

'Not a whisky, thanks,' said Lauren. 'But I'd love a cup of tea. You too, Ro?' (She decided he'd no reason to spike it yet.)

Brett got up grudgingly and went through to the kitchen, poking his head back again to ask what sort of tea they'd like. While he was out of earshot, they looked at each other. 'We can try to keep him talking for a bit,' said Lauren. 'Why don't you frame some tactful questions about the poison plot?'

Brett returned holding a tray awkwardly, two mugs with the strings of teabags hanging down their sides and a carton of milk. A far cry from their elegant dinner, thought Lauren.

'What brings you to the Wairarapa?' he said.

Lauren spoke up first. 'Just a day out–we're doing a few wineries–but since we're here, there might be some questions you can help us with.'

Ro took that as a cue, though she sounded nervous, 'There's now a lot of evidence that Kevin Driscoll administered poison to David Lange–and as Lauren told you, we think he was trying to silence us because we were looking into it. We know there were people egging him on. You were around then. You'd be in a position to give us some possible names?'

It was tactfully done, but Lauren couldn't resist. She chipped in, 'I heard you and him arguing that night I was here and he said he'd take you down with him if he was questioned again. So what's the story?'

Ro looked shocked. She hadn't expected Lauren to take him on so directly.

Brett was dismissive. 'I'm surprised at you, Lauren, snooping around. Kevin was very drunk. You've got it all wrong, these accusations about a so-called plot against Lange. You've been listening to a demented woman's ravings.'

'So you know about Judith Butler? Do you also know that that so-called demented woman is now dead, and it's become a police matter?' said Lauren.

Brett hardly reacted, raised an eyebrow and had another sip of whisky.

Ro was no longer nervous, and she wanted to keep Brett focused on the Lange plot. 'I'll remind you of the background,' she said. She began talking, lecture-style, about the backing for the Roger Douglas crew from international business.

'I know you were one of the Friedmanites who visited New Zealand on several occasions, and had meetings with the Business Roundtable and some of the government MPs who supported Douglas. You were right there when the sale of state assets came onto the agenda.'

'Don't lecture me about those times.' Brett spoke more shortly than usual for him, except that the whisky was slowing his words down. 'Yes, I was there. You make the sale of the state assets sound wicked. The government needed capital to get New Zealand out of the mire that Muldoon had left it in, and anyway, it's sensible for the state not to try and run activities that business can run more effectively.'

'That's not what recent history shows,' said Ro. 'A pity we ever sold some assets, and we've had to buy them back. And it's now become clear that fortunes were made by those business people smart enough to get their hands on the family silver.'

'Is that so?' said Brett. Lauren was sitting back, beginning to enjoy the exchange, but wondering when the political might turn personal.

'Yes, and the prime minister at the time became more and more uncomfortable about selling everything off–banks and other financial institutions, forestry, our national airline, electricity companies. Things were turning sour. Extraordinary when a prime minister has to disagree with his own government's programme. So where were you when he said it was time to stop for a cup of tea? Where were you when the Douglas camp were wanting to "roll the fat man"?' Ro drew quote marks in the air to show she was quoting and slowed down to emphasise the words.'

She paused for breath, and Brett interrupted her again. 'You lefties are always so paranoid. I'm tired of it. Let me tell you what really happened. Come into the living room, we'll sit somewhere more comfortable–and have another drink.'

26

'For we will shake him, or worse days endure'

He poured himself another whisky, added a small amount of water, and carried his glass and the whisky bottle into the living room. Lauren and Ro left their tea mugs behind, but declined the offer of a glass of wine. He gave them sparkling water from a bottle in a small fridge that was part of the drinks setup, and brought out a selection of cheeses and olives which he put on a coffee table.

He then sat in a comfortable leather armchair while Lauren and Ro shared a sofa. Lauren wondered how Brett was going to squirm out of it.

Brett mainly spoke to Ro. He said, 'Lauren knows that economics was my strong interest at Cambridge. And that I had the opportunity to go to Chicago and do some postgraduate work. There was such an air of excitement about Milton Friedman's work. We were young, things seemed poised for change...guess you lot were involved with women's lib and socialism and so on, but we thought we were bringing a brave new world into existence, too.

'New Zealand took on the new ideas wholeheartedly'–he saw

their expressions, and said, 'At least to begin with. And my specialty was international financial policy. I first visited on behalf of the bank I worked for in the City. In the end I went out on my own. My first job was to help an American company buy a portion of one of the first assets sold, a development fund.'

'What exactly does this have to do with Kevin and a plot to kill Lange?' Lauren couldn't help herself.

'It has nothing to do with a plot, because there was no plot. If you listen, I'll explain why people were upset at the thought the asset sales would stop. There wasn't nearly enough capital flowing around in New Zealand to purchase all the state assets that were up for grabs. I found I had a talent for bringing people together in a bid. I took a slice of each deal for myself, and as well clipped the companies' tickets. I took a percentage of all the large transactions that I'd organised.'

'Do you expect us to be impressed?' said Lauren. 'Was making money all you were interested in?' She remembered their conversations in Cambridge and inwardly answered her own question. 'You still haven't told us where Kevin Driscoll comes in.'

Brett said, 'Bloody Lange got cold feet just when the asset sales were going really well. Then asset sales got taken away from cabinet ministers and suddenly we were faced with bureaucrats who were far less inclined to cut deals.'

He took another sip of whisky. 'I met Kevin Driscoll at some of the meetings before they changed the rules. He was the errand boy for the Douglas crowd. I fixed him up with a cut in some of the deals so that he would keep us close to the action.'

He saw the horrified expression on Lauren's face, and said, 'All right, all right, that might seem dubious, but I was young and impetuous. When Lange made the process bureaucratic, Kevin got very upset. He had seen himself as masterminding the deals by trading information back and forth between the politicians and the purchasers. He got very nervy when the rules changed. I think he'd bitten off more than he could chew and he lost money in the '87 crash.'

Ro had been listening carefully. 'From what I've read, Kevin wasn't the only nervy one, was he? What about you money men?'

'We weren't nervy, we were disappointed. Douglas had the right idea. So yes, there was talk about rolling Lange, but that was in a political sense, you must surely understand. Lange's supporters–of whom there seemed to be very few, I might add, apart from his staff– used to say the same kind of things about Douglas.'

'So how did that political talk turn into Kevin trying to poison Lange?' Ro was not to be put off.

Brett looked at her. 'We don't know that that happened. But Kevin did get very wound up and he asked if I would help him out with his loan. I refused, of course, I had no reason to take on board his risks. I guess I did imply there'd be some reward if Lange was brought down. I was talking about a leadership challenge. Kevin maybe thought I meant something darker. So perhaps he did try to do away with Lange, but obviously it didn't work. No harm done.' He shrugged and drained his glass.

At last! Ro glanced at her phone. Yes, it was still recording. Brett saw the glance and went to speak, but Lauren interrupted. She got up from the sofa, stood close to Brett's armchair and almost spat at him. 'No harm done? Brett, that's attempted murder. And Kevin hasn't the backbone to poison someone without a lot of pushing. Misunderstood you? That'll be the day.' She suddenly understood why someone might stamp their foot.

'I tell you, there was no plot.' Brett looked offended. 'Look, I'll admit to a few backhanders back in the eighties–fruitless to investigate now, I'm sure. But plotting to kill Lange, that's ridiculous. Anyhow, the slowdown was just a hitch in the process.'

'No plot,' repeated Ro. She was with an effort staying cool. Still sitting on the sofa, and not raising her voice. 'No plot, but it was you who was encouraging Kevin to roll Lange, and offering him money if he succeeded. No plot? You needn't give us any other names. It was you.'

'There was no plot. Look, people like me, who help the super-wealthy invest their fortunes and the big institutions make lucrative investments, have to be very careful. A whiff of scandal and none of my clients would ever touch me again. That was a long time ago when I was young. It's ancient history. And of no account now.'

A whiff of scandal. That's what Lauren and Ro were bringing him. Lauren wondered, how far would Brett go to avoid a scandal? Or did he rely on those around him to deal with inconvenient facts–and people.

Brett suddenly ran out of steam. He got up to renew his drink, taking another big splash. He sat down and wiped some sweat from his brow.

Then he said, slurring his words a little, 'Lauren, I fancied you back in our undergraduate days. You were rather cool and aloof and I always loved a challenge. But I can see that it would have been a waste of time. I know about your proclivities.' He threw a rather suspicious glance at Ro.

Lauren sat back down too. She said coldly, 'I did marry and have children. I wasn't immune to charming young men. But although you had your fair share of charm, there was always something about you that I didn't trust. And now I know how right I was.'

She followed up Ro's accusation. 'We've recorded this discussion. There might be more than a whiff of scandal coming your way.'

Brett shrugged, looked disbelieving, then shut his eyes. Lauren wondered if he was falling asleep. Then he said, 'It hasn't been easy for me, Lauren.' He was starting to mumble. He looked emotional. 'My marriage might be on the rocks. Darya is a difficult woman, I think you'll appreciate that. But I'm fond of her.'

'For goodness' sake!' Lauren snapped. 'You've been fond of a few women in your time, and they haven't always enjoyed it. I know you were had up for hitting Barbara Bagstock. And what did you try on Darya, that she pulled a gun on you?"

Brett had the decency to blush, but didn't answer the question. 'A little tiger. Anyhow we've had a big row and I've sent her home–she was none too happy about it, left me behind to pack up and said she'd see me in court. Didn't realise it was for her own good, she was starting to interfere in my business.'

He got up, poured himself another glass. This time, he brought the bottle back and plonked it on the coffee table.

Now Ro snapped. 'Your business, eh? Your precious clients probably don't give a stuff about how you treat women, but your business has to look squeaky clean. It might not look so good once all this comes out.' She waved her phone at him.

Lauren couldn't help herself. She knew Deirdre would consider she was barging in. But she didn't want to hear him say yet again that there was no plot. 'It's not just the Lange plot. We have a very good idea why you sent Darya home.'

Brett's eyes narrowed and he jerked a little, apparently trying to regain concentration.

'Judith Butler died suddenly on Christmas Eve. We thought Kevin might have helped her on her way, trying to get rid of a witness.'

Brett snorted and took another gulp. Lauren continued. 'But did you know that Darya visited her nursing home on Christmas Eve?'

He startled. 'What? What are you talking about? What are you trying to say?' In spite of the whisky, he looked more engaged, more alert. He stared at Lauren, who suddenly wondered if she should continue. She did.

'Who would stand to benefit if Judith Butler were removed? Kevin, but you too, if you were involved; and that means Darya as well. And what's more,' Lauren moved in for the kill. 'Darya was seen directing Kevin on to a catamaran on the day he was last seen. There was a witness.'

Brett lurched to his feet. 'You interfering bitches!'

They sat frozen. 'Hand over that phone.' He stumbled towards Ro, bumping against the coffee table. Ro looked paralysed, but Lauren pulled her sideways and they rose hastily. Brett rounded the table, saying, 'Don't think you can get away with this,' in a slurred voice. There was nowhere to go. Brett was backing them into a corner. Ro tried to slither past him but Brett grabbed her by the arm. Ro pulled away and knocked a vase. It crashed to the floor, and broke. Brett took no notice.

'Let go of her,' Lauren cried. Brett snarled. 'Give me the phone, or

I'll...' he threatened. Ro tried to shake him off. 'You're hurting me. Let go!' As they continued to struggle, she dropped the phone. Lauren dived down and scooped it up. She made for the door and Brett dropped Ro's arm and stumbled after her. Lauren turned, thinking she should hold her ground. She looked him in the face and was shocked at the rage she saw in his eyes. They were narrowed, impersonal, looking at her as if she was no-one, a nothing.

A buzzer sounded. Brett stopped in his tracks, looked confused, swore and then made for the intercom. 'Who is it?'

They heard a woman's voice, one familiar to Lauren. 'Police. Open the gate.'

'Shit,' said Brett loudly, glared at Lauren and Ro and lurched out of the room. They heard him open the front door, heard the crunch of the police car on the gravel, and then the car door slam shut. A voice said, "Can we come in, please. We are here to see Darya Wilson.'

There were sounds of people entering the hall. Deirdre and who else? wondered Lauren. Brett shut the door behind them and his voice got louder as they approached the sitting room. 'I'm sorry, my wife is not here,' he said.

'Will she be long?' Deirdre's voice. Then Deirdre reached the doorway. She looked both dumbfounded and angry. (Lauren wouldn't have thought that was possible.)

'What on earth are you doing here?' She positively barked it. 'And who is this?' She looked at Ro as if Ro might suddenly turn into Darya. She also took in the shattered vase on the floor.

Lauren hastily introduced her. 'Rowan Wisbech, my friend who's writing about women in the fourth Labour Government.'

Deirdre ignored her, turned to Brett. 'I asked, will your wife be long?'

Brett was trying to stand up straight. 'She has gone back to England.' Deirdre's face got tighter. Her brown eyes were cold. But she didn't miss a beat as she said, 'In that case, Mr Wilson, I will need to talk to you. Jerry here will get some general information from you first.' She nodded to her offsider and said, 'Identification and so on, please Jerry.' Then turned back to Lauren and Ro. 'Meanwhile I'd like to see you two in another room, right now.'

Lauren again had that naughty schoolgirl feeling. She stood up, and with Ro, followed in Deirdre's wake, back into the dining room. Deirdre surveyed the room, the half-packed boxes with piles of stuff on the table. 'Leaving, is he? Perhaps you were here to help him pack.'

'We were just wanting to know if they were still donating to the Arts Festival,' Ro blurted. She could see why Lauren said Deirdre was scary (sexy but scary, Lauren had said). She could also see that Deirdre didn't buy that story at all. She changed it. 'And I wanted to tackle Brett about the Lange plot.'

'You what?' Now Deirdre looked flabbergasted. 'You have no evidence that hasn't already been looked at by the police. Why would he tell you anything? Ms Fraser, I have already asked you to step away from police business and the same applies to you, Ms Wisbech.'

Lauren looked at the floor rather than Deirdre. 'We thought we might trip Brett up into saying something useful. And he did. Ro has recorded it. About the Lange plot.'

'You were going into a very dangerous situation and you don't know what Brett is capable of, with or without his wife. Because you knew him from your student days, you probably had a false idea of how far he would go.' Lauren winced. She recalled again the look in Brett's eyes just before Deirdre arrived.

Deirdre continued, 'And you didn't have access to the latest evidence. Never mind the original plot: we have evidence that someone in this household is implicated in Kevin Driscoll's disappearance. And now I would like you to leave us to get on with our work. No more trampling over police business. I have told you that already.'

27

'Ambition's debt is paid'

'You must help me, Piotr.' Darya was ushered into the grand living room of her ex-husband's palatial house. She had arrived in London a couple of days earlier after an exhausting trip. Wellington to Sydney, fearing all the while that police might meet her on her arrival. Brett had warned her to take precautions, when he had all but thrown her out. An Emirates flight to Dubai was to leave Sydney within the hour and she managed to purchase a last-minute ticket.

She thought it unlikely that the UAE would have an extradition treaty to New Zealand. The Arab countries were well known in her circles. Some might have irritating laws about what women could and couldn't do, but they were not inclined to allow other jurisdictions to interfere with comings and goings.

At the airport in Dubai, she easily found a last-minute seat on a plane to Heathrow. She used her second passport, her Ukrainian one, in her maiden name. She always kept it up to date and carried it with her as it contained a long-term visa. She had never wanted to rely solely on a husband to guarantee her passage into the UK, which she now regarded as her home. The queue at Heathrow was very long and by the time she got to the immigration desk she was nervous and exhausted. But there was clearly no flag against her maiden name and she was through without incident.

Darya was now staying at a hotel in central London. She could not return home in case the police came looking for her. Brett had sent a worrying email suggesting that she lie low for a while. Then he had phoned, using a newly purchased cell phone, and had asked her to go out and buy a disposable cell phone herself. The conversation that ensued was not a happy one. Darya was tired and angry and Brett was livid. He raged at her about her interference and her recklessness. When he calmed down he told her that she would have to make herself scarce. She'd been spotted talking to Kevin on the jetty and the police had evidence that Kevin had been attacked on the boat and thrown over the side.

Brett was also furious about Judith Butler, telling Darya that Lauren had talked to the police and suggested it wasn't a straightforward death, and that Darya could have been involved. 'How dare she!' Darya had replied. Brett had told her in no uncertain terms that their life together had ended. He was not willing to cover for her and she should just disappear. 'You're on your own.'

Now she was entreating her former husband, a tall man with a beard and a full head of curly greying hair. She had taken care with her appearance, and looked as well turned out as ever. But her voice shook slightly. 'I'm in trouble, the New Zealand police are after me.'

'Why should I care, Darya? You're not my charge any more. You were not at all pleasant when we were divorcing.'

Darya gave him an edited version of her sorry tale, careful not to incriminate herself. She described it as police wanting to interview her about "something I have done". 'I need a false passport and papers, I know you can procure them quickly.' Piotr considered her request thoughtfully. 'I don't know what you have done, Darya, but I imagine that it was something very wicked.'

'I was trying to protect my husband,' Darya protested.

'Even less reason to help you. I never liked that arrogant man.'

'I'm not with him any longer.'

'Hmm,' said Piotr. He paused and walked around the room, stroking his beard and glancing at her. Then he said, 'I can probably do it, but exile will be your punishment.' Darya's face fell.

'Wait here,' he said, 'while I make a phone call.' He left the room. She paced around, trying to distract herself by inspecting artworks that were unfamiliar to her, ones that must have been purchased after their split–unless he had had them hidden away. Yes, that would have been just like him, now he felt he could get away with displaying them. It was some time later before he returned. 'Yes, I can get hold of Ukrainian papers. You will be a schoolteacher in a small village in the Ukraine.'

Darya began to protest, 'I am not a village schoolteacher! My family are nobility, you know that. Are you trying to humiliate me?'

Piotr took no notice. 'My associates will procure you a position there. You will fly out in a couple of days. Change your hotel again and I will arrange for the bill to be settled. Do not use credit cards. Here is some cash to tide you over.' He pulled out his desk drawer and gave her an insultingly small amount to spend for a few days in London. He searched around and found an envelope of Ukrainian banknotes as well. 'You will be met next Tuesday afternoon at the National Gallery, near the painting of the two Russian peasant women–you know the one. Make sure you are there, I cannot specify the time, just wait.'

He laughed as Darya screwed up her face and looked ready to spit at him. 'Hold your tongue, my dear, you should be grateful.'

28

'You hard hearts, you cruel men of Rome'

L auren was sitting at her desk pretending to work but
actually brooding about the abortive trip to the Wairarapa.
What had she and Ro been thinking? She was really in
Deirdre's bad books now and maybe they had messed up the police
investigation, although she couldn't quite see how.

She was also fretting about Brett. She had lost any vestiges of
respect for him, and that disturbed her. Deirdre was right in thinking
that she underestimated his dark side just because she had known
him all those years ago. But how pathetic he'd become under the
influence of alcohol–until he got angry. She replayed over and over in
her mind the moment Brett's drunken rambling had turned into an
attack. If Deirdre hadn't arrived just then, what might he have done?
Probably he would have done no more than shove them out the door,
but the cold, impersonal anger in his eyes kept coming back to
haunt her.

'Oh, damn,' she said aloud, and shuddered.

She thought about him again. Usually, he wouldn't need to get
angry–he left his dirty work to others. Look at Kevin and the Lange

plot. And what about Darya? Had he been involved in her crimes? His surprise when she mentioned Judith Butler seemed genuine enough.

He relied on his wealth and prestige to protect him. And Darya was motivated to take risks to defend him, because he was the source of wealth and social standing for her. There was no need for him to get his hands dirty.

She was interrupted from her reverie by the roar of a jet engine, and looked out the window. She'd always loved it that her apartment gave her a view of the flight path to and from the airport. When the wind was strong from the south and planes fought against the headwinds, she would watch them and feel grateful to be safe and warm rather than jolted around. Now the plane made her think of Darya flying out of New Zealand. The police were looking for her but she was well on her way. Would she get away with it?

Lauren sighed. She got up to make herself a cup of tea. She guessed Deirdre was strongly motivated to have Darya arrested. Extraordinary, Darya's role in the gangland murder of Kevin. But it was Judith's murder that made Lauren sad. Sure, she'd needed help with everyday things, but there was not much wrong with her physically. Lauren recalled her springy white hair, lively brown eyes and the kind of wrinkles you get from smiling not frowning. Extroverted, keen to talk. And now look what had happened. Lauren felt guilty as well as sad.

As she brought her tea back to the desk, her cellphone rang. Deirdre. More scolding on the way? For a moment she considered not answering it, but curiosity got the better of her.

'Hello?'

'Hello, Ms Fraser, it's Deirdre Nathan here.' Ms Fraser! Lauren was really in the dogbox. 'I neglected to get your friend Rowan's details the other day and I need to phone her. Can you give me her number, please?'

The formal tone chilled Lauren. She swallowed, gave her the number and tried to sound lighthearted. 'We're not in more trouble, I hope.'

'You're not,' said Deirdre, 'and I trust you'll keep it that way.'

'Deirdre,' said Lauren. It took some courage to venture the first name and she hesitated before saying again, 'Deirdre, I'm really sorry about the other day. We were out of line. We were just so shocked when we realised what Darya had done and we had a pretext to visit Brett and maybe find out more.'

Deirdre's voice changed, softening a little. 'I know you've had the best of intentions, Lauren. But your impulsiveness put both you and your friend in danger. Just as well Darya wasn't at the house. She's clearly a dangerous woman. There's no doubt she arranged a killing. And I believe you're right in thinking she helped Judith Butler on her way, not that we'll ever know for sure.

'But I don't know why you thought it would be all right to confront Brett Wilson, just because you were students together a very long time ago.'

'I know that now, I saw it in his eyes. No doubt he'll manage to slide out of any responsibility, that's what he's always done. But I can't bear it if Darya gets away with murdering people.'

Deirdre sounded astonished. 'Get away with it? Of course she won't, not for Kevin Driscoll's murder, anyhow. We have Interpol onto it and I'm confident we'll find her and have her extradited, wherever she's fled to. The lowlifes she hired to kill Kevin have given us full statements, trying to lay the blame on each other and we have a good case against Darya.'

'Still nobody from the Lange plot, though, now you haven't got Kevin to give you a statement.'

'That's true,' said Deirdre. 'You could say he's met with rough justice but we've not enough evidence to get the people who urged him on.'

'Even though we gave you the recording of our conversation? So what did Brett say to you?'

'Lauren, you're incorrigible.' Deirdre laughed. 'Please, no more questions. You're treading on dangerous ground again and I need to get on with my work.'

Lauren was emboldened by the laugh. 'Just one more question, then, Deirdre. Do you ever have time off? I'd like to take you out for a drink, let's say as an apology for the annoyance we've caused.'

There was a silence at the end of the phone, just long enough for Lauren to feel she'd put a foot wrong again. Then, 'Thank you,' said Deirdre, 'I am supposed to have time off, but my next two weeks are looking horrendous. Why don't you call me after that? You can use this number.'

~

LIKE LAUREN, Ro was at her desk when the phone rang. 'Inspector Nathan here. Is that Rowan Wisbech?'

'Yes it is.' Ro wondered who on earth was Inspector Nathan. Oh yeah, Deirdre. Lauren was on first name terms with her, but that degree of familiarity was obviously not being extended to Ro.

'I wanted to talk to you for a moment about your book. I gather it's about to be published shortly?'

'Yes, I'm putting the final touches on it right now and then it'll be off to the publisher. It'll be a few months before it's out. Would you like a complimentary copy when it's done?'

There was a pause. Deirdre was nonplussed, then recovered. 'Do you realise that the courts have the power to make an injunction preventing publication of anything that might prejudice the right to a fair trial?'

'What has that to do with my book?' Ro had a sinking feeling.

'You will not be able to publish any references to the so-called Lange plot. There is a good reason–an ongoing police investigation– that the public should not be given information. We're prepared to go to court to get an injunction to stop publication if we have reason to believe your book will include such material. We are confident it would be granted. Then, if you go ahead, you and your publisher would be subject to contempt of court and all copies of the book could be seized and destroyed. I wanted to give you advance warning. We're getting an official letter out to you shortly and I need to know your publisher's details, so I can send them an official letter as well.'

Ro was blindsided. She had not made more than veiled references to the plot in her book but she was planning to publish separately on the Lange plot. In the mainstream media with all the details. Only the day before she'd spoken to the *New Zealand Listener*'s deputy editor who had expressed enthusiasm. She had already begun to draft the article. Now what would happen? Would the *Listener* fight the injunction on behalf of an academic who wasn't known to them? Think like the journalist Nicky Hager, she told herself. How would the scourge of the establishment respond?

'That's simply impossible, Deirdre. This is a story that is in the public interest. You can't suppress it.'

'We'll see you in court then,' said Deirdre and hung up.

～

RO PHONED LAUREN. 'HI RO,' said Lauren, 'has Deirdre got hold of you yet?'

'Bloody Deirdre, she's trying to stop me publishing the Lange plot story. There's not much in the book and I can easily leave it out, but I was jacking up something with the *Listener*.' She brushed a tear away. 'She says they'll take out an injunction if I don't roll over. It's outrageous, I told her this is an important event New Zealanders should know about.'

'What was her reason?'

'Oh, I don't know–something about prejudicing the right to a fair trial. Not that they seem to have any trial going ahead, with Kevin out of the frame and Darya God knows where. The accomplices, I suppose, but that seems quite a tangent.'

Lauren was slow in replying. When she did, Ro realised they weren't going to agree on this. 'Ro, it would be terrible if they finally put a case together about the Lange plot and it failed because of something you'd published. She's told me our recording is still not enough evidence but perhaps something else might turn up. And I'm not sure how it works but if they bring Darya to trial, possibly they'll want all that material fresh, not pawed over in the media. The plot would come out in the trial.'

Ro had to concede that, and Lauren went on, 'If it ever comes to court it would be our work that helped bring it there. I've always said the Lange plot was a crime, not just history.'

Ro squirmed. *Just* history? She was still going to try to make a case for the right to publish. People should know there had been a plot to kill a prime minister.

29

'The evil that men do lives after them'

Lauren was taking Monty for a walk up Mt Victoria. It was a warm sunny day in mid-February, but the northerly was near to gale force. She felt her phone vibrate in her pocket, and called Monty to heel while she fished it out. The sun was too bright for her to see the screen, so she moved beside a tree, shady and sheltering her from the wind. Monty snuffled around the tree roots. No doubt he was smelling other dogs before him. It was a text from Kirsten.

'Will you be at home tonight? I need to talk to you.'

She and Kirsten no longer talked virtually every night as they had done in the past. The relationship was heading for the rocks but Lauren couldn't help nursing hopes. There were still enjoyable times.

She texted Kirsten: '6.30 movie then quick meal with Pam. Try me at 10.' Lauren found texting annoying. They had spoken just the night before and she had told Kirsten of her plans for this evening. She felt like adding, I told you already. But best not to exchange sharp words by text.

After a comedy that involved oldies, lost loves, misunderstandings and canal boat chases through London, and then a kebab with Pam, Lauren was sitting at home wondering what was so important that Kirsten needed to call tonight. The landline rang. 'It's me.' She sounded tense and there was no affectionate greeting.

'Hello darling,' Lauren said, mellowed by the movie and the meal.

'I've news. The firm is sending me to Sydney.'

'That's exciting. How long will you be away?' Lauren was trying to recall the date of Kirsten's next scheduled visit. She thumbed her diary. It was around ten days from now.

'It's permanent. They want me to leave in a couple of weeks. I'm sorry, I won't be able to come to Wellington. I'll be frantic, packing up my flat.'

Lauren felt a rush of emotion and tried to keep her voice from wavering. 'You didn't talk to me about it before you made your decision. Don't I matter?'

Kirsten went on the defensive. 'It's a great opportunity and I had to decide at once.'

'So what does that mean for us?' Lauren regretted the words as soon as she'd uttered them. She knew what it meant. 'No, forget I said that. No point in beating around the bush. Obviously, it's over between us.' She gathered steam. 'I've enjoyed the ride, I hope you won't be lonely, but it's your choice.'

Kirsten sounded tearful. 'Lauren, I do have to tell you something before you hear it from someone else. Bee and I have been getting close lately, and she's decided to come with me. But I'd like you and I to stay friends.'

'Oh, Kirsten, that's nonsense! It'll be a while before that happens. We'll both need a break from each other. In fact I'm hanging up now.'

She cut the connection and sat motionless for a moment, thinking about the relationship. Images came floating into her mind. The very first time she'd met Kirsten. Kirsten at their favourite café, holding out a forkful of mushrooms for Lauren to try. Kirsten, naked and in a tangle of sheets on that Greek island. She pushed away an unwelcome thought of Kirsten naked with Bee.

Everyone said it was hard to keep a long-distance relationship going and they were right. She stood up, walked out to her kitchen. A drink? No, she didn't want a drink. She wanted to tell someone, wanted a hug, wanted to burst into tears. It stung, she had been betrayed. Silly, if she was honest with herself, things hadn't been going well ever since Kirsten moved to Auckland. And Kirsten had never understood Lauren's preoccupation with the Lange plot. She had been discouraging and insulting when Lauren needed support, especially since she couldn't talk to her Wellington friends about it.

She sat back down, staring at rather than reading her novel. The phone rang again ten minutes later—just long enough for Kirsten to have poured out her heart to Bee, Lauren guessed. She didn't answer. Then a text dinged. 'I do love you.' She didn't respond to that either.

She realised that she was feeling a sense of relief as well as sadness and injured self-esteem. They had drifted apart and really, the relationship with all its ups and downs was becoming a straitjacket. She gave a rueful smile. At least it would save on airfares, and her friends would stop complaining that they never knew which weekends she'd be in Wellington.

She decided she would have a drink after all, and poured herself a glass of wine. She picked up the novel and tried to concentrate on the page.

LAUREN HADN'T EXPECTED to sleep well, but she drifted off before midnight. She woke up with a start when it was just getting light. The phone was ringing. The landline. She staggered out of bed in the half light and answered sleepily. It was Phyl from next door. She sounded short of breath. 'Sorry Lauren, but can you come over? I need help.' The phone went dead.

Lauren threw on yesterday's clothes, grabbed her key to Phyl's place and went in calling, 'Phyl, Phyl.' She found her in the living room, sitting in her favourite Lazy Boy in her dressing gown. She was leaning back with her eyes closed and her face was grey. 'I've called the ambulance, should be here soon. Can't breathe, terrible burning in my chest. Lauren, would you look after Monty? I think they might keep me in.'

'Oh, Phyl. Yes, of course I will. I'll pack up some things for you.' She headed off to the bathroom, found a toilet bag in a bottom drawer and put in Phyl's toothbrush and toothpaste. She looked around for her pills. She knew Phyl took medications for a number of ailments that she never complained about. She went into the bedroom and found pill dispensers, loaded them into the toilet bag as well, found a zip bag in the wardrobe, a clean nightie from a drawer, the book Phyl was reading and her reading glasses. In between packing, she kept an eye on Phyl, still sitting with her eyes shut.

Now she heard knocking on the door and ran to open it. A woman and a man from Wellington Free Ambulance. What a welcome sight! They checked Phyl's vital signs, talking to her quietly as they did so. The guy then went back to the ambulance to get a stretcher. 'Better if she doesn't exert herself,' said the woman to Lauren.

'Do you want me to come with you?' said Lauren to Phyl.

Phyl shook her head. 'I'd rather you stayed with Monty.' Monty had been sitting on the floor on the rug that Phyl kept for him next to her chair. As they manoeuvred Phyl onto the stretcher, he stood up and whimpered.

'It's all right, Monty,' said Lauren. She bent down and stroked him reassuringly. They watched together as the stretcher was borne out. Monty whimpered again and Lauren said, 'Come on, we'll take you to my place.' She looked at her phone. It was just seven. No time to fret about Kirsten then. There'd be too much going on.

A siren wailed from the street above as the ambulance set off for the hospital.

～

LAUREN TOOK Monty back to her apartment and made herself some breakfast. She was worried about Phyl but it was too soon to phone.

The dog jumped up and licked her face and pawed her. 'Down, Monty,' she said. She thought how very comforting dogs are when people are in an emotional state. She rubbed his ears. 'Good boy.' He must be worried about Phyl as well. She fished around in her cupboard and found him one of the treats she kept for when she was walking him.

She decided a walk would be good and being with a friend. Pam and Megan both lived within walking distance, but in apartment buildings where she couldn't take Monty. She didn't want to be in a café. She still felt wobbly after the call with Kirsten and now, with Phyl being carted off, tears were close to the surface. Better to be somewhere more private if she became tearful.

She phoned Michael, who responded warmly. 'Of course, you and Monty walk round and he can meet our new pup.' The road wound around the top of Evans Bay, a walk she normally enjoyed. The footpath was narrow and she had to be careful with Monty whenever a car went by.

Michael greeted her, cradling a pup in his arms, a sweet looking tawny Labrador with soulful brown eyes. 'This is Mandela. Mandela, meet Monty.' Monty was barking, leaping up and trying to see the pup. Michael walked through to the living room and rather trustingly, Lauren thought, put Mandela in a basket. Monty strained at the lead and Lauren allowed him to approach gradually. A few sniffs and licks from Monty and excited squeaks from the pup, and Monty established himself as top dog, but benign. Off the lead, he settled down beside the basket.

Lauren told Michael about Phyl as he made her a coffee. She didn't mention Kirsten. She was upset, but it was not just Phyl and Kirsten. Somehow the intensity of the moment released other feelings. The weight of Kevin's and Judith's deaths bore down on her. She felt responsible. If she had not been prying, they would still be alive.

She confessed her doubts to Michael as they sipped their coffees. He was a good listener, not interrupting except to murmur encouraging signals for her to continue, until she'd got it all off her chest.

When she stopped, Michael looked at her warmly and said, 'Lauren, you're a good person. You've been trying to do the right thing. Justice doesn't come without a cost. It's unfortunate that these deaths were the repercussions and it's right not to minimise them.' Lauren sniffed as Michael continued. 'Judith Butler might have been losing it, but she was still a human being and entitled to get older, well cared for and loved. She still had much to offer as your interview showed. And Kevin was foolish, self-serving and ruthless, but he didn't deserve to die. It would have been better if he had lived to be tried for the Lange murder attempt, and for hiring people to intimidate you and Ro. But Lauren, you didn't kill them, Darya did.'

Lauren bit her lip to stop her tears. Her emotions were all over the place today, quite unlike her usual self. 'I suppose what you say is true, I've just been feeling so awful about it.'

Michael grasped her hand and leaned towards her. 'Remember how helpful you were to me, when I told you about Kevin blackmailing me. I've thought about it a lot over the last few weeks and I'm starting to forgive myself. I'm sure you will come to terms with this. You just need time to get a perspective on it all.'

Lauren felt better, though still shaky. She was pleased that her talk with Michael had helped him. But now Monty was getting restless and she took her leave.

30

'The gods today stand friendly'

It was June, four months later, and Unity Books was packed for Ro's book launch. Lauren had brought along Phyl who was much recovered after her heart bypass. Now she seemed as fit and bossy as ever, although she let Lauren take over more of Monty's exercise these days.

'I'm not a Labour voter, Lauren,' Phyl said, when Lauren invited her.

'It's a book launch, not a Labour Party meeting! Anyway, you need to come because you've been a great adviser to Ro and me on the Lange affair.'

'I thought Deirdre had deep-sixed it,' said Phyl.

'Yes, unfortunately, but this is Ro's original project, a history of the women of the fourth Labour government.'

'In that case, I hope the refreshments are good.' Phyl gave her a wicked look.

The bookshop was crowded with colleagues and friends of Ro, and a sprinkling of notables Lauren recognised as involved in the party or Parliament during the years Ro's book covered. The room was abuzz with old friends and acquaintances catching up.

Ro's publisher, a young man in his thirties, managed to make himself heard and gave a brief but flattering speech about what an interesting project it was, and how good Ro had been to work with. He made an oblique reference to some excitement at the end of the project. Most of the guests looked puzzled, but Lauren smiled to herself at the reference. She knew the injunction had been upheld by the courts, so the *Listener* hadn't got their exposé. That had annoyed Ro no end.

Lauren spotted Deirdre in the crowd. She must have been there in an official capacity. Lauren winked and Deirdre acknowledged her with the hint of a smile. Since that coffee a few months back, their friendship had developed. Perhaps it would turn into something more? Lauren suppressed the thought.

Ro took to the mike and made a speech about the project, how it came about, what fun it had been, how wonderful the women she'd talked with were. She said she understood how difficult it must have been for them, given the tensions of the time. Then she said, 'You may have heard rumours...' Lauren's heart sank. Surely she wasn't going to get them into trouble. She glanced across. Deirdre was inscrutable.

Ro went on, 'I found out some things that we couldn't publish. Many people are still alive. The transcripts and voice recordings and all my notes are deposited in the Turnbull Library and sealed until 2030. I do suggest to my young historian friends'–glancing around the room–'that you put your skates on, on the first of January, 2030, and race down there, for there will be some surprising revelations.'

Lauren's heartbeat slowed to its normal rate.

'And finally,' Ro went on, 'I have dedicated the book to Judith Butler. Judith died too early, before I finished the project. She was a fine backbencher, one of Labour's best.' Lauren saw Judith's daughter standing nearby. She was smiling, but her eyes were wet.

Ro finished up, 'No event concerning MPs is complete without a political speech so I am handing over to my good friend Lauren Fraser to say a few words.'

Lauren stepped up to the mike. She was a little nervous, but she knew everyone would warm to her opening. 'Today is a special day,' she began. 'I know you're all as excited as I am about the prime minister's brand new baby. Only the second time in the world that a prime minister has given birth in office.'

Everyone cheered and clapped. Lauren continued. 'The day is special for another reason: Ro's book, that celebrates the women of the Labour Party during the Lange era.'

She smiled. 'And I'm not going to make a long political speech. But there is a postscript to Ro's book that I'd like to draw to your attention. Women in the book tell you how hard it was in the Lange government with the fierce division between the Douglas supporters and the rest–whichever faction they supported. Those divisions were fiercer than you can imagine.' She was thinking of Brett and the plot. The need for secrecy was frustrating!

'What I want to remember is how Lange ended his parliamentary career–after the fall of his government. His last speech, his valedictory speech, apologised for the excesses of his government and challenged those who succeeded him to consider the less fortunate, "those people who cannot foot it".'

She beamed. 'And here we are! With a government that's taken up that challenge, a new woman Prime Minister who wants to make our country a kinder place, a place where children flourish.'

Lauren turned towards Ro. 'Ro, one day you might write a book about the women of the sixth Labour government.'

She handed the microphone back to the publisher and stepped away. Probably not her greatest oratorical moment. But people clapped, as much as people standing with glasses in their hands can clap. One of Ro's colleagues congratulated her. 'People don't remember that Lange apologised for the economic reforms going too far. Never hurts to remind them.'

Lauren was wishing the apology could have involved some redistribution of wealth – she'd have enjoyed disbursing Brett's fortune to those in need.

~

BY EIGHT O'CLOCK, as people drifted off, the launch came to a close. A good number of books had been sold, without any whisper of the plot against Lange.

Ro was on a high, bouncing about, inviting close friends as well as her publisher to a post-launch dinner at a restaurant off Courtenay Place. People strolled towards it in little groups, clutching their signed copies in the bookshop's brown paper bags. Megan, who was walking with Lauren, said, 'A pity your friend Michael wasn't at the book launch, given that he was an MP at the time.'

'It was a shame,' agreed Lauren. 'He and Kiano had an electrician coming in this evening specially to finish doing their lights. They wanted to be there to check the placing. They want to make sure their paintings are lit properly and that they're both happy with the colour effects of the other lights.'

She laughed. 'They're perfectionists! Kiano is going to be right behind the electrician, touching up the walls. It's their housewarming on Saturday.' Privately, she thought it might also be that Michael was still reluctant to mix with colleagues from that time.

The housewarming. She could hardly restrain herself from giving a little skip. She'd plucked up courage and invited Deirdre to come with her. Made it sound casual. 'You know, he helped you break the Kevin Driscoll case with his eye witness account. He'd love to meet you when you're just enjoying yourself out of the office.' They'd been having a drink at the end of Deirdre's work day. In March they'd gone to the Arts Festival opera that Darya had wanted to sponsor. Lauren noted that the Wilson name was on the programme but there was no big splash of the sort that Darya would have wanted.

Deirdre had been a discerning companion and, since then, they'd been out two or three times. Not that Lauren was counting, she told herself firmly. It had been odd seeing her at the book launch, being professional. They hadn't talked at all.

TWO NIGHTS later she was preparing for the party. Deirdre would be there soon. They'd arranged that she would bring her car as far as Lauren's place and they'd walk to Michael's together. Senior policewomen shouldn't be caught over the limit!

Absentmindedly she checked her laptop as she passed. Two or three emails: one from Greenpeace, something from her old college and an email from Rachel. She checked the time–still time to look at a couple. She'd read the Greenpeace one later. The college email was a reminder that the research study into ageing was ongoing. 'This is to advise that your next annual data collection will be carried out over two days in Melbourne, Australia, on Monday 30th September and Tuesday 1st October, 2018. Air fares will be reimbursed and accommodation has been arranged. It is expected that there will be ten graduates in the group.'

A shame that there would be no freebie to Cambridge next time, but Melbourne was great to visit. And not so far from Sydney, she could be maternal and visit Martin there. And Kirsten? Would they be on speaking terms? She made a face. Not with Bee there.

She turned to Rachel's email, with an attached photo. Rachel and she weren't frequent correspondents but caught up with each other's news two or three times a year. It was only a month since she'd last heard.

'Hi Lauren. Thought you'd like to see this straight away.' Lauren looked closely at the photo of a building entrance. It was their old college library. It boasted shiny new signage: the Brett Wilson Library. Lauren continued reading. 'The man himself was at the opening, and you'd never guess who was hanging off his arm. Charlotte! I caught her by herself for just a moment. She reckons he's a reformed character. They're going to spend time on his new property in the New South Wales Highlands. Charlotte's excited about the horse-riding. I hope it works out. He seems to me much the same as ever, still polished and pleased with himself.'

Lauren snorted, remembering his drunken ramblings. She glanced at the time. There was a knock on the door.

'Hi, Deirdre. Will you come in or shall we go straight there?' Deirdre was looking particularly attractive. Her brown eyes matched a patterned silk scarf swinging casually across her shoulders and black leather pants accentuated her slim legs. 'Let's go straight away,' she said.

As they took the path to the street Lauren thought briefly about Brett, about Darya, about Kevin. Kevin was dead, Darya was wanted by Interpol, Brett was in the clear. He was the one that got away.

She needed to put it all behind her now. As they walked on, she linked arms with Deirdre.

AFTERWORD

The idea for this work of fiction came to us after yet another conversation deploring inequalities in New Zealand. Both of us lived through the era of Rogernomics and were aware of the tensions in the Fourth Labour Government. Lois, who had been a political candidate herself in the late seventies and early eighties, was acquainted with David Lange.

The central motif of the book, a plot to kill David Lange, is of course fictional, as far as we know! We did read widely about the period and have otherwise kept close to the facts. There was a fire in David Lange's flat and his health, particularly his stomach pains, did cause concern to his staff and associates before his heart condition was diagnosed and treated. There were huge tensions amongst rival factions in Cabinet, the Labour caucus and the Party and it is a matter of historical record that Roger Douglas and his colleagues joined forces in Lange's second term to topple him. Some of the phrases we use, including 'let's roll the fat man', were reported in memoirs of the time, although they clearly referred to staging a coup not an assassination. Although New Zealand has never had a prime minister assassinated, it is worth recalling that David Lange himself told television news that former US Vice-President Dan Quayle had said Lange would have to be 'liquidated'. Apparently our Security Intelligence Services assessed the threat as not credible. Lange, demonstrating his characteristic jokiness, told CNN that he did not feel at risk from someone who couldn't spell 'potato', referring to a blunder Quayle had once made.

Key sources for the history of the Lange government were:

David Lange, *My Life*. Auckland: Penguin Books, 2006.

Margaret Pope, *At the Turning Point: My Political Life With David Lange*. Auckland: AM Pub., 2011.

Harvey McQueen, *The Ninth Floor: Inside the Prime Minister's Office: A Political Experience*. Auckland: Penguin Books, 1991.

Margaret Clark (ed.) *For the Record: Lange and the Fourth Labour Government*. Wellington: Dunmore, 2005.

Thanks also to Auntie Google for endless help with research and fact-checking.

We wish to acknowledge with gratitude those who helped make this book possible. For comments on drafts, Saffron Gardner, Paul Haines, Claire-Louise McCurdy, Lynn Scott, Penelope Todd, Sarah Welch, Jim Welch. For assistance on police procedure, thanks to our contact. For manuscript assessment, thanks to Fleur Beale. Jim Welch copyedited, James McDonald designed the cover and title page and Christine Borra from Your Books gave us helpful advice. Constance Fein Harding (www.cfeinphotography.com) allowed the use of her artwork for the cover.

We'd like to acknowledge our Shakespeare Reading Group. They sharpened our ear for Shakespeare and his relevance to modern life. The quotes at the heads of chapters are all from *Julius Caesar*, a classic account of betrayal and political thuggery.

ABOUT THE AUTHORS

Jennifer Palgrave is the pen name of writing partnership Lois Cox
and Hilary Lapsley. Lois and Hilary divide their time between
Wellington and Waiheke Island. This is their first Lauren Fraser
novel.